"You don't even kno

How can you say so confidently what I will do or not do?"

"I've watched you for some time, Miss Lantz. I have a pretty good idea."

Rose put a hand to her cheek as the blush came again.

Dear Lord, how is it he can keep doing this to me? I wish we were at my house but it is still another half mile. I swear I will die if this keeps up.

They walked in silence a few minutes. Rose finally leaned forward to pat Delaware's neck, the pressure on her legs making her flinch.

"I am surprised to find you here in October, Mr. Daniels," she said. "I thought you stayed out in the western mountains until first snow."

"Often I do."

"Why is this year different?"

He was quiet and did not answer her for several steps. "I needed to be here."

"For what?"

"For whatever is going to happen. Perhaps I can help. Perhaps not. But I will be close at hand."

Born and raised in Canada, **Murray Pura** has lived in the USA, the UK and the Middle East. With over two dozen works of fiction and nonfiction to his credit, he has published with HarperCollins, HarperOne, Baker, Barbour, Zondervan and several other publishing houses. He works in many genres, including historical fiction, classic or literary fiction, romance and Amish fiction. Currently, Pura lives and writes at his home by the Canadian Rockies.

THE ROSE OF LANCASTER COUNTY

Murray Pura

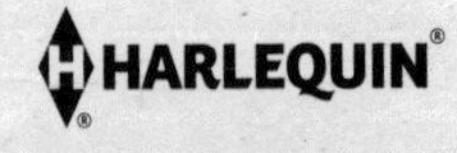

Recycling programs for this product may not exist in your area.

ISBN-13: 978-1-335-49006-3

The Rose of Lancaster County

First published in 2013 by Murray Pura.
This edition published in 2020.

This edition published by arrangement with Harlequin Books S.A.

For questions and comments about the quality of this book, please contact us at CustomerService@Harlequin.com.

Harlequin Enterprises ULC
22 Adelaide St. West, 40th Floor
Toronto, Ontario M5H 4E3, Canada
www.Harlequin.com

Printed in U.S.A.

THE ROSE OF LANCASTER COUNTY

Volume 1

The Rose Garden

The gate creaked. The young woman looked up from the large Bible that was open in her lap. All around her red and white roses grew higher than her head, preventing her from seeing who had entered the garden. She waited a moment, listened to the footsteps, used a maroon strip of cloth as a marker, and closed the Bible gently. A smile played over her lips.

"Rosa?" came a voice.

"Ja?" the young woman responded. *"Wo bist du?"*

"Im Rosengarten." In the rose garden.

"Die Rosengarten?" Which rose garden?

"Nehmen den Weg auf der linken Seite." Take the path to the left.

"Ach, ich so verwirrt." Oh, I get so confused.

The young woman stood up. A white shawl covered her soft brown hair and her green eyes glinted with amusement, her fingers going to her mouth to keep from laughing out loud. "Lydia. You have been coming to this garden for weeks and still it is a mystery to you. How will you find your way into heaven?"

A tall woman with black hair, black shawl, and deep blue eyes walked into the enclosure where the woman in the white shawl stood. Hands on her hips she glanced about.

"Heaven will be clearly marked," she replied. "And Jesus will be my guide. Here there are no signs and if our Lord is walking about I have not seen him." Suddenly she smiled. "But who cares? I am here and you are here and everything is good. We have not seen each other for a week. I've missed you, Rose. The days drag if we cannot quilt together and tell stories."

"I feel the same way."

They embraced, Rose pulling back after a moment to laugh. "What did the nine mice say?"

"Who has a wedge of cheese big enough for all of us?"

"So Jakob Ammann has. He must provide cheese to feed a thousand followers meeting in his kitchen."

Lydia's blue eyes glittered. "I hope we are not quilting in his kitchen today, Rose."

"We are not. He is too old and frail to handle the likes of us."

"Still I would like some of his cheese."

"Oh, we have a wedge good enough for us and the nine mice. Mother picked it up from Mrs. Ammann's friend but it was made by the Ammanns. It is the holy recipe." She grinned. "Come."

She led the way through a wooden archway intertwined with the same white and red roses.

"I can't get over how large this rose garden is." Lydia

glanced about her as she passed under the arch. "You'd think your family had lived in Lancaster twenty years."

Rose grinned. "Not even ten. But Mother, the first thing she did, she planted the rose bushes she had brought on the boat from Switzerland. And God made them grow."

She stopped in another enclosure of flagstones underfoot and roses overhead—roses grew over arbors that shaded the area from the sun. A quilt was spread on a long wooden table, a wedge of white cheese wrapped in paper had been placed in the middle of the quilt, and right next to the cheese sat a black cat.

Lydia erupted with laughter. "Nitz. She guards the quilt and the cheese. So the nine mice can nibble on nothing."

The cat spoke a soft meow that had a question mark.

Lydia picked her up and cuddled her. Nitz's vivid green eyes closed and purring made her body vibrate.

"You are such a baby." Lydia kissed the top of the cat's head. The rough tongue licked her fingers. "If only you could stitch our quilt would be finished much sooner."

"Oh, we are not in a race." Rose took a small knife from a pocket in her long black dress and cut a sliver of cheese from the wedge. "Here. A workman is worthy of his hire."

"I haven't done anything yet."

"You will. Come. Let Nitz hunt and let us stitch."

Lydia put the cat on the flagstones. Nitz immediately slipped into the rose bushes.

"So." Rose sat on one side of the table and picked up a needle that had already been threaded. "Yours is just by that other chair."

Lydia studied the quilt before sitting down. “It looks well. Have you done more work on it by yourself?”

“Very little. The night of the big thunderstorm I spent some time with it in the parlor. I did a few of the roses on the edges.”

“Rose’s rose quilt.”

Rose shook her head and pushed the needle into the fabric. “Rose and Lydia’s rose quilt. It will be a warm one with the lamb’s wool. And the roses and green leaves will make you think of spring even if the snow is piling against the door.”

Lydia took her seat and lifted her needle. “I still think the first quilt should be yours.”

“Why?”

“Well. The theme is roses.”

“And I am named after the Rose of Sharon in the Bible—is that it?”

“It’s not just that. You are going to be married in December. You and your beau should have a warm covering for the frosty nights.”

“Oh, Juerg and I will be warm enough.” Rose’s cheeks turned a light pink. “But my mother and the other ladies are making two quilts right now. One is very thick and it is for the Ammanns so they can be warm as toast all winter long. I am pretty certain the other is for me and Juerg but Mama will not say. *Es ist nicht fur Sie zu wissen. It is not for you to know.*”

“I saw Juerg on the way here. Such a gentleman. Doffed his hat. He was driving a cart piled high with hay.”

Rose smiled as she sewed. “Always a gentleman. As if we were in Bern or Geneva. That will be the final cutting of hay. In a few weeks it will be time to begin the harvest." She glanced up at Lydia. "What about you? When will we see you wed?"

"I am in no hurry. I am more than two years younger than you after all."

"But Ernst has his eye on you."

Lydia let out her breath in a loud puff. "All the eyes in the world will not help Ernst win my hand. He is too rough and ready for my liking. Always dirty."

"Lydia. What do you expect a blacksmith to look like after a day banging together plowshares and wagon wheels?"

"No, he is like that when we gather for worship too. The barn floor is cleaner than his hands."

"His hands are rough and dark from good, hard work. No soap will get all of that out. And it should not. Any woman would be proud of Ernst's work ethic."

"Hmm. Well, Any Woman can have him then." She held up her corner of the quilt and examined it.

"What about Hans?"

"He's only a boy."

"Martin?"

"No, not Martin. He is too short."

"My goodness." Rose set aside her needle and carved off a slice of cheese for herself. "Who then?"

Lydia pulled her needle through a quilt square and did not reply.

Rose tried again. "There must be someone God has put in your heart."

"You will not approve."

"I will not approve?" Rose chewed her cheese slice rapidly and swallowed. "What are you talking about?"

Lydia kept her head down and sewed. "You won't."

"Who is it I will not approve of? I like all the men in our colony. The short ones, the tall ones, the heavy ones, the ironmongers, the dairymen, the ones who care for our horses and make the harness—" She stopped. "Ah." She shook her head. "You cannot mean the man I am thinking of."

Lydia pinched her lips together. "I don't read minds. If you want me to know who it is you will have to tell me plainly."

"It is not him. Tell me it is not him." Lydia kept sewing.

Rose tilted her head. "Lydia. He is not a follower of our ways. He does not care what Jakob Ammann teaches. Why, he is not even a disciple of Menno Simons."

"I told you that you would not approve."

"Why, he is gone for months at a time, dresses like an Indian, has this big long gun on his shoulder and skins on his back—you complain about Ernst being rough and ready? What is Ethan Daniels? And you say Ernst is dirty? Why, Ethan is black with dirt when he comes back from the western forests."

"A bar of soap and he is as good as new."

"He is not one of us, Lydia. He was raised in the Virginia colony. They say he turned his back on his parents and their wealth just to run around half-naked in the woods."

Lydia refused to look up. "He is a great hunter. Even my father has admitted that. Ethan has great respect for the land and its inhabitants, including all the Indian tribes. And he tells me he believes in a God who created the mountains and rivers and wilderness."

"Our God? The Father of our Lord Jesus Christ?"

Lydia shrugged. "He is very kind. Very gentle."

"How can he be? A wild man like that?"

"You have never spoken with him."

"And please God I never shall."

Lydia lifted her head. "Is that any way for a Christian to talk?"

Rose tried to respond once or twice and picked up her needle and thread again. "I apologize. I will pray for him. That is the best I can do. But you cannot get serious about—about—this man they call Long Hunter. Not unless he takes up our ways and settles down." Agitated, she put her needle aside and fidgeted with a corner of the quilt. "What kind of life would that be for a woman? Filthy and starving and running around the forests after a man who is part beast—"

"Rose." Lydia's blue eyes sparked. "He is not a beast. He is a man God has made. And if you ever got close to him you would see how handsome he is."

"I have no intention of getting close to him."

"His eyes are a perfect gray. Like the sky is just before sunrise. A clean and cool morning gray. You would love them."

"I would not. Juerg's eyes are good enough for me. He is a man of God. And a farmer besides. He knows how to settle down and raise a family and keep those eyes of his on Jesus Christ."

Lydia shook her head and returned to her stitching. "I did not come here to argue."

"Nor did I." Rose picked up her needle. "How is it you have words with him anyways?"

"Father buys his meat. And his skins. Some of the

skins Papa takes to Philadelphia to trade. Others we use. They are expertly tanned, Papa tells us. So smooth and soft. I have a blanket of deerskins from Ethan, from Long Hunter. I will use them with this quilt on the coldest nights."

Rose snorted. "Suit yourself." She placed a hand on the wedge of cheese. "Would like some more of the Ammann recipe?"

"Very much."

"I will cut you a large piece to gnaw on." She brought out her pocketknife. "So. Are you still my bridesmaid?"

"If you wish it."

"Of course I wish it. Ethan Daniels is not going to come between me and my best friend."

Lydia smiled. "I don't think he wants to, Rose."

"Good. Then he and I can agree on that." Rose tossed Lydia a large chunk of cheese. "You will not ask him to the wedding, will you?"

Lydia bit into the white cheese. "Why? Are English allowed to be present?" She chewed and turned the cheese over in her hand. *"Ach, dies ist so sehr gute."*

"Sometimes Jakob invites them to things. Who knows? But you will not ask Long Hunter to my wedding, Lydia, will you? Please. Martin, Ernst, Hans, they are all good. And if it must be an Englishman, I can settle for Adam Peachtree, but—"

Lydia stopped eating and looked at her friend in horror, her blue eyes large. "What? Adam Peachtree? Do you think that is a joke?"

"I don't know. He's not so bad, is he?"

"And you criticize Ethan Daniels? Adam loafs around his father's store in Lancaster and when he sees a young woman he leers. The Lord forgive me but there is no other word for it. I cannot go in there with Mama, not so much as to buy a spool of thread. Always he is lurking. You get this strange sensation and you look and there he is behind the shelf of coffee pots and his eyes are running all over you. Ugh." She shivered. "That is not even funny, Rose Lantz. I once asked Papa to consider moving out of the county just to avoid Adam and his father's store but Papa says no, he likes Penn's Land, he likes the spirit of liberty and tolerance. *Just to another county*, I pleaded. No, he likes Lancaster County and the church here. And of course Jakob Ammann is also here. And you." She smiled. "So I must put up with Adam Peachtree. But I do not go to the store if I can help it. And no, I will not be inviting him to your wedding. You can be sure of that."

"I see."

"Better your Long Hunter than Adam Peachtree."

"Lydia Beiler. You can be most annoying. He is not *my* Long Hunter. And I would be most grateful if you came with a cousin, if you must have an escort, rather than him."

"All right. But if you change your mind—"

"Most certainly I will not change my mind."

"If perhaps you run into each other and you talk at length or he—"

Rose's green eyes flared. "Run into each other? Talk at length? What sort of dark and stormy night are you imagining in your head, Lydia? I will not be running into Ethan Daniels anytime soon. Indeed, quite the opposite is the case—if anything, you will find that I am running away from him." She plunged her needle into the quilt. "Though I should never give a villain like him the satisfaction of seeing me run. I would walk swiftly and with an erect posture."

Lydia laughed. "*Villain? Erect posture?* What sort of man do you think he is? Your language is rather bold regarding a person you have never met. Why would you have to flee from him? Are you a deer that you should be so intimidated?"

"Oh, my goodness, I am not intimidated by the likes of Ethan Daniels. I simply don't care to have him in my vicinity." She rethreaded her needle. "Enough now. We don't see each other for seven days and all we can find to do is quarrel about a man who spends half the year living off acorns in the forest?"

"Rose—"

"Tell me where you have been reading in the Bible. I have spent my week in the gospels. Especially Luke. What about you?"

"Why, I have been memorizing verses in Esther. That she was born to do something special, to stand up for others and save them—*geburtig fur eine solche Zeit, wie diese." Born for such a time as this.*

"Yes, I love that story. Whenever I—"

"Rosa? Rosa?"

Rose looked at Lydia, raising her eyebrows in surprise. "I'm here, Mother! With Lydia in the last garden! Working on the quilt!"

Her mother bustled into the enclosure, a short stocky woman with brown hair pulled back into a bun so tight it stretched the skin on her face. She clapped her hands together. "Quickly now. Your father and the other pastors must meet and they love to use this part of the rose garden in fine weather."

Rose and Lydia jumped to their feet.

"You did not tell me anything about this." Rose gathered up the quilt. "I thought we agreed Lydia and I had all afternoon. Until the milking."

"I did not know the leadership were meeting. Neither did your father until five minutes ago. Jakob Ammann is in the parlor with Pastor Philip. Pastor Ulrich has been sent for."

"What is this about?"

"I don't know. Grandfather Ammann is friendly enough but his eyes are hard. Something is troubling him."

"Perhaps he is ill." Rose helped Lydia with the spools and scissors. "They say he is getting more and more frail."

Her mother dragged two more chairs to the table. "Who gossips such nonsense? He is healthy as a horse. This has nothing to do with a weak heart or a sore back. He is worried. So prayer and godly talk will clear his mind of whatever it is."

Rose and Lydia rushed out of the enclosure and practically ran over Jakob Ammann.

"Oh, Grandfather, I'm sorry," said Rose. "We were in such a rush to clear a place for you and the pastors."

The slender man with an untrimmed white beard and bright clear eyes smiled. "It is all right, daughter. In truth, I wish to speak with you and young Lydia. Please remain with us for a few minutes, if you will."

"Why—of course."

Rose's father and two other men joined Jakob Ammann under the arbors. All four were dressed in black with black hats and the pastors had untrimmed beards like their leader except theirs were brown. Rose's mother pulled two more chairs to the table and smiled. Jakob nodded his thanks.

"Martha, you are just like the sister in the Bible," he said. "Always getting things done decently and in order."

"Danke, Grossvater." Thank you, Grandfather.

"But you also have Mary in you because I know how often you sit at our Lord's feet. So you are a double blessing."

She bowed her head. "I serve all of you as I would serve the Lord." She left.

Jakob sat but did not use the chair at the head of the table.

The three men arranged themselves on either side of them. Rose pulled back the chair he had ignored and dragged it to the opposite side facing him and the pastors. She caught his eye. He smiled and she sat, gesturing for Lydia to sit beside her. She still held the quilt bundled up in her arms.

"What have you been working on, daughter?" Jakob asked Rose.

"It is to be a quilt for Lydia here."

"Not for your own wedding?"

"I wished my friend to have something first."

"Ah. Glory be to Jesus Christ."

"Amen," the three pastors responded.

Jakob looked at Rose's father. "Pastor Johannes. Will you open in prayer?"

"Ja." He stood up, removing his broad brimmed

hat. *"Moge Gott uns gnadig." May God have mercy on us.* He continued to pray in Swiss German for several minutes, then pronounced the *amen* which the others echoed, and took his seat again.

"Pastor Philip. Pastor Ulrich. Pastor Johannes. I have called you together because there are important matters we must discuss and pray about. You may wonder why I have asked Fraulein Rose and Fraulein Lydia to remain with us. That is because what we must resolve touches on them. Indeed it touches on all the women of our church, young and old."

The men nodded and waited for him to continue.

Jakob leaned back in his chair and stroked his beard. "We left Switzerland and Alsace because our desire to follow God with a pure heart was not tolerated there. In the English colonies we found much freedom to walk in Christ's steps as we felt was right. William Penn's Land has especially been kind to us. We have not been here ten years and we have lived and worshipped our Lord in peace."

"Ja, ja," agreed Pastor Ulrich.

"Now and then, perhaps, they have wondered about our Swiss German language and our practice of baptizing adults and not children. They are curious about our foot washing. And our church discipline. But on the whole we have been left to ourselves. There is no persecution as we experienced it in the old countries, oh, no, nothing like that, we thank God. No beatings, no imprisonments, no torture, praise be to God."

"Amen," the pastors responded together.

"So but human nature is still human nature and it is corrupt without the saving grace of our Lord Jesus

Christ that makes us new men, born a second time from above. And it is in human nature to be suspicious of what is different and not understood. Sometimes the English mutter, *What are these people talking about when they speak with one another in their language? What are they saying about us? What is it they are planning to do?* Thus I am not surprised when this spills over into something like superstition—*Perhaps they are putting spells on us. Perhaps they are uttering curses. Perhaps they mean to drive us off our land and take it for themselves.*"

"God forbid we should act in such a manner," Rose's father replied.

"Nevertheless." Jakob leaned forward and put both his hands on the tabletop. "Some of the business leaders in Lancaster have approached me. Some of the ministers of the various churches as well. They are concerned that there are those among them who think a number of our people practice witchcraft. They were anxious that we do all we can to dispel such rumors by our words and our deeds."

"Witchcraft." Pastor Philip shook his head. "No, no, no."

"We are bound to take it seriously," Jakob Ammann continued. "It is not so long ago people were put to death in the Massachusetts colony for this offence. Before our time, yes, in 1692 and '93, but our own law against witchcraft in Penn's Land was only enacted in 1718, scant years before we arrived. Who knows what mischief the devil could stir up here? I believe there is witchcraft, of course, in these colonies, just as there was witchcraft in Switzerland and France. But it is my understanding some of the men and women executed in Massachusetts were most certainly innocent. That is what the business leaders in Lancaster have told me. There has been repentance in Massachusetts for condemning many who they now realize were not guilty. There has been monetary compensation. People have admitted Satan deluded them. I have heard that some deliberately accused their neighbors in the hopes of thereby gaining their land after those accused were found guilty and hung. Most malicious, oh, most malicious is the work of Satan on the human heart. But we already knew that from the way we were treated in Europe. All of us have lost friends whose only crime was to ask to be baptized as Jesus was, fully covered by water and fully aware of what they were doing—adult baptism, believer's baptism. Oh, yes, dark are the workings of the devil on the human spirit. What happened in Massachusetts and in Switzerland could happen here."

Rose felt like ice. Lydia reached for her hand and Rose gripped it.

Jakob tapped on the table. "My daughters, first I ask you this, as your spiritual father in Christ—have you seen anything of witchcraft among our people? Have you known, in particular, of any of our women casting spells, or conjuring up demons, or placing the evil eye on our English neighbors?"

Rose found her mouth was dry. She fumbled with her words. "I—I have not—no, never—all our women revere Jesus Christ and wish to be his disciples—not the devil's—"

Jakob's eyes rested on Lydia. "Daughter?"

Lydia's face was as white as many of the roses that

grew over her head. "No, Grandfather, I have seen nothing like what you describe. Our women are God-fearing people. They would not wish to risk their souls consorting with the devil and his legions."

Jakob tapped on the table with his fingertips again. "What about the men? What have you seen? What have others told you?"

Lydia shook her head. "Oh, no, the men follow the holy example of their pastors and of you. I have seen no darkness. I have heard no imprecations. They love the Lord. They wish to be like him."

"What of men outside our fold?"

Lydia whitened even further. "No, I have heard nothing."

"The Long Hunter?"

"No, oh, no, he is just a hunter and a trapper, he wants nothing to do with the devil."

Tap tap tap. "Some will say he is successful on his hunts because he consorts with Satan in the forest. That he makes sacrifices there. Holds Black Sabbaths. And the devil rewards him with meat."

Lydia shook her head. "No, Grandfather, it is not right to say such things or think such things. He is not one of us but one day he may be. I know he cares about God and God's words and this world that the Lord has made."

"He has told you so when you had conversations with him?"

"Very brief conversations—yes."

Tap tap tap. "That he would be baptized and join our fellowship of believers?"

"Yes. Yes."

"My daughter, do not be alarmed. I am bound to ask

these things because others may ask the same questions with dark intent. I wish you to be prepared for such pitfalls and snares."

"I understand, Grandfather."

His eyes returned to Rose. "I see I have reminded you of the evil days in Europe. I am sorry. It is only that I wish you fortified against the assaults of those who may seek to trip you up and do you harm—you, and Lydia, and the rest of our church. So the authorities treated us in Switzerland and so they may treat us here."

"Yes." Rose felt weak. "Of course."

"What have you seen or heard of the men? What devilry have you heard they have been up to?"

"I have seen or heard nothing. Our men are pure."

"What of this Long Hunter? Ethan Daniels?"

"I know nothing of him. I have never spoken with him." Tap tap tap.

"Do you desire to do so?"

"No. Never."

"Why? Do you think he is evil?"

"I—I—" Rose struggled with her tongue again. "He—he is not one of us—I have no interest in him or his ways—I love Juerg, the man I am to marry—I do not think the Long Hunter is a wicked man—I wish him no harm—but he is not the sort of Christian man I find honorable—"

"Hmm." Jakob looked from Rose to Lydia and back. "And both of you are innocent of such charges? You do not call out to the devil for help? You do not collect plants for magic or for potions?"

Nitz jumped onto his lap.

Startled, Jakob's face quickly darkened. Then the cat

rubbed its head against his hand and his features relaxed. He smiled and his fingers scratched the cat's ears. "Ah, Nitz. You were only a kitten on the ship. Now see how you have grown." The cat meowed. "I know. I know. Such unpleasant talking. Such an unpleasant topic."

"Nitz," Rose called.

"No, no, daughter, let her remain with me." Jakob petted the cat and looked up. "Your hearts and your words are clear to me. In your eyes I see fear of persecution but not the look of guilt. Thank you. You may leave us. I hope you will still have time to carry on with your quilting before your evening chores demand your attention."

"Danke, Opa." It was the tender word for grandfather that Rose sometimes used.

"Pastor Philip will pray for both of you before you go."

Tall and broad-shouldered, bald but with his beard still a rich dark brown, Pastor Philip stood up. He smiled at the two young women. *"Do not be afraid of the terror of the night or the arrow that flieth by day or for the pestilence that walks in darkness or the destruction that wasteth at noonday."*

"Amen," said Jakob Ammann.

Pastor Philip bowed his head and prayed for their protection and for the blessing of God's angels and his Holy Spirit. Then he said his *amen*, which was repeated by the others, including Rose and Lydia, and sat down. The two women got to their feet.

"May God be with you as you discuss these matters." Rose gathered up her quilt once again. "It is surely not a pleasant task."

"No," replied Jakob. "But it is the Lord's task. He

will give us the strength we need. And the wisdom. They who honor him he will honor."

"Amen." Rose began to walk out of the garden. "His blessing be upon you."

"Yes," agreed Lydia. "May his countenance shine upon you and give you peace."

They had hardly taken another step before Rose's mother rushed in. "I am sorry, I am sorry, but the sheriff of Lancaster is at the door."

Jakob raised his head sharply. "What is the matter? Who does he wish to see?"

"You. And the pastors." She swung her troubled eyes on Lydia. "And you."

Rose felt fear make a fist in her stomach.

"Why?" Jakob stared at Rose's mother as if she were part of some plot against them. "What has she done?"

"He did not tell me very much. Only that it is serious and that he must see all of you this minute."

Jakob pushed his chair back and stood up and the pastors with him. "That is all he said? He demands to see us on short notice and that is all he says to you?"

"He—he did tell me one other thing."

"And what was that?"

"That he must question Lydia. And all of you. The Peachtree boy from the store has lodged a complaint."

"A complaint? What sort of complaint?"

Rose's mother stared at Lydia with large dark eyes. "He claims that Lydia has made him fall in love with her. That he cannot eat or sleep or even pray. He says she has cast a spell on him. That she is a witch."

Volume 2

The Covenant

The sheriff was dressed in a black frock coat and stood in the hallway by the front door. His tall black hat was in his hand. Beside him were Lydia's mother and father, their faces and bodies rigid. Jakob Ammann and the pastors approached them by a hall that led from the back of the house and the rose garden. Rose's mother followed and then it was Rose and Lydia. The two young women were holding hands as tightly as they could.

"Sheriff. What is this we hear?" Jakob Ammann was a head shorter but spoke as if he were towering over the sheriff. "You come to lay charges against one of our women? Charges of witchcraft?"

The sheriff held up his hand. "I bring no charges with me, sir, and no papers of warrant and arrest. A complaint has been lodged and I am bound by Pennsylvania's laws to investigate. I am sorry to trouble thee but the more quickly we deal with this matter the better."

He looked at Lydia and Rose. "Forgive me. I do not know either of thee. Who is Lydia Beiler?"

"I am, sir," said Lydia.

"I will have thee and thy father and the male leadership. May we use the parlor, Mrs. Lantz?"

"Of course, of course. It is just through this door here."

"I would like to have my friend by my side," Lydia spoke up.

The sheriff shook his head. "Thy father and the men who govern the church. No one else. I must ask thee a number of questions. It is not for thy friend to hear my questions or thy answers."

Rose quickly kissed her friend on the cheek. "Go. I'll be here when you are finished."

"There is a meal." Rose's mother smiled at Lydia. "We shall eat together once the sheriff is done. You will see Rose then. And your mother."

Rose's father opened the door to the parlor and the men went inside. Lydia followed her father into the room, glancing back at Rose with the eyes, Rose thought, of a hunted deer. Then the door was shut.

"I have some things prepared. Martina, I will need your help." Rose's mother led the way into the kitchen. "The stew is on the stove. But also the corn needs to be boiled and the carrots sliced."

Lydia's mother picked up a knife. "I will see to that."

"Danke, Martina. Rosa, hier ist ein Korb fur Sie." She handed her daughter a large wicker basket. "From the garden I need dill. From the fields some wild mint and wild onion. And mushrooms. Be careful now to collect only the good mushrooms."

Rose nodded and left the house with the basket over

her arm, one hand clutching her shawl, her head down. The sun was lower in the sky but there was still plenty of summer light left. Among the beets and carrots tall green stalks of dill moved in the light breezes. She took her knife from her pocket and cut several, laying them carefully in the basket. Walking away from the house she passed through their yard and a stand of old oak trees and emerged into a glade of uncut grass encircled by more oaks. Bending down, she looked closely for mint and onions and mushrooms.

Lord, I ask you to be with Lydia in a special way. How frightening this is for her.

All because of an unkind boy. You know the truth. Please make sure it comes out.

She cut some onions and plucked up mushrooms after turning them so she could see under their tops. After searching the entire glade she had not found any mint and went through the oaks on the far side to where a stream ran through the brush. Following the stream she passed by a covered bridge painted red, hunting for mint in spots she had always found it before. One part of her mind was on wild mint plants while another was on what was happening in the front parlor of her home.

She wandered across a meadow and through a cluster of white birch trees. Spying mint by an old fallen tree she hurried to gather it up.

Thwack. Thwack. Thwack.

Startled by the sound of chopping Rose peered around. Fifty yards away, through a screen of sugar maples, she could see a tall man wielding a double bitted axe. His hair was long and he was stripped to the waist in the warm weather.

Beyond him was a small log cabin. She got to her feet and moved away quickly.

Of all things, Rose Lantz. Why weren't you paying more attention to where you were going? You practically walked into that wild man's front yard. And him half-naked. Isn't the renegade supposed to be in the western forests this time of year?

"Meowrr!"

A black cat sprang out from under her feet and she almost screamed. Hand on her heart she began to laugh. "Nitz! Did you follow me out here? You scared me to death!"

The cat rubbed against her long dress and kept meowing until Rose picked her up. "Whatever is the matter?" The cat put her face to Rose's and purred. Rose carried Nitz in her arms and headed back to the farm. Passing by the bridge again she saw a wagonload of men on the road. They paused to gaze at her. Dropping her head she hurried on through the oak trees and back into the glade.

"Why, there's a patch of wild mint right here." She knelt, cat in her arms. "Why didn't I notice it on the way in, Nitz?"

Her basket was full. She carried on across the glade, passed into another stretch of oak trees, and came out in view of her house. The sheriff was just mounting his horse. She quickened her pace. He saw her as he walked his horse from the farmyard to the main road and tipped his tall black hat with its wide, flat brim.

"What has happened?" Rose burst into the kitchen. "Is all well?"

Her mother and Lydia's mother glanced up, their

faces scarlet from the heat of the cooking. Her mother pointed with her chin. "So she is in the rose garden waiting for you. The men are praying."

Rose put down the basket. "I should help you here."

Her mother shook her head. "Ah, no. Go to her. We are all right. The meal will be another half hour yet but everything is done."

"Are you sure?"

Her mother waved her hand. *"Gehen Sie!"*

Rose found Lydia back at the long wooden table they had used for their quilt.

Lydia shot to her feet and threw herself into her friend's arms. Nitz leaped from Rose with a squeal of protest and darted into the rose bushes.

"Oh, it was terrible, terrible."

Rose smoothed Lydia's dark hair. "It's all right. Our whole community will stand with you. This Peachtree boy cannot say whatever he likes out of spite and get away with it."

"So many lies he told. That I went to the store so I could see him and bewitch him. That I made eyes at him. Whispered his name when no one else was listening. Tried to take his hand or kiss him on the lips. Lies, lies!"

"He is jealous. That's all. He cannot have you so he will try and hurt you. So some men do." Rose led Lydia back to her seat. "How did you respond?"

"Of course I denied all of it. Grandfather and the ministers were very good. They pointed out it was my word against his and that Adam Peachtree's standing in Lancaster was not such that his accusations ought to be given more weight than my defense. Your father reminded Sheriff What-God-Will of improprieties that had been laid at Adam's feet in the recent past and that they always involved women."

"Good."

"But there were all these questions that had nothing to do with Adam Peachtree. What did I do on the nights that had full moons or no moons? Did I have a cat? What color was the cat? Did I have a broom? Did I ride it?"

"What?"

"So my father quipped that at the witches trial William Penn presided over many years ago Mr. Penn had said there was no law against flying on broomsticks."

Rose burst out with a laugh and put her hand to her mouth. "Oh, my goodness, how did the sheriff take that?"

"He made a sour face and said it was nothing to joke about, that flying brooms was something only witches did, and that many people, including a number of peaceful Quakers, were upset that milk was going sour in the milking pail and that foals and calves were not living through the summer."

Rose made a face. "Oh, come. Livestock die all the time. Surely a poisonous weed is to blame or an illness that went through the horses and cattle."

Lydia smiled. "He wouldn't have liked having you there, no, he wouldn't have liked your spirit. Of course I admitted to nothing so Grandfather asked him again if he was going to lay charges. The sheriff hemmed and hawed and finally said he was bound to investigate the complaint, had done so, that I had denied casting any spell on Adam Peachtree or that I had the slightest amorous inclinations towards him." Lydia twisted up her mouth. "Ugh. Adam even claimed I had tried to entice him to the kissing bridge by entering into his room in the shape of a spirit. Imagine, Rose, meeting Adam Peachtree at the covered bridge and kissing him there."

Her whole body shuddered.

Rose had both arms around Lydia as they sat side by side. "Praise God, it's done then, *ja*?"

"Unless he lodges more complaints."

"What else can he say? It's finished with."

"Oh, Rose, who knows? Who knows what people will say if the harvest is not good? Will they point the finger at me again with my long black hair? Will the ones who defended me today stand up and defend me tomorrow?"

"The pastors will never turn their back on you. Neither will Jakob Ammann. Neither will I. That you can be sure of."

"Sheriff What-God-Will said I had the witch's look because of my black hair and blue eyes."

"What? Why, that is nonsense. You are a child of God and the most beautiful woman in the county."

"Oh, Rose, I am not."

"You certainly are. Think of how handsome your sons will be and how lovely your daughters. God has blessed you. And we are blessed by that blessing."

"You exaggerate but thank you."

"No one is going to trouble you again. Believe me."

Lydia chewed on one of her fingernails. "Who can say? What does Grandfather tell us about the heart of man? That it is deceitful above all things and desperately wicked?"

"Yes, Jakob Ammann and the Bible say this. But people are righteous too, Lydia. The wicked are not the only ones who dwell on this earth." She took her friend's hands in hers. "This is what I want to do. Let us make a covenant. Like the Lord made with Israel. Like he made with us in Jesus Christ."

"What do you mean?"

"We will never turn away from each other. No matter what you may be accused of. Or I, for that matter. We shall both uphold one another in the Lord regardless of what people say about either of us. We will never betray our friendship. Always, always, will we support one another, defend one another, and speak well of one another."

"I like the idea. But I don't want to cut myself or anything."

"Oh, no, nothing like that. Let our yes be yes and our no be no as Grandfather admonishes us. But maybe—" Rose reached up, pinched off a red rose by its stalk, and lay it down so that it was in her lap and Lydia's. "Maybe this rose can be a symbol of our faithfulness to one another. I'll press it and keep it in the big Bible in my room."

Lydia nodded. "All right."

"Let's hold hands over the rose."

Rose's fingers curled around Lydia's and Lydia's around Rose's.

"I promise to be a faithful friend forever." Rose smiled into her friend's blue eyes. "Nothing will come between us."

Lydia nodded. "I agree. I will be your faithful friend forever, Rose Lantz. I will never forsake you. That is the covenant I make with you today."

"Amen."

"Amen."

They hugged each other tightly. Rose stood, taking

the rose in her hand. "Come. Let's go up to my room and place it in the Bible." She pricked her finger on a thorn and laughed, putting the finger in her mouth. "Hurry. The next thing you know they'll be calling us in to eat."

Lydia got to her feet. "Thank you for your love for me, Rose. It means the world, oh, it means far more than the world. I felt so scared an hour ago and now I feel as free as a lark. Praise God."

"I'm glad. Yes, may the Lord be praised. So. What part of the Bible should we press the rose in? Old Testament? New?"

"Oh, Ruth and Naomi?"

"Yes, that's a good place. Or should it be where Jesus is saying something like, *Greater love hath no man than this, but that he lays down his life for his friend?* Or, *Beloved, let us love one another, for love is of God and everyone who loves is born of God and knows God*?"

Lydia laughed as they half-ran through the rose garden to the house. "Or the greatest commandments, *To love God and to love your neighbor as yourself?*"

"There are too many verses to choose from. God wrote such a good book. What are we going to do?"

"Oh, pray all night until an answer comes to us."

In Rose's room they turned over page after page of the large Bible she had brought with her on the ship from Europe. Just as they were called down to the afternoon meal they decided on Lamentations: *It is of the Lord's mercies that we are not consumed because his compassions fail not. They are new every morning. Great is thy faithfulness.* They placed the rose there and closed the Bible carefully on it.

"So in the same way we shall be faithful to one another, Rose Lantz," said Lydia, taking her friend's hand.

"Amen. So be it." Rose grinned. "Now let's run downstairs before the men gobble everything up. I'm starved, aren't you?"

"Famished!"

The men and the two mothers, along with Rose's younger brothers, Nathan and Hans, were sitting quietly as Lydia and Rose raced along the hall, stopping just before they entered the dining room. Rose's mother frowned but Jakob Ammann smiled and got to his feet.

"I thank God you both have so much spirit in you. It has been a trying afternoon."

"Yes, Grandfather." Rose's face was flushed from the running but she smiled at Jakob Ammann in return. "We have prayed together and read the Bible together and recommitted ourselves to each other as sisters in the Lord Jesus Christ. His compassion never fails us. Every morning it is another sunrise in our hearts, *ja*? Great is his faithfulness. So we are not afraid any longer."

"Amen." Jakob nodded towards their chairs. "I shall thank our Lord and we shall eat of the goodness he has given us from the earth." Once the two young women were in their seats he began to pray, bowing his head of silver-white hair. *"Herr, wir danken Ihnen fur Ihre Anmut und Ihren Schutz. Lord, we thank you for your grace and your protection. Remain with us in these days when dark thoughts travel abroad. Deliver us from the evil one and his minions. Deliver us from the crimes of man. May Christ reign in our hearts and in our church. For your faithfulness we thank you. For the food you give us so that we may serve you on this earth we thank you. In the name of Christ Jesus. Amen."*

"Amen," the men and women responded.

Jakob took his seat and immediately began to butter a heel of rye bread that was on his plate. He glanced up at Lydia. "You comported yourself well with the sheriff, my daughter. You were civil and respectful, your replies to his questions brief and to the point. I do not think there will be any more trouble from Master Adam Peachtree."

Lydia smiled and sipped from a glass of water. "Thank you, Grandfather."

"There is no telling, of course, what others may say and do. Stay constant in prayer and maintain righteousness morning and night as a woman after the Lord's own heart." He helped himself to a large kettle of stew that sat in the middle of the table, ladling the meat and broth into a bowl in his hand. "Serve your mother and father and siblings with gladness. Do not let the harshness of this day diminish your walk with God in any way. *Enter his gates with thanksgiving and his courts with praise.*" He sprinkled a generous amount of pepper onto his stew. "I had the opportunity to look at the quilt you and Rose are working on. It was folded on a chair in the hallway. I find great beauty in it. And great peace. *I am the rose of Sharon and the lily of the valleys*—the rose speaks of our Savior and Lord. I should lie most comfortably under such a quilt when the snow fell thickly upon our fields."

"Oh, Opa, lassen Sie uns fur Sie," said Rose excitedly, putting down her spoon.

Jakob smiled and waved his hand. "No, no, don't

trouble about me, my old quilt from Bern continues to serve me well."

"Aber es ware ein Segen, es su tun."

"A blessing for you to do or not, do not trouble yourself. I am quite content with what I have."

Three days later Lydia and Rose were back in the garden with their quilt. "It is silly for me to have this," Lydia said as they stitched. "You are getting married first."

"Not this argument again. We agreed the first would be yours weeks ago."

"I don't know how we came to such a decision."

"Well—"

"And now I am worrying about Grandfather. And his wife. Grandmother Verena is thin as a hoe handle. Even my father and mother say so."

"I told you our mothers and many of the other women are working on a quilt for the Ammanns. They will give it to them before the snow flies."

"But it will not be a rose quilt." Lydia pouted. "Grandfather truly loves our rose quilt."

Rose stopped sewing and sat back in her chair. *"Ja, ja,"* she sighed. "Perhaps I should speak with Mama. We make the rose quilt for Grandfather and Grandmother. And they make that first quilt for you."

"Or you."

"No, no, I told you. The women are making another quilt for Juerg and I."

"So—"

"So this one we give to Grandfather. And the women give their first quilt to you."

Lydia shook her head. "It makes no sense I should be given one."

"It makes perfect sense. You will have no husband this winter. I will. You have no one to keep you warm. I do. So you get the first quilt. Just to be sure you will not freeze to death on us once the snowflakes fall."

"Ha." Lydia broke into a sharp laugh. "I may surprise you."

"Oh, ho, how will you do that? No one can court you fast enough to be ready for a December wedding."

"Why not?"

"It's almost September."

"Three months. A lot can happen in three months, Rose Lantz."

A smile flickered over Rose's lips and she put down her needle. "Who do you have your eyes on?"

"You'll find out."

"Tell me."

"I can't. But you will be the first to know if anything comes of it."

Rose went back to work with her needle. "You and your secrets. I just hope it is not that wild man Ethan Daniels."

"Suppose it were?"

"Baptized into our church? Accepted by the brethren? Betrothed to you? All in three months' time? Perhaps the Lord will turn the water in your well to wine too."

"Ha. You'll see."

Through the rest of August and into September the two young women were able to quilt together at least once a week, sometimes two or three times. Their needles glinted in the sunlight as they talked and laughed and stitched. Harvest began in the fields around Lancaster and wagons piled with oats and barley and wheat moved back and forth along the roads, raising dust Lydia and Rose could smell in the air and taste on the tips of their tongues. Rose had been accustomed to seeing Juerg several evenings a week but now she did not see him at all as he worked hard to bring in his family's grain. Even under the light of the full moon he worked just as many of the other men did.

How much better, she thought, *to wed a man of the soil and the farm than to be attracted to a man of the woods and the wilderness, a man with no roots, carried by the wind in every direction. I hope Lydia is not serious about Ethan Daniels. I pray it is a good-hearted farmer who loves the land and loves his God that she is beginning to have feelings for.*

The roses were still sturdy and full of color when scarlet and orange leaves swept across Rose's path on her walks. The oak trees near the Lantz farm and the covered bridge turned copper and bronze and caught fire in the sun. The robins had not left, they still hopped from branch to branch in the chokecherry bushes by the creek, gorging themselves in preparation for their flight south, but the ragged Vs of wild geese in the afternoon skies made it clear that the first hard frosts were not far off.

"Soon we will have to move indoors," Lydia said on a morning that was chillier than the others. "It's too bad."

"You and I shall be fine, sister. We'll use the parlor and the parlor has a wonderful woodstove that will keep us toasty warm."

Thump. Thump. Thump thump.

Lydia stopped sewing and smiled, listening. "So the hunters. My father and yours are out together this morning. Perhaps God has blessed both our families with venison."

"Or geese. Or turkey. Smell that?"

Lydia sniffed. "You have your smoke house going. What do you use? It is a pleasant scent."

"Mama favors wild apple wood. She says it imparts a delicate taste to the meat. She has ducks in there today."

"And maybe deer this afternoon when the men return." Lydia tried to peer out through the rose arbors. "Is Juerg out with his musket today?"

"Ah, no. He must get in the last of the crops. He will hunt for his family later in October."

Lydia was still craning her neck. "There is line of gray smoke. So Ethan is in his cabin. I would have thought he'd be out with the others."

Rose stitched more quickly. "Why? He hunts all year. That's all he does. Why would he need to hunt now? Let others have the deer and bring in food for their loved ones. He has only one mouth to feed and he has probably cured the meat of a dozen stags this year."

"Oh, Rose, you surely have it in for him. How would you know how many deer Ethan has brought in this year?" Lydia returned to her stitching. "I take it you are not aware he brings meat to the widows in our church?"

Rose stopped using her needle. "What did you say?"

"And not just our widows. He brings meat to the English widows too—deer, goose, duck. All cleaned and cured."

"How long has this been going on?"

"Since the spring of '27. So almost two years."

"Father and Mother have never mentioned it."

"Perhaps because they know how you feel about him and that you would not welcome any news of Ethan Daniels."

Rose began plying her needle again. "And so I don't. But I am glad to hear God has been able to place some decency in his heart."

"Often he plays with the children who have no father. This is mostly the English families where the men have been killed in Indian raids."

"Now you are making things up."

"No, I am not teasing you. I've just never told you about him because you always fly into a temper."

"I do not fly into a temper."

"The boys and girls will gather at the English schoolhouse on an evening and he will play hide and seek with them while their mothers or older brothers watch. Not all the children who show up at the school have lost their fathers but many have."

Rose looked up. "You have gone to these game nights, haven't you?"

"I took Little Mary, my cousin, and young Ludwig just last week. Ethan taught the children lacrosse—"

"Oh," interrupted Rose, "an Indian game, of course."

"—and he showed us a game I had never seen before. Stickball, Ethan called it."

"What is that?"

"You throw a ball made of a deer hide at a person and they have to hit it with a hickory stick. The farther you hit it the better. If you swing and miss three or four times your turn is over."

"It doesn't sound very exciting."

"Oh, the children loved it. You run after you hit the ball."

"Run where?"

"In a circle. You try to finish the circle before someone catches the ball you hit and throws it at you."

Rose rolled her eyes. "Throws it at you? Of course this would be the sort of rough game a man like Ethan Daniels would teach the children."

"You never heard such squealing and laughter. The ball is soft, Rose. It's not like a rock or stone, it does not sting so much when it strikes you. Oh, it was such a time."

"So you played too."

"And I hit it! I had so much fun."

"Good for you."

"And then there is a fire he builds and he tells the young ones all these stories he has in his head. You should hear the tales he spins."

"I'd rather not."

"He tells Bible stories too, Rose. Last week it was Daniel in the lion's den. My goodness, none of the children moved a muscle they were so intent on listening to everything he said."

"Very nice." Rose stopped to rethread her needle, closing one eye in a squint. "Why are you telling me all this?"

"You have such a low opinion of him. I thought you should know."

"And this is the man you are going to marry?"

A flush came to Lydia's face. "Did I ever say so? Of course not. He has never asked for my hand. I hear he is a confirmed bachelor."

"Is that what you hear? Then I thank God. No woman in Lancaster will have to chase after him through the woods for the rest of her life. Now let us speak of better things."

"Rose—"

"Yes, better things. Are you feeling well these days? Adam Peachtree has not gone to the sheriff again? No more talk of broomsticks and spells and goats' blood?"

"Ah, I thank God, no." Lydia's face opened into a sudden smile, her blue eyes catching the morning light. "It is as if that happened a hundred years ago."

"Good, good, the Lord be praised. And our quilt is not so far from being finished. Mother has said yes, we can give this to the Ammanns, that will be all right. By November, it will be ready, don't you think?"

"Perhaps not the first of November. I hope he will like it."

"Of course he'll like it. He already likes it. Didn't he tell us so?"

Four days later the sun was bright and warmed the day until the afternoon was comfortable and Rose found she could sit outside with needle and thread and quilt. Lydia was supposed to join her after her chores but she did not appear. Rose expected to see her the next day instead but she did not come to the rose garden then either.

"I don't understand, Mama." Rose stood in the kitchen, her face pinched, her hands restless. "This has not happened with Lydia before. Not so many missed days in a row and no message."

"See to the milking." Her mother wrapped a dark shawl over her shoulders and head and went to the door. "The women are meeting and doing some quilting for an hour or two. I will find out from Martina Beiler if anything serious is going on. There is also the cabbage soup on the stove you can keep an eye on. Father took Nathan hunting for the first time today and I think they will be late."

Eight-year-old Hans worked with her in the barn. She found she was snapping at him when he made mistakes with the cows or spilled milk from his bucket and the fat tears that started down his face made her stop everything, scoop her little brother into her arms, and tell him how sorry she was. Then they worked side by side and she refused to indulge in sharp words again.

"I like this better," he said.

"What is that? How we are milking together?"

"Yes. And this mood. I like this mood very much."

"So do I."

Her father and Nathan came through the door just before sunset.

"Ah, Nathan." She smiled at her brother. "So how was that? Did you get a deer?"

Nathan returned the smile and shrugged. "We only had the fowling piece."

Her father removed his tall black hat. "Ducks. Mallards. Our boy caught several on the wing. They are already cleaned and plucked and hanging in the smokehouse."

"On the wing! You have a sharp eye, Nathan."

"Hans." The father knelt and hugged his youngest son. "How is it with you?"

"Will I hunt soon, Papa?"

"Hunt? Nathan is twelve and you are only eight. Should we not wait a few years?"

"But other boys—"

"Other boys. Well, let us see how tall you are next year. If you are a good deal taller than you are now we may take you with us."

The boy brightened. "So if I drink lots of milk?"

"Sure. Lots of milk. That will do it." He got to his feet. "Where is your mother, Rose?"

"There is a quilting."

"A quilting, *ja*." He clapped both of his boys on the shoulder. "Go and play, you two. We'll call you when supper is ready."

"May I show Hans the ducks, Papa?" asked Nathan.

"Yes, go ahead, just be sure to close the smokehouse door when you are done." The boys ran out of the house and he turned to his daughter. "Your mother will be late. So I met Pastor Ulrich on the road. The women have stopped their quilting and are praying. In an hour the church will be gathering here. I agreed that would be good. Jakob Ammann has called for a night of prayer."

"What? A night of prayer? Why?"

"This trouble with the English has started up again. Two farmers were badly injured last week bringing in their barley crop. Another family claim their milk has gone bad in the pail just as it did during the summer. Someone else says they saw a cat turn into a crow and fly across the face of the moon."

"But this is nonsense, Papa. Superstition. And they are blaming us?"

"The Quakers, no, not so much. But others—" He put his hands in his pockets. "They point the finger at your friend Lydia."

"No. Not Adam Peachtree again."

"Master Peachtree has nothing to do with it. No one speaks of love charms or bewitching a man. They say she is after those who are not German or Swiss or Dutch and that she wishes to take revenge on Lancaster because of how she was treated by Sheriff What-God-Will."

"Oh, no. Has the sheriff come for her?"

"Not yet. That is why we pray tonight." He looked at her gloomily, his eyes black behind his dark beard. *"Es ist wie Europe alle immer wieder." It is like Europe all over again.*

The door flew open and Rose's mother rushed in. "I am sorry I am late. There is all this to-do about witchcraft. The women were praying."

The father nodded. "I was telling Rose. I met Pastor Ulrich on the way back from the hunt."

"The families will start to arrive by six-thirty. Let us wash up and eat and prepare the house for them." She went to the kitchen and put on her large apron. "Rose, how is the soup?"

"It is well."

"Call your brothers. There is fresh rye bread cooling on the sill here. And cheese in the cupboard." She set out pewter bowls and spoons and plates. "Grandfather calls for an all-night vigil so the children and infants will be here. Many will bring bedding. He will excuse those who rise early for the harvest even though most are finished with their crops. Some have the milking and the chores so they leave when they must as well."

Rose went to the smokehouse and brought her brothers back to the house. The Lantz family washed, prayed, and ate quickly. Rose and the boys cleaned the dishes and kettle and went to the barn to milk the dairy herd.

Her father tended to the horses and helped his wife set out candles and oil lamps in every room. As darkness settled in over the fields every window was golden with light. Rose had never seen so many candles and lanterns in any house at night.

"It's beautiful," she said. "I just wish it were for a better reason."

Her mother shook her head and clicked her tongue. "There is no better reason than prayer and worship."

Juerg was the first to arrive. Taking off his hat he smiled and nodded at everyone as he stepped through the door. "Christ's blessing on this home."

"And on those who enter," responded Mr. Lantz. *"Velkommen."*

Rose clasped the hand of the tall and slender young man with blond hair. "It's good to see your smile. I've missed you."

He shook his head. "Even tonight I cannot stay, my Rose. I have to finish with the oats before the frost. Father is not well, nor my brother Walter, so it makes things that much harder. But I wanted to come by and tell you I will be praying at the same time all of you are praying. And I wished to see you and tell you how much I love you. I am sorry for your friend."

"Thank you, Juerg. I don't understand why Lydia is being picked on by the English. But I am going to ask God to set everything right."

"I as well will pray that. I plan to see you after worship on Sunday. Will there be time for a ride in the wagon?"

"Of course."

"A long ride?"

She gave him her best smile. "Of course."

"God bless you and be with you." He slipped outside, hat still in his hands. "The leadership, they know I will be harvesting."

"Good. God bless you and be with you, my love."

She watched him walk swiftly to his horse, mount it, and ride into the night.

I feel like I hardly know you anymore. Where has the autumn gone?

She was still standing in the light of the doorway when the Beiler wagon drove up. Lydia sprang down and ran to her friend, crying as soon as Rose took her in her arms.

"I don't know what to do anymore, Rose, I don't know what to pray that I haven't prayed a hundred times."

"Shh. Come to my room. Let us have a few minutes before everyone arrives." She led her up the staircase to the second floor, arm around her waist, and brought her into the bedroom, closing the door tightly. "Here. Sit beside me on the bed." The creak of wagon wheels and the jingle of harness came through the open window. "Now. So." Rose held both of Lydia's hands. "You are not alone. Our whole church stands with you. God stands with you."

"God?"

"Of course God. He sides with the truth. And the truth is you are no witch working evil spells on the English."

Lydia hung her head. "Sometimes I wonder. Have I hated people? Cursed them without realizing it? Do I think bitter thoughts and do these thoughts turn into spells?"

"Oh, no, no, Lydia Beiler, do not let your mind take you to such places. You are one of the kindest souls I know. Even Adam Peachtree you never cursed and you had plenty of reasons to do so."

"How do you know what I do in the privacy of my room? How do you know what I say in my sleep?"

"I don't believe it. If that were true why hasn't Adam Peachtree been harmed? Why hasn't he been thrown from his horse and broken a leg or had a shelf full of cast iron kettles drop on his head at the store?"

"I don't know."

"You do know. You are upset by what he has accused you of but you have never wished any evil to befall him. Or the sheriff. Or anyone in Lancaster County, English or not. Remember who you are, Lydia Beiler. A child of God, blessed and redeemed by Jesus Christ our Lord. Don't let anyone take that away from you."

Lydia leaned her head against Rose's shoulder, tears making streaks down her face. "I don't understand. I don't understand why they are against me. I wish I did not have such black hair or such blue eyes."

"That's the way God has made you and you are beautiful, beautiful."

"If I could change my hair color—"

"Don't even consider it for a moment. You are perfect the way you are. It's other people who have to change, not you, and they have to change in their hearts." Rose kissed the top of her friend's head. "Now remember our covenant. It doesn't matter what anyone says or does, I shall remain faithful to you, I shall never turn my back on you or forsake you. Yes?"

"Yes."

"And you? How do you feel about me?"

"I—I feel the same way. I will never abandon our

friendship. I will never fail you. Through Jesus Christ our Lord."

Rose hugged her. "Amen. We will make it through the darkest night, sister."

There was a soft knocking on the door.

"Rose?" It was her mother's voice. "Are you in there? Is Lydia with you?"

"Yes, Mama."

"Jakob Ammann is here. We are ready to begin."

The house was full as the two young women came down the staircase. Some of the older children were running back and forth outside by the light of lanterns but most sat with their parents on chairs or couches or on the floor. Infants were already asleep in their mother's arms. Rose's mother and father were serving coffee and tea and Rose and Lydia went to help them. There were people in every room.

"I do not expect them to come after us with torches and pikes." Jakob Ammann stood up in the front parlor. His voice was strong enough to be heard in all of the rooms where people waited and listened. "This is still William Penn's Land, not Germany or Switzerland. Nevertheless man's heart is what it is regardless of where we dwell on this earth. So we appeal to the Lord our God for his protection and his abundant mercies. As the night wears on and you must sleep, then lay your head down and do so. If you must tend to chores, leave quietly and do so. But I hope many of you will still be awake and praying with me when the sun rises."

He began. People bowed their heads. The coffee pots and teapots were returned to the top of the stove to remain warm. Lydia and Rose sat on stools in the kitchen.

They could hear Jakob Ammann's words clearly. When he had finished Pastor Ulrich stood and carried on. After him it was Rose's father, Pastor Johannes. Then Pastor Philip. He was followed by all the men of the community who were there. At nine o'clock Jakob Ammann began to sing a hymn on his own while he sat in his chair. After several lines the entire house joined in. The hymn was slow and spoke of suffering for Christ and the honor this bestowed. When it was finished Jakob stood up again.

"We will have a short break to refresh ourselves. There is coffee, there is tea, there is milk. Good Mrs. Lantz tells me she has rye bread and butter for those who feel hunger. We shall begin our prayers again in ten minutes. God bless you all."

So the night went. Lydia put her head in Rose's lap and fell asleep at one o'clock. By two many were lying down with their eyes closed, a number with blankets pulled up around their chins. All the children were sleeping on the carpets on the floor with their pillows and quilts. More hymns were sung at three and four and the men prayed out loud in between. Pastor Ulrich wept as he called out to God to deliver their children from persecution. Lydia's own father prayed for more than half an hour just before Rose nodded off at four-thirty. Her mother gently shook her awake as dawn found its way in through the windows.

"Come." Her mother was whispering. "Help me cook the sausages and bacon. Then you must do the milking."

Rose rubbed her eyes. "Where is Lydia?"

"Jakob Ammann brought her forward so she could be prayed over in the midst of the congregation. So she is sitting in the parlor with him now." She put a finger to her lips. "Shh. They are just finishing the praying and then there is a final hymn."

Mother and daughter worked alongside several other women at the stove.

Soon the scent of fresh coffee and cooked meat and baking bread filled all the rooms.

Singing rose up and many who had been sleeping woke and joined in. Rose could hear Jakob's voice as he brought the prayer vigil to a close.

"All night we have cried to the Lord and sung hymns and spiritual songs to his praise. Now morning has broken and we give him the rest of our lives and those of our children and grandchildren. Do not be afraid for he is with us. So we will share in a simple meal together and carry on with the day. Some of you have not rested and you will need to rest once you have returned to your home. But rise no later than noon, complete the work the Lord has given you, prepare an early supper, and go to your beds when the birds go to theirs. And may Christ Jesus be with you."

"Amen," the people responded.

Rose laid out platters of bacon and fried eggs and then hurried to the barn, dragging a sleepy Hans and a grumpy Nathan with her. Lydia waited and helped clean the Lantz home and kitchen. Once the milking was done Rose walked with her friend along the road to the Beiler farmhouse as the sun climbed higher and warmed the cool morning.

"So on the Thursday you will come and we will work again on the quilt?" asked Rose as they made their way past the autumn fields and trees.

"Yes. Yes, I will."

"And you feel up to it?"

"Well, I am pretty tired right now, as all our people must be. On the other hand, the prayers have blessed and encouraged me. I feel God is warming my soul the same way his sun is warming the day. I will be there. We can rejoice in our friendship and in his love for us."

"Amen," Rose replied.

The week went by swiftly. The sheriff did not appear at the Beiler house and gossip about witchcraft seemed to drop off in Lancaster. When Lydia was driven to the Lantz home Thursday afternoon she alighted with a smile on her face and, as she told Rose, great hope in her heart.

"I feel I am shielded." Lydia threaded her needle as they sat in the rose garden. "That the Lord has put a wall around me."

"That is good. Still, remember what Grandfather told us on the night we prayed—*The Lord may well grant us peace for a season but we may also be tested further. Let these prayers fortify you as well as liberate you.*"

"Yes, I remember. The Bible is by my side at my house. I have taken to sleeping with it under my pillow. And there is always a prayer in my spirit and on the tip of my tongue."

Rose smiled, pulling the thread up and through the quilt. "That is so good to hear. It blesses me."

"Praise God." The needle flashed in Lydia's hand. "So tell me what mischief your brothers have been up to this week."

"Oh." Rose laughed and put a hand to her mouth. "Did I tell you what happened with the two of them and the fox and the smokehouse?"

"A fox? Your smokehouse? No, I know nothing of that."

The afternoon was hot and Rose's mother brought lemonade out to them as they stitched. At four-thirty the young women rolled up the quilt, placed it in the house, and began to walk to the Beiler homestead, white shawls over their heads, talking constantly, holding hands. Carts and wagons passed them coming and going. One stopped just ahead of them. It was filled with children.

"Hello, boys and girls!" Lydia called out as they approached. "How are you this happy day?"

Several of the children scowled. "Witch!" shouted one.

"Black-haired witch!" yelled another.

One boy threw a clump of mud that hit Lydia on the head. "Go away, you wicked woman!"

Lydia gasped and put her hands over her face.

Rose wrapped her arms around her and snapped at the children, "Shame on you! My friend loves God! She's no witch!"

She hurried Lydia past the wagon and looked up at the driver, a clean-shaven man. "Your children misbehave and you do nothing?"

"They do not misbehave," the man growled.

"Shame on you too, sir!"

Rose and Lydia walked quickly. A cart came alongside them that several young men were riding in. One leaned out and spat on the road.

"Why don't you two fly?" he taunted. "Isn't that faster? Or does your magic only work at night?"

"Don't speak like a fool!" Rose glared at him. "We are good Christians just as you are. We have no interest in witchcraft."

"You're not Christians!"

The young men jumped out of the cart. Two of them carried axe handles.

They blocked Rose and Lydia's path. Lydia's head was down but Rose stared at them defiantly.

"Let us by!" she demanded. "We have not done you any wrong!"

One of the men sneered. "Oh, you've done us wrong. Stillborn calves last spring. Milk curdled in the bucket. My little brother dying with a high fever as we stand here. You're trying to kill us all. But we'll kill you first."

Rose's face lost its blood. "Kill? What are you talking about? We haven't done anything to you or your brother!"

"Oh, yes you have—witch!"

He swung his axe handle at her head. She ducked and it struck her on the back. She cried out and staggered but kept her arms around Lydia. Another of the men stepped in and swung at her knees. There was a loud crack and white pain shot up through her legs. She fell, still trying to protect Lydia from the blows, covering her friend with her body.

"No broomsticks to get away on." The men gathered around Rose and Lydia as they lay in the dust. "No full moon to give you your powers. No devil out in the light of day. We have you where we want you."

"Please." Blood slipped from Rose's mouth. "We're Christians. We love God. We love God's people. We only wish to be left in peace."

"Oh, we'll grant you your wish all right. You're going to rest in peace, witch." Rose saw axe handles being lifted. "If there's any peace in hell. In the name of God, go to the devil!"

A shot cut through the air. One of the men yelped as his axe handle snapped in two and went flying from his hand.

"Put the other one down." Rose did not recognize the voice. Only that it was a man's. "I carry two rifles, as you can see. Put the other axe handle down."

Rose saw it drop into the dirt.

"Get back in your cart and leave," came the voice. "Leave now."

"These are witches."

"They're not witches. They're good Christian women. Go."

"Suppose we don't go? There are five of us and only one of you. Of course you have a gun."

Rose sat up, wincing, as a long barreled rifle was laid in the roadway. She saw the men tense as they faced the stranger. One yanked out a knife from his boot.

"Who is it we have the pleasure of addressing?" snarled the bearded man with the knife. "Who is it we have the pleasure of slicing up and giving to Satan?"

Rose looked at the tall man in deerskins whose long hair was pulled back behind his head and tied off with a leather strap. His eyes were as cold and hard and gray as any eyes she had ever seen in man or beast. They looked like iron. He braced himself for the attack and his hands were rock steady by his sides.

"My parents gave me the name Ethan Daniels," the man replied. "But it is the Indians who have given me my other name. I am called Long Hunter. And I am ready for you."

Volume 3

The First Frost

The men rushed Ethan Daniels in a group. Rose could not stop herself from crying out his name as they attacked, frightened of their faces and the flash of the long knife in the leader's fist.

"Ethan!"

He ran straight for them and seized the arm of the man with the knife, twisting it sharply so that the man yelped and dropped the weapon in the dust. Ethan kicked the blade away, picked the man up, and hurled him at two of the others. Then he whirled, snagged the hair of the other two men, and smacked their skulls together so that there was a loud snap of bone striking bone. Rose watched them drop like sacks of onions. Her mouth open she saw Ethan spin and face the ones behind him—the leader lay in the road, groaning and holding his arm, but the final two men had pulled their own knives and were about to lunge. Ethan jerked a tomahawk from the belt around his waist and sprang.

His arm was a blur in Rose's eyes. A red line of blood appeared on each man's wrist and they yelled in pain. Their knives were suddenly on the ground.

"No one moves that fast," whispered Rose to Lydia. "A stag in the forest does not move that fast."

Ethan shrieked a war whoop and the men ran away as fast as they could, eyes bulging. He let them go and stood over the leader who was still nursing his arm as he sat in the dirt. Tucking the hawk back in his belt he said, "Get in your wagon and leave."

"You broke my arm. I can't lift the other two in."

"It's not broken. But you'll need a few days before you can chop a cord of wood."

Ethan picked up the men sprawled in the dust, one after the other, and dropped them in the bed of the wagon. Then he helped the leader up into the seat and handed him the reins.

"Go home and put some ice on it," Ethan advised.

The bearded man sneered. "Home? I'm going straight into Lancaster and laying charges against you with the sheriff."

"That doesn't surprise me. When cowards can't get their way by violence they run to the law for help. Go ahead. Tell the sheriff one man bested five of you. Tell him how you assaulted two young women. See how people respond to that when the word spreads through Lancaster County."

"Witches!"

"The daughter of Mr. Beiler and the daughter of Pastor Lantz. Upstanding men in the community. Citizens held in honor and in the greatest esteem by those of their church and those outside their church. See how that broomstick flies when people find out you attacked these girls with axe handles and beat them to the ground. Perhaps you'd best move on to the neighboring county, friend."

The man growled out a curse and flicked the reins. His two horse team started forward. Ethan watched the wagon rattle along the track. Then he knelt quickly by Rose and Lydia.

"How is it with you two?" he asked, his voice suddenly soft.

"I am well," responded Lydia with a small smile. "I thank you."

"Miss Lantz? They hit you on the back and across the knees."

"I'm fine—fine." She did not know what to say. He was so close she could smell the scent of spruce resin on him along with that of earth and water and forest. "Thank you—thank you. We'll be on our way."

"You had best let me check your legs for broken bones. Will you lift your dress to your knees?"

Her face flamed. "I certainly will not, sir. My bones are perfectly fine."

A flicker of a smile came and went in his gray eyes. This irritated her further and she pushed her hands against the dirt and began to stand up. Pain roared through her legs and she cried out and collapsed. Ethan caught her before her head struck a rock. He lifted her up in his arms.

"Put me down, sir." Rose felt the heat burning her face. "I can walk."

"You can't, Miss Lantz. We must get you to your

father's house and Miss Beiler is not able to lift you onto my horse."

He carried her fifty yards down the road to where his dapple gray mount was nibbling clover in the ditch. She clenched her hands in her lap till they were white.

The heat in her face intensified. She took in the smell of rough soap from his skin and wood smoke from his tanned deerskin shirt and turned her head as far away from him as she could. A sudden urge to fold herself against his chest and let him take care of her made her furious. She closed her eyes and grit her teeth.

Oh, please, Lord, let it be over, let it be over.

With a jolt she was suddenly in the saddle. He put the reins in her hand. "Delaware is easy going unless there's a fight. But the fight's over so your ride will be peaceful enough."

"Thank you, Mr. Daniels. I think I know how to handle a horse."

Again a smile flitted across his eyes. "That's good to know. If he bolts while I get Miss Beiler I reckon you'll deal with it."

"Does he bolt often?"

"He doesn't cotton to wasps or anything with wings."

She gripped the reins tightly as a bee drifted near. Delaware lifted his head, snorted, and pricked his ears forward. The last thing Rose wanted was to have the stallion break into a run and throw her head over tail into the ditch. The indignity of it in front of Ethan Daniels mattered more to her than the thought of adding a broken arm to her leg injury. She tightened up on the reins even more and Delaware, annoyed, stamped his front hoof. Praying as hard as she had ever prayed in her life, Rose closed her eyes and thanked God in German when the bee headed for some daisies by a fence post.

"Why is your face like that? Are you in pain?"

Rose opened her eyes. Lydia was standing beside the horse. "How did you get here?" asked Rose.

"I walked with Ethan."

"*Ethan.* You act as if he is a personal friend."

"How should I act towards a man who in all probability saved my life and yours?"

"Don't exaggerate, Lydia Beiler."

"Exaggerate?" Lydia gave a jump and settled herself on the saddle behind Rose. There were no stirrups. "Did you see the look on those men's faces? They had already hit you twice and were going to strike you again. How do you think your body would have held up to a half dozen more blows from a pair of axe handles?"

Rose watched Ethan pick up his rifles with their long barrels and curly maple stocks. One he slung over his back and the other he held in his hand. Fascinated by the way he moved, so light on his feet yet with so much strength, she barely heard Lydia's next comment.

"Besides you used his Christian name yourself."

"What?"

"You called him by his first name."

Rose glanced quickly away as Ethan turned towards them and caught her eye. "I did not."

"Oh, yes, you did." Rose heard the smirk in her friend's voice. "You thought they were going to hurt him."

Rose remembered and the heat came into her face again. "There were five of them. It was a natural reaction."

"Why didn't you call out, *Mister Daniels*? Or just, *Watch out?*"

"I confess I don't know. It won't happen again."

"Is that true, Rose Lantz?"

"That's true, Lydia Beiler."

Ethan came up beside the horse. It nuzzled his arm. "Let's head towards the Lantz farm."

Delaware turned and followed him.

Lydia spoke up as they moved along the road. "Thank you again, Mr. Daniels."

"No man could do less, Miss Beiler."

"But to take on five others in order to protect us."

"I'm grateful they weren't Mohawk or Tuscarora. The fight might have had a different ending."

"Oh, no, you would have handled them too."

Ethan smiled. "You have a great faith in my abilities, Miss Beiler."

"I do, sir, I do. My parents will not know how to thank you enough."

"Well, bear in mind there may be others who are thinking along the same lines as those five men. I would advise you both to travel in the company of your brothers or fathers or the men of your church in the future. When farmers and townsfolk get riled like this there's no telling what mischief may occur. Large groups do not always bring out the best in our race."

Rose looked at him. "Do you mean that, sir?"

"I do."

"But what is wrong with church meetings? Or picnics?"

"If those men had been inviting us to pray or sing a hymn or tuck into a plate of venison and potatoes and greens, why, nothing, Miss Lantz. But that was not their intent." He looked up at her, his eyes a dark gray. "Nor will it be the intent of others. Do not walk alone till this tempest passes."

"Tempest? One attack by a gang of scoundrels hardly amounts to that, Mr. Daniels."

"There is more coming."

Ice pricked her spine. "How can you say that?"

"I hear it. I see it. They are looking for something to blame for bad crops, bad milk, and illnesses no medicines can cure."

"And you think they have settled on us."

"On Lydia, yes. And her friends as well if those friends stay true."

Rose sat more erect, though it made her wince as she straightened her legs. "No fear of that, Mr. Daniels. A whole mob from Lancaster could not persuade me to break off my friendship with Lydia."

The quick smile of his eyes, there and gone like a flash of wings. "If you had a tomahawk or firearm I might fear for the mob, not you."

Lydia burst out with a laugh but Rose glared.

"What is that supposed to mean?" she snapped. "Our faith in Jesus Christ is not a faith in violence."

"No. It is a faith in love—the love of God and love for one another. Your love is great. When a love is great it will go to great lengths."

"You think I would fight for Lydia like you just fought?"

"In your own way, yes. I believe you would lay down your life for her." The words startled both of the women.

"I, sir?" Rose responded.

"Yes."

"You don't even know me. How can you say so confidently what I will do or not do?"

"I've watched you for some time, Miss Lantz. I have a pretty good idea." Rose put a hand to her cheek as the blush came again.

Dear Lord, how is it he can keep doing this to me? I wish we were at my house but it is still another half mile. I swear I will die if this keeps up.

They walked in silence a few minutes. Rose finally leaned forward to pat Delaware's neck, the pressure on her legs making her flinch.

"I am surprised to find you here in October, Mr. Daniels," she said. "I thought you stayed out in the western mountains until first snow."

"Often I do."

"Why is this year different?"

He was quiet and did not answer her for several steps. "I needed to be here."

"For what?"

"For whatever is going to happen. Perhaps I can help. Perhaps not. But I will be close at hand. If either of you require my assistance just send a message. You know where my cabin is."

"I appreciate that, Mr. Daniels, but I think you take this far too seriously."

He shifted the weight of the rifle in his arms. "I do not do it only for you, Miss Lantz, or for you, Miss Beiler. I had family at Salem in 1692. An aunt who died long before my time. Long before my time and long before her time. She was accused of witchcraft. On the strength of the words of a few wild girls they killed her for that." He did not shorten his stride. "I'm here for her as well."

Rose felt the air leave her body. "I'm sorry. I'm so sorry."

"It was a long time ago. But perhaps not long enough. We are not yet free of that thinking." He glanced up at her, his eyes the iron color she had come to recognize. "I thought the law came with Moses, Miss Lantz, and that grace and truth came with the Messiah."

"Yes, that is so, Mr. Daniels."

"Then why do our colonies still live under the law of Moses rather than the grace of Christ?"

"I—I don't know." She surprised herself by smiling. "But I am glad you stayed here for us. I thank God for that."

"Well, I believe it was God who nudged me in your direction. I wasn't sorry to follow his leading."

"Even though it took you away from your mountains and woodlands?" Rose found herself teasing him, surprising herself still further. "You must have been a little bit sorry."

"Not to see your beauty and Lydia's. I have marveled at the splendor I have seen in the wilderness—the waterfalls, the hills, the rivers, the sunsets. But the beauty you and Lydia hold is better and rarer."

The blood was in her face once more. "Surely you just mean Lydia, sir. Her beauty is famous in Lancaster County."

He smiled at both of them. "It is a special beauty, that's true. Lydia is the most wonderful night with stars. But you have a great beauty too, Miss Lantz. You are like a fire in that night."

Rose struggled to reply, the heat running through her whole body now and not just her face. “You—you cannot mean that.”

“I do mean it. Has no man ever told you? Do you not have a fiancé?”

“Of course, but he is a moderate man, a man of few words and not given to—to excesses.”

For the first time Lydia and Rose heard Ethan Daniels laugh. He threw back his head. “As I am? Do you find me excessive?”

“I find you perfect,” Rose heard Lydia whisper.

“It doesn’t trouble me, Miss Lantz, to hear you say that. For I find that God is excessive. Every day on the frontier I see his excesses—the rich green of the leaves, the swiftness of the deer, the blaze of flowers no man is there to see. Isn’t all that far more than we need? I revel in his excesses. So you pay me a compliment.” He nodded with his head. “Here is your farmstead.”

Rose protested that she could dismount on her own. But her legs gave way when her foot touched the ground and Ethan caught her and carried her again. Lydia opened the door and when Rose’s mother came running from the kitchen she led the way to the bedroom, Lydia explaining what had happened on the way. The blushing continued for Rose as Ethan brought her into her room and laid her gently on her bed, making sure her head rested fully on her pillow. Soon her father and brothers were there and then the pastors and Jakob Ammann and neighbors with tense, tight faces and German words of blessing and concern. Several older ladies put blankets over her and probed her legs and knees with their fingers, muttering to themselves. Nothing was broken but her knees were swollen, it would be several days before she could walk again. An ointment that smelled like spearmint was rubbed into her legs as she grimaced. Jakob Ammann prayed. All the pastors prayed. Her father prayed.

Every time she looked for him she saw Ethan standing alone just inside the door while people swirled about him, leaning on the barrel of the rifle he had slung over his back.

Why, you're a rock in the middle of fast water.

"Rest, you should rest now." Her mother was tipping a cup against her lips. "A strong tea. Half a dozen herbs. Drink. It will relax you. Come, Father, you must ask our good people to leave the room. Our child must sleep and we must pray."

"Yes, my dear, we are gathering downstairs for the praying."

"Ask him to stay." Rose brought her head off the pillow. "Ask Mr. Daniels to stay with you, Mother. He saved us."

"I know he saved you, dear, Lydia has told us everything, I thank God, now lie back."

"Please ask him to stay."

"Of course I would ask him to stay but he is gone."

"Gone? Where? When? He was just by the door."

"I do not know when and I do not know where. I have been too busy with you. He is like a ghost. You do not even know he is there. He will come by and see how you are another day. Now you rest."

Rose lay looking at the door after her mother had shut it behind her.

Where did you go, Ethan? Why are you not here?

She looked up at the ceiling. *Oh, why should it matter? He is out running through the forest. Juerg will be here soon. He is my man. He is the one who must come to me and comfort me. He will be here in the morning. That is who I must wait for.*

That is who I must long for.

She shut her eyes. It was Ethan's face not Juerg's. *Lord, forgive me, forgive me.* She thought she might drift off but the pain in her knees sent stinging darts up and down her legs. *I am sorry to be so weak. I don't know why my mind is filled with his face and his eyes.* She looked at the red sunset in her window. *No man said I was beautiful before. Certainly not as beautiful as Lydia Beiler. No man.*

She did not sleep well that night or the next. The third day her mother rubbed a different ointment into her knees and legs. It made her skin tingle.

"What is that, Mama?"

"We are going to try it. He says it has hawthorn in it. Usually people drink hawthorn for the heart but he tells us it is good for sores and wounds as well. Of course yours is not an open wound."

"He says? Who says?"

"Shh. Do not get wrought up."

"I am not wrought up. Who gave you this ointment?"

"He did. Mr. Daniels. Long Hunter."

She propped herself up on her elbow. "He came by the house with it?"

"Yes. Hours ago."

"Did he—did he ask to see me?"

"He wanted to know how you were. Then he gave me this and left."

"On his horse?"

"On foot." Her mother clicked her tongue. "Why so many questions?"

"Has—has Juerg come by?"

"No, no, remember he is hunting all this week and the next. You will see him in November."

Rose lay back. "I wish I could see somebody."

"Lydia will be over this afternoon. She wonders if you are strong enough to work on the quilt with her here in your bedroom?"

Rose sat up, wincing and smiling at the same time. "Yes, yes, I would like that."

"Shh. Calm yourself. She will be here at two."

"Wonderful, oh, wonderful, someone to talk to."

"Good, but I hope you will pray with her."

"Why, of course, Mama, we always pray." She sat up further. "What is it? Has something else happened?"

"No, nothing like the afternoon on the road. But there is still the talk, the complaints about crops, you know, it is the way the English are. Pray with her, that will be good."

Lydia brought the quilt up from downstairs along with a large sack when she arrived. Rose saw that while her face smiled her eyes did not.

"Guten tag," Lydia greeted her, kissing her on the cheek. Their arms went about each other's necks. "You look so much better."

"*Danke.* What is this you have along with our quilt?"

Lydia spread the quilt over the bed while Rose dug through the sack. "Wonderful cloth from our neighbors."

"No. Not our neighbors. The English? Truly?"

"Some of the English. The Quakers." Lydia sat on the bed. "See how rich the reds are? How expensive the cloth? It is too much, really, but I could not turn away their graciousness. They feel so badly about what has happened and want to make it up to us. How are your knees?"

"The swelling has gone down. I'm going to try to get up and walk in a day or two." Rose pulled squares and rectangles of cotton cloth out of the bag, admiring them. "Our roses are going to look like the real thing. It was Mr. Daniels' hawthorn. I drank some of his hawthorn tea and Mama used the ointment on my legs."

A spark came into Lydia's eyes. "Ah. The good Mr. Daniels."

"What? It was just ointment."

"So I never saw you blush so much in my life as the other day." Lydia grinned and put a finger in her mouth. "You blushed for two hours."

Rose's cheeks reddened. "I did not."

"Sure you did. Every time he looked at you your face went the color of this Quaker cloth." She held up a burgundy square. "He comes to my house to speak with my parents and me just yesterday and ask after my health. But who does he really want to know about? Rose, Rose, Rose."

The heat was all through Rose's face and hands. "I'm sure that's not true."

"Oh, it's true. If you were not my best friend I would push you down a well. Since you are my best friend I will only be jealous and pull your hair." Lydia laughed and threw a handful of bright red cloths at her friend. "When he talks about you his eyes change color."

"Lydia Beiler, the nonsense you spout!"

"Look at how you blush. The gray eyes always lighten when your name comes up. They become soft like a robin's feathers, the feathers underneath the wings. He is quite a man, isn't he, Rose?"

Rose dropped her eyes and fiddled with the squares in her hands. "I freely admit I misjudged him. I have taken that sin to God."

"Yes? I am sure you have. And a few other things."

Rose looked up, startled. "What do you mean?"

"Clearly he cares for you."

"No, no, he only—"

"He tells you he has had his eye on you a long time. He returns early from the western frontier he loves because he is worried about you."

"He said he came back for both of us."

Lydia shook her head, lips curving into a rich smile. "I am used to getting compliments from men. Not our church men, of course, they are too modest. The Englishmen. So I hardly listen anymore. But no one has ever compared me to flames in the night."

"You are stars in the darkness, he called you that."

"Very sweet. I adored it. Until he said you were the fire in my night." Lydia's eyes danced light and dark. "I know a man's flattery when I hear it. And I know when he means it. Ethan Daniels does not say insincere things. He doesn't know how to do it. He is not a man of ballrooms and mansions and plantations. Ethan Daniels lives among oaks and stones and brooks and skies." She tugged on a strand of Rose's shining brown hair. "He meant what he said. You're the fire in his heart."

"I am not."

"You will have to choose between Juerg and Long Hunter."

"I will not."

"You will."

"Now, you two, no stitching done yet?" Mrs. Lantz bustled into the room with two wooden bowls into which wooden spoons had been planted. "I have a stew here. I hope you have some hunger." She stopped and started at her daughter. "My goodness, child, are you coming down with a fever now? Just when you were ready to get up?"

"I don't have a fever, Mother."

"No? Look at yourself in the mirror. You're burning up." She put a hand to Rose's cheek and forehead. "I don't understand. What brought this on?"

"I'm not sick, Mama. Truly, I feel fine."

"You're on fire and you feel fine?" Lydia began to giggle.

Mrs. Lantz swung her eyes onto Lydia. "So it's funny, Lydia Beiler?"

"Excuse me, *Frau Lantz*. I do not mean to laugh but—" She clamped fingers over her mouth and broke into a laugh.

Mrs. Lantz scowled, lines deepening around her eyes and in her cheeks. "Funny, funny. What is going on between the two of you?"

"Nothing, Mama. I'm perfectly fine. I'm just excited to see Lydia and all the Quaker cloth she has brought us. I am." She reached out with her hand. "What is that you have? More of your bean soup? I have had it all week but to show you I am healthy as a horse I will take another bowlful."

Her mother tilted up her nose. "What's wrong with my bean soup, hm?"

"Nothing is wrong with your soup. And to prove to you there is nothing wrong with me I will eat some more of it."

Mrs. Lantz sniffed. "It is not my soup."

"Well, what is it then?"

"Your Long Hunter was here again. Slipping in and out like a bird on the wing." She put a bowl in Rose's hand. "He made you a venison stew."

"What?"

"It is his special recipe, he said. So it will put you on your feet again." Her eyes narrowed. "There. Red splotches again. What has come over you?"

"I am—I am—"

Lydia spoke up. "Mrs. Lantz, was Mr. Daniels just here?"

Mrs. Lantz contemplated her daughter. "*Ja, ja.* In and out. Rifle in one hand, kettle of stew in the other. Steam still rising when he gave it to me." She sat down on a chair. "So. That's what it is. Not a flu. Not fever." Her hands were braced on her knees. "The Lord help us. A man. A man who is not one of our people."

"Mother—"

"I thought this blushing of yours had ended when you were twelve. It takes one wild man to bring it back."

"I—I had better eat." Rose spooned the stew into her mouth. "Oh. Hot." She moved it around swiftly in her mouth. "But good. Don't you think?" She looked at Lydia for help.

Lydia brought up a spoonful and blew on it twice. "It smells perfect."

Mrs. Lantz shook her head. "So I should have seen this coming. Juerg gone. A man different from any man you have ever known saves you from harm. Brings you tea and ointment. Roses and meat. He probably shot that deer just this morning for you and prepared it. I wouldn't be surprised."

Rose stopped eating. So did Lydia. "Roses, Mama? What roses?"

"As if you do not see roses enough every day. I have them in water in the kitchen. Do you want them?"

"Of course I want them."

"There is nothing special about them. Ours in the arbor have much more blossom to them."

"Please, Mother."

"Oh, ja, ja." She pushed herself to her feet. "You crazy girl. Your head is spinning and spinning." She moved her finger in a circle in the air. "Watch or one day it will spin right off."

"I can get those flowers for Rose, Mrs. Lantz."

"All right. That will save me a trip back up the stairs." At the door she looked at her daughter again. Lydia and Rose both saw the smile come and go over her lips. "I am bound to thank God for how Mr. Daniels protected you. I see how straight and tall he is. So be giddy for a season, if you must. Then marry Juerg and settle down. *Ja?*"

"Yes, Mama."

Lydia returned with a wooden urn spilling over with roses that made Rose's eyes widen with their brightness.

"Why, they almost look like gold." She took the urn in her hands and put her nose to the blossoms. "What breed are they?"

Lydia sat on the bed. "I don't know. They look to be a blend of peach and yellow. Truly beautiful. I suppose he is saying something to you with them."

"Hush, Lydia, my mother is worried enough."

"So if she wants you to marry Juerg she should be worried."

"It is only a kindness."

"Well, that is something new."

Rose looked up from the flowers. "What is? His kindness?"

"You have not blushed since I gave you the bouquet."

"Oh. Only because it is not a bouquet as you say. Just something for a sick person."

Lydia cocked a dark eyebrow. "Really?"

"Yes, that is all it is. Where do you suppose he picked them?"

"He tends a rose bush at his own cabin."

"No."

"My father has been to the cabin many times. He told me about the bush years ago."

"That is something for a man."

Lydia nodded. "Especially a real man like that."

"Like what?"

"Hunter. Woodsman. Frontiersman. Fighter. But also a cook and a gardener. Would you let such a man slip through your fingers?"

Rose had her nose in the blossoms again. "Don't talk so crazy. Why do you think my mother said the roses were poor? They are as full as any of our own."

"Why do you think?" Lydia's eyes slanted and darkened in mischief. "Oh, silly me, I forgot this." She handed a small slip of paper to Rose. "It was stuck on one of the thorns. I doubt your mother noticed it."

Consider the roses of the field, how they grow. They toil not, neither do they spin. And yet I say unto you, that even Solomon in all his glory was not arrayed like one of these. Wherefore, if God so clothe the grass of the field, which to day is, and to morrow is cast into the oven, shall he not much more clothe you?

"He struck out the word lilies and put in roses, hm?" Lydia played with a strand of her friend's shining hair again. "So it's not a bouquet?"

Rose's cheeks had grown pink. "It's just a verse from the Bible."

"Yes. A verse from the Bible with one little word changed." Rose put the urn on the table beside her bed. "We should quilt."

"*Ja*, we can quilt but you will still dream about him."

"Be quiet, Lydia Beiler, I am not going to dream about anyone." She picked up a rectangle of maroon cloth. "I am going to use this for some of the rose petals."

"That's fine with me." She laughed to herself as she threaded a needle. "I had some fear when I came this afternoon. You know, from the English talk. But an hour with you and Ethan has cured it."

"*Me and Ethan*. How you go on."

"Well, it is not *me* and Ethan, my dear." Lydia began to stitch the stem of a rose.

"It should be." Rose put the end of a thread in her mouth. "You are so beautiful. Dazzling blue eyes and gleaming black hair. Just like a brook running under the shadows of the leaves."

"Thank you. That's very nice. Now if I could only get Ethan to say that to me." Rose cut her maroon cloth with a pair of scissors. "I am sure he is dying to."

"Ha. If he is dying to he must have died already because he's had a dozen chances to say it."

"A man needs the right moment."

Lydia laughed and shook her head as she sewed. "A jar of hawthorn ointment and a bowl of stew and suddenly you are an expert on the ways of men? How did this happen?"

"I am not an expert. I just see he chooses his time. Tomorrow there may be a gift waiting for you."

"No, Rose Lantz, you are very sweet, but the next gift will be for you as well. And the one after that." She lifted her eyes and winked. "Perhaps he has a brother just as cute? Back in the Virginia colony?"

"You will have to ask him, won't you?"

"Perhaps I will. For you, everything is sewn up."

"Oh, sewn up. Yes, if you mean I am going to marry Juerg and be a farmer's wife."

"Hm. We'll see, won't we?"

The next morning when Rose woke up there was a staff carved out of wood resting against the side of her table. The smell of the oak tree it came from was still fresh. She gripped it and pushed herself out of bed. Her knees sagged but the staff kept her up. There was a bit of pain in her legs but not very much. She thumped to the closet, put on a white flannel gown, and opened the door. Her father was halfway up the staircase.

"I heard the noise," he said. "Are you all right?"

"I am using this staff to help me walk. Did you make it for me, Papa? It is just like something you would do."

He smiled and nodded. "So I would. But someone else beat me to it."

Her cheeks grew warm instantly. "Who was that?"

"Who do you think? Your cook and medicine man."

"When?"

"At four. I had just gotten up to get ready for the milking."

"Oh, Papa. I can do that now, I'm much better now."

"Well, we'll see, we'll see. Can you make it down the stairs without any help?"

Clutching the staff she came towards him step by step. Each time the staff struck wood there was a bang. "I'm sorry for the noise, Father."

He smiled. "That is nothing. Everyone is up. No, it's nothing. Make all the noise you like. It's wonderful to see you on your feet again."

Her mother came to the bottom of the stairs, wiping her hands on her apron. "Be careful, my dear. How are you feeling?"

"Much better, Mama. My legs are only a little sore."

"I praise the Lord. Still, do not try to conquer the world all at once. Will you have some oatmeal for breakfast?"

"*Ja*, I'd love some."

When she reached her father he hugged her. "Good girl, good girl." He whispered in her ear. "Do not go anywhere unless I am with you. No more of you waking alone or walking with Lydia. No riding alone. Do you understand?"

"Of course, Papa. But I don't think anything like what those men did will happen again."

"You don't know. If there were only Quakers and followers of Jakob Ammann in Pennsylvania it would be fine. But people still wag their tongues. The English are restless. Nothing is good when the English are restless."

"All right, Papa."

After she ate her mother chased her out of the kitchen and she thumped her way into the farmyard. Sunlight ran hard and bright over the barn and geese and wagons. Eventually she found herself staring in the direction of the open fields and oak trees and covered bridge. She was well aware there was a small cabin in the woods just past the bridge.

A few weeks ago I ran because he was wielding his axe and chopping firewood. God forgive me, now I wish I could go back to that moment and walk into his yard and ask him for his help in locating wild mint.

"How goes it with you?"

She turned so quickly she almost stumbled. He reached out a hand to steady her.

"Easy. I did not mean to startle you. I am so used to treading silently in the forest I do not know how to walk noisily among farmers and townsfolk anymore."

"Mr. Daniels." Rose's mind was whirling as he stood there in his deerskins with his long hair tied back and a long barreled rifle cradled in his arms. "I want to thank you—I want to thank you for your gifts to me. All the gifts. You have been most kind."

The smile was in his eyes. "I was happy to bring the gifts, Miss Lantz. It's good to see you up on your feet. And there is nice color to your face."

"Oh." She put her free hand to her cheek. "I feel much better. A combination of prayer and rest." She realized his eyes *were* a softer gray as he looked at her, just as Lydia had told her. "And hawthorn. And venison. And roses." The heat was all over her but she managed a small smile. "Thank you, sir." She remembered the oak staff she was clinging to. "And this. I would not be able to move around our farm without it."

"It came to mind last night. I should have thought of it sooner."

"No, no. I wouldn't have been able to use it until today. You were right on time, Mr. Daniels."

"I'm glad to hear it. What will you do with your day?"

"Lydia will come over this afternoon. We'll quilt in the rose garden. This evening I hope to get back to milking our dairy herd. And there is laundry to do."

He glanced up at a sharp blue sky. "There will be frost tonight. A harsh one with the full moon. This may be the last time you see your summer roses unblemished."

"I—I did not know you kept your own rose garden."

"Hardly a garden. A very large bush. But it did well this year. Likely because I was home earlier than usual and could prune it." The smile in the eyes. "Thanks to you."

She dropped her eyes. "And Lydia. You wish to protect us both, yes?"

"I do."

"The roses you gave me were, well, they were a great blessing. And the Bible verse as well."

"Good. I must go." He reached out a hand and squeezed her shoulder gently. "Don't stray far."

She watched him move off into the meadows and oak trees she had been gazing at, vanishing in the shadows.

Her shoulder tingled where he had touched her as if someone had rubbed hawthorn into her skin.

Lord, I'm sorry, I don't know what to do. Of course I realize I am betrothed to Juerg, of course I realize we are meant to marry and raise crops and have a family. But it's very difficult to turn my back on Ethan. He is so kind and gentle and strong. I feel safe with him. I feel more beautiful than I am.

She and Lydia laughed and teased their way through the quilting session in the rose garden that afternoon. In the evening she milked along with her brothers and was able to move from stall to stall easily with the help of the staff. Alone in the dark of her room she thought about Ethan.

He picks me up with one arm and holds me close to his chest. I take in the scent of the forest and the wood smoke that is on his deer hide shirt and on his skin. His lips brush mine.

"Oh, stop it, Rose Lantz!" she said out loud.

She rolled over on her stomach. Her knees ached. After a few minutes she flipped on her back. Then she went to her stomach again.

Go away. Go away.

But when images of him faded she whispered, "Don't go, Ethan. Come back to me."

Finally she prayed. *God, I don't know what to do about this. I can't get Ethan out of my mind. I should be thinking about Juerg but I can't. I should be praying for Lydia's safety but it seems I can only do that for a few minutes before I dream about Ethan again. I'm sorry. Perhaps I should talk to Grandfather.*

She got up at four, exhausted, saw the dark rings

under her eyes in the mirror, and went as quietly as possible down the staircase with her staff in her hand.

What would you think of my beauty now, Ethan? I look like a wagon wreck.

The early morning was silver. Frost was on the barn roof, on the fence posts, and on the shrubs by the door—the veins of every leaf were etched clearly. When she finished milking she made her way to the rose arbors. Tiny spikes of ice were on each blossom, white on red and white on white. She sat at the quilting table as sun cut the haze open and turned silver to bronze and bronze to brilliant yellow. The spikes of frost became round beads of water she could see her eyes in. It looked to her as if the dark rings were gone and her eyes were changing color from a meadow green to an earth brown to a sun rising in the sky. She closed her eyes as sunlight flashed over the arbors and thanked God for everything around her. She asked for peace and she asked for strength. When she opened her eyes again she saw that dozens of roses overhead had brown edges to their petals and that many of them had begun to curl inwards.

Now I am starting to see things like Ethan and use words like Ethan.

"We are grateful for this day and for our family and the harvest. Give our bodies strength with this food and, yes, our souls also. In Jesus Christ our Lord. Amen."

"Amen," echoed Rose and her brothers and mother. Her father opened the black Bible by his plate.

But we have this treasure in earthen vessels, that the excellency of the power may be of God, and not of us. We are troubled on every side, yet not distressed; we are perplexed, but not in despair; persecuted, but not forsaken; cast down, but not destroyed; always bearing about in the body the dying of the Lord Jesus, that the life also of Jesus might be made manifest in our body. For we which live are always delivered unto death for Jesus' sake, that the life also of Jesus might be made manifest in our mortal flesh. So then death worketh in us, but life in you.

"From the Word of God, Second Corinthians, chapter four and verses seven to twelve. Amen."

"Amen," Rose and the family responded again.

The plan was for Lydia to arrive earlier that day so the two friends could quilt through the morning, share lunch with Rose's family, then continue on in the afternoon until it was time for the milking. Lydia's father dropped her off, spoke about half an hour with Rose's father and mother, then drove away. Wearing thick sweaters along with their woolen shawls the young women sat down at their table in the arbor, blew on their fingers, and began to stitch.

"I see many of the roses have died," said Lydia. "I am sorry for that."

"Mama picked some of the best ones yesterday and has them in vases in all of the rooms of the house. Hopefully some of them will still be alive once we have to move indoors."

"When will we do that?"

"I don't know. A week? Two weeks?"

"The front parlor?"

"Ja, ich denke so."

"That's my favorite room. It feels like I'm in another country every time I sit in there."

"That's because Mama has filled it with Swiss

things. It reminds you of when we were children. Papa is supposed to fix the clock this winter."

"The cuckoo? Really?"

"Yes." Rose stopped sewing and smiled like a little girl as she glanced across the table at her friend. "The goatherd comes out, remember? The bird is on his shoulder."

"But at noon all the goats come out behind him. And at midnight he arrives with a lantern that glows and a baby goat in his arms, a kid."

"So my father has a lot of work to do. He thinks it is just a matter of replacing a few springs but he's not sure."

Lydia struggled with a stitch. "Sometimes I think of Switzerland and I wish we had never left. Then I remember why we left and I thank God we are in the American colonies. So but now I feel the fear I felt in Europe."

Rose put down her needle. "I am so sorry. Of course this is like a north wind that goes right through your coat and sweater. Let me pray for you."

"All right."

"Give me your hand."

They held hands across the quilt and bowed their heads. Rose prayed in High German for protection for Lydia and for a strong resolve to stand by what she believed and who God had made her to be.

"You must understand how beautiful you are without and within," Rose said to her, still holding Lydia's hand. "Your eyes and hair do not make you a witch any more than your faith in the Lord Jesus Christ does. God gave you those eyes and that hair. They are a blessing. Do not let cruel people twist you out of shape."

Lydia squeezed Rose's hand and released it. "*Danke.* Coming here is so good for me."

"And for me."

"The Lord delivers us from all the afflictions of the righteous."

"Amen." Rose picked up her needle again. "And he has many ways and means of doing so."

Lydia glanced up as she rummaged through the bag of Quaker cloths. "Oh?"

"Of course. I am not saying anything new."

"You've seen Long Hunter, haven't you?"

Rose's cheeks colored. "What makes you say that?"

"Well, your face now. But the way you spoke your words a moment ago."

"It's true, God does have many ways of blessing and defending his people."

"When did you see him? Our defender from God?"

Rose stitched rapidly and would not lift her head. "He was here this morning. Very briefly. He mentioned protecting us"

"He mentioned protecting *you.*"

"No, Lydia, both of us, not one or the other."

"Did he bear you any more gifts?"

"No, he did not."

Lydia laid three cloths of different shades of red side by side on the quilt. "What do you think?" She picked up a square that was very dark. "Are you going to tell Juerg once he returns?"

Rose bit her lip. "Tell him what?"

"That you are falling in love with another man?"

Rose's face was instantly scarlet as she jerked her head up. "I am not. I am not."

"How much do you think about Ethan Daniels? And how much do you think about Juerg?"

"No, it's just that Ethan—Mr. Daniels—is a new friend in my life—and there was the fight on the road when he came to our defense—and the hawthorn ointment—so naturally he has come to mind—but I am not falling in love with him, not at all, I am not—"

"Have you dreamed about kissing him?"

Rose threw several rectangles of crimson cloth at Lydia. "Stop it. Talk to me about what you read in the Bible this morning."

"Yes, I will, but only after you answer my question. And remember to lie is a sin, especially between friends."

"Lydia Beiler, you can be the most irritating person."

"Have you dreamed that dream?"

Rose bent her head and thrust her needle into the quilt.

Lydia nodded. "You have, haven't you? Do you think such a thought makes you less of a Christian?"

"I am betrothed to Juerg!"

"But not married. And betrothals can be broken. In peace and in grace."

"I am not going to break anything."

"Is it fair to Juerg not to tell him about Ethan?"

Rose let out her air in a rush, threw her head back, and rolled her eyes. "All right, Lydia of the Book of Acts, the dyer of purple cloth and lover of God, tell me what to do."

"You think Juerg is God's man for you but that is

because you never allowed our Lord to speak to you about Ethan. You despised Ethan and treated him with contempt. It took you almost getting killed to open your eyes. But now you see him. There is Juerg standing next to Ethan now. Finally you can pray and make a proper choice. Which man will you wed?"

"This is the most ridiculous idea you've ever had. Who is talking about marrying Ethan Daniels? He hasn't even proposed to me. And he is not even one of us or a member of our church."

"And if he was?"

"*If. If.* What does my mother say? *A small word with a big meaning.* So even *if* all these things happened I still don't know what I'd do."

"Not at all?"

"No. Certainly not."

"Close your eyes."

"Why?"

"Close them."

Rose rolled her eyes again, folded her hands in her lap, and bowed her head. "Fine. They're closed."

"I'm going to say three words. Tell me the first thing that pops into your head when I say each one."

"Lydia, this is silly. We have work to do."

"Three words. It will take only three seconds. Do it for me."

Rose twisted up one side of her face. "Very well."

"So you're ready?"

"Ja, ja, ich bin bereit."

"Man," said Lydia.

"Man?" Rose responded.

"Ja, Mann."

Rose was silent.

Lydia spoke softly. "Marriage."

"Lydia!" Rose protested, "This is an utter waste of time!"

Lydia spoke the third word. "Love."

Tears jumped onto Rose's cheeks. "I cannot. I cannot." She balled her hands into fists. "God forgive me."

Lydia got up and came around the table. "It's all right." She knelt and took her friend in her arms. Rose cried into her shoulder. "Really. It's all right."

"It's not all right!"

"It is. You must know God's will for you in Christ Jesus. Even if it is difficult for you or others to accept. You must find out God's will. Not Grandfather's. Or your mother's. His will." She kissed the top of Rose's head and her shawl. "What is in your heart?"

"The heart is deceitful above all things and desperately wicked."

"What has the Lord put in your heart?"

"I don't know."

"When you pray, when you read his Word?"

"A woman can be infatuated. That does not mean it's the work of the Lord God of hosts."

"What is the pure desire of your heart?"

Rose cried harder. Lydia tightened her arms and rocked her.

"Oh, it's too much, it's too much," Rose managed to get out. "How do I know how Ethan feels about me? What about Juerg? What will my parents think? And our church people—what will they say? It's impossible. I can't, Lydia."

"A home together. His arms around you. His prayers

in your ears. His strength when you're weak. His love. Every day. All your life."

Rose started to laugh. "Oh, shut up." She hugged Lydia back. "You say the craziest things. *His arms. His prayers. His strength. His love.*" Tears were still making their way over her face. "You should be a preacher."

"There are no woman preachers."

"Well, when there are you get to go to the head of the line." She kissed Lydia on the cheek. "Really, you are crazy. The things you say. I'll bet you think about him, too."

"I do. But he's the one who's thinking about you, my dear."

"You can't say that."

"Food? A walking stick? Roses?"

"He's just a nice person."

"Rose!" Lydia tilted up her friend's chin with her fingers. "If he had given those gifts to me what would you be telling me right now?"

"Well, I don't know."

"You do know."

Rose leaned her head into her friend's shoulder. "My world is inside out. Thank goodness God gave me you."

Lydia smiled and patted her back. "So I feel the same way." Suddenly there were loud voices from the house.

"This is still my home! You can't go marching through it as if you own it!"

"And I am still the law, madam! The law goes where it wills and where God wills!"

Footsteps approached through the garden. Rose felt her friend tense and she took her hand. They both got quickly to their feet. The sheriff broke in upon them with a silver-topped cane in his hand. Two men in Quaker black with white tabs at their throat were with him. Behind them, her hair unraveling and her face an angry red, came Rose's mother.

"Lydia Beiler!" snapped the sheriff.

Lydia straightened her back. "Yes."

"Adam Peachtree is dead, killed in a fall from his horse this morning. Last night witnesses say they saw thee fly across the face of the full moon. Other witnesses say thou held forth in the forest and did burn a Bible and call upon Satan to strike down thy enemies and wreak havoc in Lancaster County."

"No!" exclaimed Lydia, the blood rushing from her face. "I did none of these things!"

"What else would a witch say?" The sheriff lifted his cane and pointed it at Lydia, touching her face with its silver top. "I arrest thee in the name of the king. I arrest thee in the name of God. For murder I arrest thee. For consorting with the Devil I arrest thee. For witchcraft I arrest thee." Chains rattled in the hands of his assistants. He nodded, his eyes like slits. "Bind her hand and foot. If any stand between her and her jail cell, bind them too. We'll put all hell behind bars if we must. This very day Lydia Beiler's wickedness shall be put to an end."

Volume 4

A Rose Among Thorns

A bearded face glowered at Rose and her father as it squinted through a barred window in the jailhouse door. "What is it thou want?"

"We have come to see Lydia Beiler," Rose's father responded.

Rose could see it was the sheriff when afternoon sunlight fell on his eyes and cheeks.

"All right," the man grumbled. "Come in if thou must." The thick oak door swung open with a moan.

Rose hugged the quilt to her body, white shawl over her head, as she followed her father into the Lancaster jailhouse. She had no intention of letting the sheriff or any of his constables take it from her. Jakob Ammann, her father, and the other pastors had visited the magistrate and obtained permission for Lydia to be visited regularly and frequently but that did not mean Sheriff What-God-Will would look favorably on her bringing needle and thread into his jail.

"She is here," growled the sheriff, leading them down a short corridor, Rose limping as she moved along without her staff. "Well away from prisoners so that she may not bewitch them."

Rose's father made a face and spoke up. "Are we no longer under the law of King George II then?"

The sheriff, towering over the pastor, gave him an angry look. "Pray, sir, whose law should we be under but his and God's?"

"I am glad to hear it. Under such law a person's guilt must be proven. Have you proven Lydia Beiler's guilt, sheriff?"

"To my satisfaction."

"To yours. What about your oath to the king? Have you presented the evidence and the argument he desires?"

The sheriff shot him a dark look.

"She is here," he rumbled. "In the last cell. Thou have an hour."

Lydia sat on the edge of a small cot. When she saw Rose her face broke into a smile and she jumped to her feet.

"I am not staying, sheriff," Rose's father said. "I leave my daughter in your hands in good faith. I shall return from my errands at three."

"She takes her life in her own hands once she enters the cell," the sheriff retorted.

"But she is always in the Lord's hands, do you not think? She will be safe."

The sheriff glared. "As thou say so may it be."

"Rose!" Lydia was at the bars. "I did not think you would come!"

Rose immediately folded one of her hands over her friend's as it curled around an iron bar. "How could I not come? You are my friend and my sister in the Lord Jesus Christ."

"But this is a jail. And an ugly and dank one at that."

"I don't care. We made a covenant together. I am in this place because of my love for you and because of Christ's love for us both."

Rose's father smiled. "How is it with you, Lydia Beiler?"

"I slept poorly. With more prayer and Scripture reading I hope to have a better day and a better night, thank you."

"I shall pray with you," said Rose. "And I will read the Holy Bible with you as well."

"Did you bring a Bible?" asked Lydia.

"Why, no. Do you not have one here?"

"The sheriff will not permit it."

Rose's father looked at Sheriff What-God-Will. "I don't understand. You are a Christian man."

The sheriff tilted up his chin. "We will not have a witch despoil the Word of God or use it in her foul enchantments once our backs are turned."

"Do you object to a person reading the Bible to Miss Beiler?"

"I do not. But the Bible cannot stay in the cell."

"May my daughter have the loan of your jailhouse Bible for the hour?"

"It is in use."

"Father." Rose put a hand on her father's arm. "We have so little time. Let me begin my visit while you tend to your errands. There is much of the Holy Bible I have memorized. Hasn't Grandfather Ammann encouraged us to do this? And I have taken him at his word. We will be fine. Tomorrow I will bring my own Bible with me on my visit."

Her father nodded. "*Das ist gute.* I will be back at three."

The sheriff unlocked the cell with a key from a large ring. "Step back." Lydia moved to her cot. The sheriff narrowed his eyes at the quilt in Rose's arms. "What is this?"

"Why, a quilt as you can see, sir. We are sewing it together."

"How many needles have thee?"

"Three or four."

"Show me."

Rose brought four needles out of the pocket in her dress.

"Thou will show them to me when thou leave," the sheriff warned. "If I find any needles on the prisoner's person or in her cell after thou have gone I will hold thee responsible. I shall go to the magistrate and thou will be barred from further visits."

"I understand."

"And if thou take the quilt into her cell thou must leave it there."

"Why?"

"She may place a spell upon it. Thou will not take it forth from here. It remains with her until she is hanged. Or set free. If set free she may take it with her when she leaves this place. If hanged it will be set on fire in order to completely destroy its enchantments."

Rose's father had not yet left. "I can take it with me, daughter."

Her green eyes had gone dark. "That will not be necessary, Father. The Lord will use it to warm Lydia at night. If she slept badly last night tonight she will sleep like an angel with it wrapped around her."

"An angel!" spat the sheriff.

Rose's eyes ignited. "Yes, an angel! This quilt is covered in prayer and the Word of God and cloth sewn in love and Christian charity. Some of the cotton used comes from Quaker hands and Quaker homes."

The sheriff ground his teeth and his jaw moved back and forth. "Thou have fifty minutes left. No more."

Rose stepped into the cell with the quilt. "I thank God." The sheriff slammed the cell door shut and locked it.

"I will see you soon, child." Her father smiled. "God bless you and Miss Beiler."

"Danke, Papa."

He and the sheriff moved off and down the corridor, their boots making a snapping sound on the rough wooden floorboards.

Lydia threw her arms around Rose's neck and began to sob. "Why, why is this happening? They blame me for Adam's death. I did not like him but I never wished his death."

Rose pulled the quilt over her friend's shoulders and held her close. "It is as Grandfather says. Yes, and other wise men before him. When people's hearts are not filled with God they will be filled with whatever ill thoughts come their way."

"They point the finger at me because of my hair and eyes!"

"Your God-given hair and eyes. The women are jealous because they do not have your beauty in their own faces. The men are envious because they cannot take your beauty in their arms and call you wife. So both point the boney finger."

Lydia giggled as the tears continued to come. "The boney finger?"

"The long crooked boney finger."

"I am supposed to have one of those, aren't I?"

"Well, you don't. You are a child of God and your finger is long and smooth and straight. And holy. Because God dwells within you through your faith in Jesus Christ our Lord."

"Last night Grandfather and Grandmother came to visit—yes, isn't it surprising? She got out of the house and came with him. Pastor Philip drove them here. And Mother and Father came also. They did not enter the cell but sat outside on stools for a half hour and each read the Bible to me, passages they felt the Lord had put on their hearts, and they prayed as well, our fingers touching through the bars."

"How beautiful."

"Grandfather reminded me that our people had been persecuted in Europe and that I should make the Lord's Word my bread and meat, sing hymns, offer up prayers like incense, and call for the true Judge to deliver me out of the hands of wicked men." She laughed. "I suppose I got so caught up in doing all of that I could not rest when I put my head to the pillow. My mind spun round and round with prayers and accusations. Every time an accusation popped into my thoughts I prayed it away. Once I had finished another accusation would come so another prayer was required. This is the way it went until dawn."

Rose kissed her cheek. "Let us ask our God for a deeper rest tonight. *He grants sleep to those he loves.* And how he loves you, Lydia Beiler."

"Do you know that?"

"His own Word tells us. *Beloved, let us love one another. For love is of God and everyone who loves is born of God and knows God. He who loves not knows not God for God is love.* And this also—*We love because he first loved us.*"

"Ah, danke schon."

"But there is more."

"So does Rose Lantz have the whole Bible memorized?"

"Not that. I meant this." Rose tugged the quilt further around her friend's shoulders. "He gives you our rose quilt for peace and comfort. Remember how Paul asked Timothy to come before winter? And bring Paul's books and parchments? And his robe?"

"No."

"So it is in the final chapter of Second Timothy. This—" She tugged on the quilt again. "This is your robe. And I have come well before winter. So you will be blessed as Paul was blessed."

"Thank you." She clasped the quilt to her throat. Her tears dry, she smiled. "I feel like a queen."

Rose admired Lydia's beauty—the dark shine of her hair, the sky blue eyes, the crimson color in her cheeks from the crying. "You are a queen. God's queen. Queen Esther."

"You shouldn't have brought our quilt into the cell. Now what will become of it?"

"What will become of it? It will warm you and help you sleep. Even in the daytime it can be Paul's robe about your shoulders. We will add more stitches each time we meet. Little time will be lost. Remember Tabitha? In Joppa? How she made robes and clothing for the believers there? So you and I will be Tabitha."

"She died."

"Peter prayed and God raised her from the dead."

Lydia let the quilt fall to the floor. "I'm afraid."

Rose hugged her as tightly as she could. "I know you are. But you are not alone. It is not just those of us who follow Jakob Ammann who are praying for you. The Quakers are. I know they are."

"Sheriff What-God-Will isn't."

"Oh, he is a sour man who has never had a wife or child to sweeten his heart. We are going to pray for him right now before we do anything else. Then we will quilt while we still have time. And encourage one another's hearts."

"How can I, who am a prisoner and weak, encourage you?"

Rose cocked her head. "Why, by the blessing of your smile, Lydia Beiler, how else?"

The smile came.

"You do not ask much," said Lydia.

"Of you? No. But of the Lord I will ask a great deal. Not only your freedom but a healing of the hearts arrayed against you. Especially a healing of the sheriff's soul and the souls of Adam's parents who are grieving today."

"So we pray for our enemies."

"If you wish to call them that. We pray for much love and because of that much love will pour into us and out of us from the Lord. This will give you considerable peace. *For perfect love casts out fear.* There will be so much of God's good cheer in you the fear that gnaws on you will have to go find a boney finger to gnaw on far from your jail cell."

Lydia threw back her head of gleaming black hair and laughed. "Oh, praise the Lord for that."

They began by holding hands and praying for the sheriff as Rose had said they would. Then they went on to pray for the town, the county, and their own people. Finally Rose prayed for Lydia for several minutes. After that they sat on the floor and worked on the quilt, talking and quoting Scripture and laughing as they plunged their needles into the cloth. Sheriff What-God-Will came at three o'clock and ordered Rose out. She hugged Lydia, left the cell with the rose quilt spread on the floorboards, the sheriff asked to see the needles, the cell was locked, and Rose was escorted to the door and practically pushed outside just as her father drove up.

"How was that?" he asked.

"The Lord blessed our hour together, Papa." She tugged her shawl tightly around her head and climbed into the wagon, wincing as she bent her knees. "But the breeze is surely as cold as Haman's heart. Or Sheriff What-God-Will's."

"Rose. *Let your speech always be with grace and seasoned with salt.*"

He clicked his tongue and the two horse team started forward.

"Well, we prayed for him, Father, which I doubt he does for us, and I will continue to pray until his attitude improves, at which point mine will likely improve as well. Forgive me."

"Hmm."

"Imagine not giving her a Bible."

"*Ja.* It reminds me of Switzerland."

Rose grew quiet as they moved through the traffic of carts and wagons and horses. The hard-edged sunlight made her draw more of the shawl around her shoulders. For weeks she had pushed back memories and suddenly her father's words unleashed them all. The army dragging their neighbors from their home and boarding it up. Both parents thrown into a lake and drowned because of the Mennonite practice of re-baptizing adults. An older man from their community tortured with hot pokers and molten drops of lead and being released so others could see his wounds and turn back to the state church. A woman singing a hymn, finally screaming it, as she was burned at the stake in the town square. Hearing the cries and smelling the burnt skin long after her mother had shut her window and drawn the curtains in her bedroom.

I swore then I could see the flames on my ceiling. Now my mind tells me I stood there in my bare feet and nightgown, a doll clutched in one fist, and watched the fire catch in her hair and explode with a bright light.

Rose leaned forward and pressed a hand to her eyes.

"My girl, what is it, what's wrong?" asked her father.

"I—I feel sick to my stomach—"

"I hope you are not chilled. The jail was like an ice-box. I thank God he made you leave the quilt with her. We must get you home."

"I thank God for that too. But it is not the cold of the day that has affected me, Father. It is the coldness of the human heart."

"Do you mean the sheriff?"

"My memories of the persecuted and the tortured have come back to me. From before we crossed over to the British colonies."

"I am sorry, so sorry for that, my dear. Prayer and hot soup will help. You must always remind yourself we are far away from all that."

"Are we? Look at what is happening to Lydia."

"It will be over in no time. The magistrate told us the trial would take place in a week, less than a week now. Once that is over and done and Lydia is free this nonsense will blow over."

"It did not blow over in the Massachusetts colony."

"That was forty years ago. The magistrate questioned Lydia with the sheriff and constables present and felt there must be a trial but mostly to clear the air and prevent a mob from forming over this witchcraft matter."

"What if Lydia is not freed?"

"I believe the magistrate wishes to find her not guilty. Have faith, my daughter. Prayer and hot soup and good hard work with the milking cows and you will feel much stronger. You will see."

When they reached the farmhouse Rose's mother came out into the yard as the wagon came to a stop.

"So and how was that? How is our Lydia holding up, Father?"

"She is cold and lonely but ask your daughter. She spent the hour with her while I did the errands."

Rose climbed down from the wagon slowly. "Mama, we prayed, we quilted, we quoted Scripture, and when I left I know she felt the Lord was very close."

"Praise God."

"We left the quilt because the sheriff felt once Lydia had handled it she might put a spell on it."

"What?"

"He would not let us walk out with it. But this was a blessing for her, Mama. The jail cells are like ice. Now she is warm as a stove."

Her mother nodded and smiled. "So the Lord works when we least expect it." The smile remained. "Are you hungry after all that?"

"Well, I—"

"Soup." Pastor Lantz began to unhitch the horses. "She is feeling a little ill. Soup would be best. Is there not some left over from yesterday?"

"With Hans and Nathan in our house?" Mrs. Lantz put her hands on her hips. "But there is soup just the same. As I have said, so the Lord works when we least expect it." She looked at her daughter, the smile still on her lips and in her eyes.

Rose stopped walking as she caught the look. "What is it?"

"Your friend has brought us soup."

"My friend?" Rose felt heat creeping up from her neck.

"It is an old recipe from Virginia. Bacon, ham, and hare. The broth is very good. The boys and I have had two bowls each. But there is still plenty for you and your father."

"You mean Mr. Daniels, Mama?"

"*Ja*, Ethan Daniels, who else brings you food? He asked how you were walking and how your friend Lydia was. But mostly he managed to steer the talk to talk of you."

Rose's face was on fire. "Oh."

"Well, do not just stand there. Come and eat. All of us are blessed by his good will but he makes this soup for you."

She sat down and prayed and her mother put a steaming bowl in front of her. She blew on her first spoonful, well aware her mother was watching. Sipping it, the flavor was so rich and full she could not keep a smile of pleasure from her lips.

"Gute, ja, gute?" her mother asked. "Yes, Mother, it's very good."

"Ja, ja, ja." Her mother nodded her head. "You have a problem on your hands, my girl."

Rose kept eating the soup.

"What will you do, hm? What will you do?"

Rose was grateful her father entered the kitchen.

"So we have company. No, no, keep eating, you need the soup, I will have some after."

"Who is it, Papa?"

"Grandfather. And the man who will defend Lydia Beiler at her trial."

"Why are they here?"

Jakob Ammann walked into the kitchen followed by a short man with red hair who was wearing dark Quaker clothes. Rose began to rise but Jakob shook his head and sat in a chair across from her. He removed his broad-brimmed hat.

"Don't trouble yourself, my dear. Finish your food. You were at the jailhouse with your father? How is our Lydia?"

"She mentioned how you visited her last night with Grandmother. Yes, and with her mother and father and Pastor Philip. It was a great blessing to her."

"I thank God."

"We prayed, we spoke Scripture out loud to lift one another's spirits."

"Gute."

The red-haired man sat next to Jakob. He also placed his hat on the table.

Rose's father took a seat near his daughter. Mrs. Lantz began to brew coffee.

"So this is Obadiah Frankling," said Jakob. "He will be what is called a defense attorney for Lydia Beiler. For many years there has been very little of this but the magistrate has agreed to permit his presence at the trial. Mr. Frankling will argue against the one who prosecutes, that is to say the district attorney, and against the witnesses the prosecutor brings forward. It is difficult to say how much Mr. Frankling will be allowed to do but we shall pray for him." Obadiah Frankling inclined his head.

Jakob folded his thin white hands with their blue veins on the tabletop. "Daughter, you know we do not let our people take oaths or prosecute one another in court. We believe such prohibitions are in keeping with the Lord's will for his people."

"Yes, Grandfather." Rose's soup sat untouched.

"So but now this is a different matter. In Europe we had no opportunity to defend ourselves before the Lord. Now in America we do. Not to take others to court. But to stand up before Caesar and say what is true and what is not true. Paul of Tarsus was on trial many times, was he not?"

"There is much in the New Testament about that, Grandfather, yes."

"We will do the same. God willing we will help our sister stand before Caesar and give a true account of her life in the Lord Jesus Christ before the whole community."

"Amen."

"Mr. Frankling may not be allowed to bring anyone forward to give testimony on Lydia Beiler's behalf. But if Judge Hallowell does agree to it he hopes to have two or three speak well of her and of her Christian character. It is hoped that you will find it is in God's will for you to stand up and say such words."

"Me, Grandfather? But I am only a woman. I have never done any public speaking."

Jakob nodded. "Naturally not. Yet you are truly the friend God has given her. Do you not both see your Christian love for one another as precious in the Lord's sight?"

"We do."

"Therefore I feel it is important you speak of her heart, you speak of her soul."

Rose glanced down at the cold soup in her bowl. "Of course, Grandfather."

"If I may." Obadiah cleared his throat and coughed into a handkerchief. "I am extremely hopeful you will be given permission to speak in defense of your friend. There is very little I can do if that is denied."

"I understand," responded Rose. "I will do my best."

"It is a witchcraft trial. They could find her guilty and have her put to death." Rose clenched her hands in her lap.

"Judge Hallowell will not be the only magistrate at the trial because the charge is so serious. That can work in our favor. What one judge disallows another may approve. If there are three of them two may grant you the right to speak and that will be enough."

Rose nodded, still looking down.

"There is the matter of mobs and riots. These are a pestilence in all the colonies whether it is about taxes or contested elections or some issue of morality. Judge Hallowell has given us a trial date of next Monday. That is because if we leave too much time between the arrest and the court proceedings people may become restless and begin to gather. The more swiftly we move ahead the better."

Rose nodded again.

"But this gives us little time. I should like to meet with you each day until the court date to discuss how you may best use the few minutes allotted you."

"If it is permitted," Rose replied, lifting her eyes to his.

Obadiah nodded. "If it is permitted."

Jakob laid his hands flat on the table. "That is what we will pray for. Lord, grant that our sister Rose Lantz may be able to speak your words in defense of her friend through Jesus Christ our Lord." He stood up and bowed his head. Mrs. Lantz sat and bowed her head along with everyone else. Jakob Ammann prayed in German for five or six minutes. Then he pronounced the amen which the others echoed.

Sitting back down he smiled at Rose's mother. "Now, Martha, what a blessing some of your coffee would be right now."

She went to the stove. "Of course, Grandfather."

"Mr. Frankling? Will you share a cup with Pastor Lantz and I this afternoon?"

"Thank you, Mr. Ammann. I would like that."

"Daughter, I fear your food is cold and uneaten." Jakob spread his hands. "Forgive us."

"It is all right, Grandfather."

Her mother bustled over with the kettle in one hand and a ladle in the other. "Here. Let me take care of that." She dished hot soup into Rose's bowl. "The coffee I will bring and the cups."

Rose pushed back her chair. "I can help."

"No, eat." Her mother returned to the stove. "I am able to take care of a coffee pot."

Jakob gave a small chuckle. "So you should eat." Rose picked up her spoon, smiling. *"Danke."*

"Do not fret, my girl. God will see us through this."

"Yes, Grandfather."

She put spoonful after spoonful in her mouth.

Jakob nodded. "Someone has made you a good soup. We thank God for our mothers."

Mrs. Lantz banged several pots together with a clanging that made everyone glance her way. Her cheeks pink, Rose returned quickly to her bowl.

"Yes, Grandfather," she said as she ate.

After Jakob Ammann and Obadiah Frankling had

left Rose went to the barn on her own to milk. Out of the sun the November air was sharp and she had put a forest green cloak on over her shawl. She enjoyed the quiet of the barn and the gentle ways of the cows for it put her in the mood to think and to pray. The visit to see Lydia in the jailhouse, the sheriff's harsh words, the talk of court and trial and execution all left a dark feeling in her heart.

I am alone, Lord, but for you. Lydia is in jail, Juerg has not returned from the hunting, Opa wants me to speak at the trial, I, who shy away from crowds and talk—it is too much, you ask too much of me. I do not even have my quilt to sew. How can you lighten my heart?

The cow she was milking gave a low murmur and turned its head. Rose felt a prickling sensation along her spine. She looked up from the milk bucket. A tall figure was in the doorway.

"How goes it with you?"

Heat sprang into Rose's face. "Mr. Daniels?"

He walked closer, one rifle slung over his back, the other in his hand. "Do your knees still vex you?"

"Yes—no—I am much better, I thank God—I walk without the staff now—"

"And when you must sit or kneel or bend over?"

"Well—I admit I feel some pain then—but it is not much—"

"May I help you?"

"Help me?" Rose knew her face was as red as blood. "Help me with what?"

"My family in the Virginia colony has dairy cattle." He unslung the rifle on his back and propped it against the barn wall along with the one in his hand. "I started milking when I was five. I was tall for my age." Picking up a bucket and a milking stool he went to the cow next to Rose. "What is her name?"

"Her name? That is Clover."

"Ah, Clover." Ethan began to milk. "What do you have for me today, young lady?"

Rose hoped he was talking to the cow and leaned forward to return to her task. For a minute there was only the sound of cows moving their legs and milk squirting into the buckets. Rose tried to pretend Ethan wasn't there but she found that impossible. Her whole body was leaping with feelings she had never experienced before. A barn that had felt like ice only minutes before she found strangely warm and comforting with Ethan only a few feet from her shoulder. Her face continued to burn as she tried to avoid looking at him.

I could control this situation, whatever on earth this situation is, if I could only control my blushing. It's ridiculous that I should act like a schoolgirl around this man. He's just like any other man and I certainly don't act this way with Juerg.

"Oh!"

A sharp pain lanced through her right knee. She almost toppled off the stool and spilled the milk in her bucket.

Ethan was at her side instantly, gripping her by the elbow with one hand to steady her, putting the other on her back. "Easy. Let me set you up against the wall so you can stretch out your legs."

"Ethan—Mr. Daniels—I am perfectly all right—" Another spasm shot through her knee and she cried out, grasping his arm with both hands and digging her fingers into his deerskin clothing.

"You're cramping up. I expect you tried to do too much today." He scooped her up in his arms.

As if I were as light as goose down.

"I'm fine, I'm fine, Mr. Daniels," she sputtered. "Pray put me on my feet."

The scents of wood smoke and deer hide and spruce resin pricked her senses just as they had the day he carried her on the road.

"If I put you on your feet you'll fall like a chopped elm." He placed her by his rifles, her back against the rough boards. "Stretch out now. That will ease your muscles."

Her legs felt better the moment she could straighten them. "Thank you, Mr. Daniels. I will only need a minute."

She closed her eyes for a few seconds and saw his face, his eyes, his arms. "The hay you're sitting on looks fresh."

"Nathan and Hans laid it down this morning."

"May I rub some hawthorn into your knees? I have it in my bag."

Her eyes sprang open. "You certainly may not."

He pulled the deerskin bag off his shoulder and brought a small jar out of it. "Here then. Put some on with your own hand. I'll finish the milking."

"I will be up in a moment. There is no need for you to do that."

"Miss Lantz, you are done for the day. Your legs are seizing up and you require rest."

"Nonsense, sir."

He stood up, smiling. "I admire your sand but even a brave spirit like yourself must tend to her own needs if she is determined to help others. Rest easy. When I'm done I will take you inside your house."

"You will not need to take me inside. I can walk for myself."

He emptied both their buckets into a large milk can and went back to Clover.

He sat on his stool. "How did you find Miss Beiler's spirits today?"

"Why—well enough."

"The gossip in Lancaster and among the farmers has you standing up for her at her trial."

"How words travel. Do people approve?"

"Not those who are convinced Lydia Beiler practices black magic." Milk squirted into his bucket. "But there are many who thank God. That is how they put it at the farmers' market in the town square."

"I'm grateful. Not that what people think matters to me one way or the other." On an impulse she asked, "Do you approve?" Then she wished she had bitten her tongue.

He said nothing for a long minute and she wanted to crawl into a hole like a mouse. Finally he got up and moved to another milk cow. As he settled down on the stool he glanced her way.

"I think a great deal of you, Miss Lantz. What you are doing is right. My prayer is you are permitted to stand. The prosecutor will not like it and will protest. Often such protests are heeded by the magistrates." He turned to his work. "However if my prayers are heard in heaven, you will stand."

A warmth moved into her chest. "Why, thank you, sir. Though I confess I have no idea how anything I can say will make any difference in the matter whatsoever."

"They will make all the difference in the world."

"How can you say that?"

"You have a presence."

"I have a presence?" Rose had started to rub the hawthorn ointment into her legs. She stopped. "What do you mean?"

"Once you begin to speak, people will listen. Most importantly, the magistrates will listen."

"Mr. Daniels, you can't know that."

"I can."

"You scarcely know me, sir."

Ethan continued to milk and did not look her way. "I recall a time you were in the Peachtree dry goods store. I was purchasing some powder and flints at another counter and was out of your line of sight. Mrs. Peachtree had asked you a question about your faith and Jakob Ammann. It was not nicely put. But you answered calmly and with a great deal of grace. I lingered over the flints with Mr. Peachtree so I could hear your entire response. You use words well and your spirit of goodness is infectious. I did not buy the flints until you had finished and left the store. That was two years ago."

Rose's mouth hung half open. "I see" was all her mind could think of to come up with.

Ethan emptied his milk bucket and moved on. "Then there was the April wind."

"The April wind." Her thinking seemed absent. "What April wind?"

"I was on Delaware and heading west through town.

I was packed and primed and ready for the mountains and the frontier. However a gust blew through the square and stirred up the dust and leaves of the autumn before. Hats and bonnets were rolling along the street. And your shawl was flying through the air like a white bird. I watched you chase it. When it snagged in the branch of a tree you stretched and stretched and finally got your hand on it."

"I see," Rose said again and could have kicked herself.

She saw him smile to himself. Without willing it, she found herself smiling too. To her astonishment, she teased him. "I imagine a shawl blowing through the air was an exciting moment for a frontiersman like you."

He laughed. "It was. Especially when your hair unraveled." The heat was instantly back in her face and on her neck.

Ethan continued to milk, still smiling at the memory. "This was several months after the incident at the dry goods store. The pins simply blew loose as you reached for the shawl. All your hair came undone. With one hand you clutched the shawl so you would not lose it again and with the other you tried to hold your hair in place. You could not do it, of course. The wind was too strong. Your hair was down to your knees. I admit it was one of my most profound answers to prayer."

Rose put a hand to her chest. "Prayer?"

"Your hair is the most unusual blend of browns I have seen—light, dark, golden—like earth, like water under trees, ponds in the heart of the woods, oak wood split open and shining in a rainfall." He got up. "One more."

He did not look her way. Rose was grateful he did not. Even in the dark of the barn she was sure her face would look as bright as a bonfire.

"Do you know what you remind me of?" he asked. Rose did not answer.

"I am following a deer trail hundreds of miles from here. There is no sign of white men or any of the tribes. I'm completely alone. I come upon this flower—small, hidden away, unnoticed, almost missed as I track the stag. I decide to crouch by it because its petals are unusually delicate and the colors, well, they seem to have been hand painted only minutes before. The flower is precise and exquisite. But sturdy. It survives on a windward slope. Has no one thought to pluck it, no man, no deer?"

Rose found her voice. "Are you making that up?"

"No. I saw the flower." He glanced at her. "Now I see it again."

Rose let out her breath. "Thank you. But you shouldn't be speaking to me in this fashion, Mr. Daniels. And I believe you are not sincere."

"I am not sure what fashion I should be speaking to you in, Miss Lantz. For I mean every word I've said. You are a remarkably beautiful woman. Others may not have noticed you under that shawl with your quiet ways. But since the dry goods store and the April wind, I have seen you in a thousand ways, thanks to God."

Rose stared at him.

No man has used words like that with me. No man.

Ethan got to his feet and emptied the milk bucket. "I need to take you in. Did you like the Virginia soup I brought to the house?"

"I—thank you—the soup was good—" She braced her hands against the wall. "I can stand on my own." She pushed herself up and her knees buckled. Crashing down onto the straw she felt tears start in her eyes. "I don't understand. I was so much better."

His arms were around her. "You did too much today. A night's rest and you will be up and around again."

"Mr. Daniels, you must put me down."

"Are you going to crawl to the farmhouse, Miss Lantz?"

Again the carry. Again the scent of his clothing and his hair and his skin and the warmth of his body and the strength of his arms. Again wanting to fold herself up against his chest. Again the softest of grays in his eyes for her where for others the color was hard and impenetrable.

"Mrs. Lantz!" He held Rose in his arms at the doorway. "Your daughter's legs have given out! I must get her to her room!"

Her mother came rushing out. "Mr. Daniels. How is it you are here?" She looked at Rose's face. "My poor girl. Where did you find her?"

"She had collapsed in the barn where she was milking."

"Please, yes, put her in her room. Oh, I thought she was better."

"She is better, Mrs. Lantz. She did too much today, that's all."

Rose did not look at him or her mother as he carried her up the stairs but fixed her eyes on the ceiling. His hair brushed her face as he laid her down and she closed her eyes.

Really, God, this is too much. You must do something about this. I have to tell him he cannot visit me again.

"Thank you, Mr. Daniels. Should I rub her legs again?" Mrs. Lantz glanced about the room. "I think we used up all the hawthorn."

"Here is another jar." He handed her the one from the barn. "I must be on my way." He smiled at Rose, who still had her eyes screwed shut as if she was in pain. "May I call on you tomorrow to see how you are faring, Miss Lantz?"

Rose clenched her hands into fists, her eyes still closed. "Mr. Daniels, thank you for all you have done, but I think—"

"*Ja, ja*, come, come. Please. Our door is open to you." Mrs. Lantz followed him out of the room. "We are grateful for your concern for our daughter. The meals, the ointments, we thank God."

"It's the least I can do. Your daughter is a grace to our community."

"Ah. How nice of you to say that, Mr. Daniels."

Mrs. Lantz watched him cross the farmyard to the barn. He entered it and came out with his rifles and a leather bag that he quickly tugged over one shoulder. Then he walked under some trees and was gone. She stood and prayed a moment before climbing the stairs.

"So. Shall I bring you up what's left of the hare and bacon soup?"

Rose put her arm over her face. "I'm sorry, Mama, I'm sorry."

"For what? If your legs are still weak there is nothing you can do but wait on the Lord. I will bring up a bowl, the last bowl."

"I mean that I'm sorry Mr. Daniels was here again."

"Sorry? Do you control his comings and goings?"

"I am betrothed to another, Mama."

Mrs. Lantz nodded. "Juerg is back. I understand he will come by after supper with some meat. All these men bringing us food because of you. *Mein stilles Mauschen.*"

"I wish I were a quiet little mouse. Then Mr. Daniels would not have noticed me."

"So he has spoken words to you?"

"A little."

"But he knows you belong to another?"

"Of course he knows. He doesn't care." She moved her arm and looked at her mother with bright green eyes. "No man has ever spoken to me as he does, Mama. I'm sorry, forgive me, but it puts a fire in my heart."

"Ha. I'm not surprised. So the English men can do."

"I must tell him not to call again."

Her mother nodded. "*Ja.* That would be best. He is not one of us." She sighed. "So but he has been very sweet to you."

"I know." Tears slipped down her cheeks. "Why do you think it is so difficult?"

"All right. Shh. Shh. I will get the soup. Soon Juerg will visit and you will remember why you love him and everything will be in its proper place again."

"I don't want the soup."

"Don't be foolish. You need the soup."

"I don't need the soup. His hands touched everything that went into that kettle."

"Let God give you some nourishment from his hands, all right? It is not the end of the world if you should eat the last bit. You need to be strong in your body and your mind for Lydia Beiler. I will get the soup."

Rose sank her head back on the pillow and let out a long breath of air. "Oh, my dear God," she moaned. "I'm doomed."

When she closed her eyes and tried to nap it was Ethan's face she saw. She forced Juerg's face over his but it did not work. Her mother brought the soup and she tried to ignore it. Finally she took the bowl off her bedside table and went at it with her spoon because her stomach was grumbling. Just as she'd thought, eating the soup made matters worse. She imagined Ethan in his cabin slicing the bacon and ham, chopping the onions, heating the whole mixture on his woodstove, tasting the soup with a large wooden spoon and *putting his lips to it.*

Lord! Help me! What am I going to do? Ethan Daniels, er macht mich verruckt!

As if I was not crazy enough before he came to the barn today!

"How is it the cows came to be milked?" her mother had asked when she brought the soup to Rose's room. "I send the boys out to finish your work and they come back and tell me the cows are dry."

"Who do you think, Mother?" she groaned.

"What? He milks the herd? A woodsman?"

"His family had dairy cattle in Virginia."

Her mother shook her head slowly, hands on her hips. "*Ach, Gott gibt dir einen Engel und man kann nichts dagegen tun.*"

"*God gives me an angel and I can do nothing about it.* Thank you, Mama, that helps, that lifts my spirits."

"Shh, now. Your mood will improve. The soup will help."

"The soup will not help."

Juerg arrived after dark. She heard his voice as he spoke with her father and mother downstairs. Then he came up the steps. The lamp was lit by her bed and the light fell on his face as he opened the door.

"Ah, Rose." His hat was in his hands and he was dressed in his best clothing. "How are you?"

It was, thank goodness, pleasant to see his smiling face, and she relaxed, smiling warmly in return. "Welcome back, Juerg. It's so good to see you. I heard you were successful with your hunt."

"The Lord was gracious. Your father and I hung the deer in your smokehouse."

"A whole deer? Ah, wonderful. Thank you so much."

"There were two other deer already there. Quite large."

"Yes? My father's deer?"

"Not his, no."

"Oh." Her mind began to spin. "I am so glad to see you."

He pulled up a chair by her bed, sat, and took her hand. "And I you, my darling. I have missed you terribly. First there was the harvest and then there was the hunting." He nodded. "*Ja*, but I thank God that now I am back for good."

"Amen."

"How are your legs?"

"I was doing very well until this afternoon. Then they gave way while I was milking. I tried to do too much too soon."

"I am glad you are resting. Did your father carry you to your room?"

Rose felt heat on her neck and ears. "No. A friend."

"A friend? The same man who protected you from those villains on the roadway?"

She hesitated before answering. "Yes."

Juerg's face darkened. "So I am grateful he helped you. On the road and at the barn today. But—" Rose saw the muscles in his jaw tighten. "I am your man. I will defend you."

"Why, of course. But you were not there, my love."

"Nevertheless. I am your betrothed. Isn't that right?"

"Yes."

"So that is my duty. Not his." He got to his feet and began to pace. "The attack should never have happened. You should not have been with Lydia Beiler."

"Juerg. She is my best friend. Where else should I have been?"

"She is accused of witchcraft. There will be other incidents. You know how the English are. People who side with her will be in danger. I am your betrothed. In another month your husband. I must insist you break off your friendship with her."

Rose shot up to a sitting position. "What are you saying? Now is when she needs my friendship the most."

"Nevertheless you must break it off." His hat turned like a wheel between his fingers, over and over. "Is it true you are going to stand for her in court?"

"If the magistrates permit it."

He shook his head once. "Never mind the magistrates. I do not permit it."

"What?"

"The English think Lydia is a witch—"

She interrupted. "Is this what you think?"

"It does not matter what I think. What matters is what the English believe. If they find her guilty they will hang her or burn her. Then they will look around to see who she had close friendships with."

"I'm not afraid of the English, Juerg."

"Then start to be afraid. They could come after you as well. God will not save you from foolishness."

"Foolishness?"

He looked out her window at the darkness. "I have not done my duty, God knows. I have been absent from your side for too long. I repent of that. But now we must set things right." He stared at her. "Bear in mind I make my living off the English, both here and in Philadelphia. I sell them my family's grain and I make a good profit and everyone at my house is blessed. I wish it to be the same for my wife and our new life together."

"Of course."

"So two things must happen immediately. You can never see this other man again. All right? I am your protector, not he. I am your husband. You must break off with him completely."

"Yes. I feel the same way."

"Gute. Gute." Juerg stood over the bed. "So you cannot see Lydia Beiler again either. You must not go to the jailhouse and you must not stand for her in court. Are we agreed?"

"But Juerg! Even Grandfather wants me to appear in court!"

"I don't care. He is our leader, yes, but I am your husband. You endanger yourself when you go to Lydia's aid. You endanger our future. Who will I sell to if the English shut me out because of you?"

"We must have faith. We must pray."

"Yes, yes, we will do all that, but first there must be obedience. No more of Lydia Beiler. Let others see to her needs. Let the Quakers rush to her side. But not you. You will cut yourself off from her. *Ja?* You are my wife and before all things there must be obedience. I am the head of the home as Christ is head of the church."

Rose was silent but a roaring grew louder and louder within her head. She wanted to bite her tongue but she could not.

"I am not your wife yet," she said, her eyes burning a green light.

Juerg narrowed his eyes. "What did you say?"

"We are betrothed. Not married."

"In one month—" he began.

She cut him off. "If the Lord wills."

"If the Lord wills?"

"A husband may be head of the home. But Christ is head of the church. I obey Christ before I obey any man. I will go to Lydia's side again tomorrow. And the day after. And the day after that. I will stand for her in court of the judges allow it."

"I say you will not!"

Rose's face was flushed. "I say I will! God says I will!"

"God says?"

"Ja. Gott sagt."

"I tell you I have prayed about this a great deal. It is my place to tell you what God says you will do."

Rose's small hands were fists. "No, it is not. I must

answer to God for my actions, not you. I will go to Lydia and I will go to court. That is God's will for me in Christ Jesus our Lord."

"*Nein.* I do not accept this."

"You must accept it. I stand before Christ with this commitment in my heart. I will not desert my sister in the Lord in her hour of greatest need, Juerg."

"Others will defend her. God will defend her."

"God has asked *me* to defend her. And I will do it."

"I say again, *you will not.* Rose, do not cross me on this. I have thought about it long and hard. I warn you."

"And I have prayed about it long and hard."

"You must obey me. You must. You are my wife."

"I am not your wife!" Rose's face was aflame. "And you are not my husband!" Her eyes were fire. He glared at her and then nodded his head.

"So you make your choice. Right now you make it."

"I do."

"We are finished. You understand that? Once I leave this house I go to Jakob Ammann. I tell him the betrothal is broken, over, done. I cannot marry a woman who rebels against the good will of her husband. I only wish to protect you."

Her face softened. "I know that. But you must trust me. You must let me follow God and go to Lydia Beiler."

"You are not following God if you go to Lydia Beiler. You are not obeying his will."

"I am, Juerg."

"You are not. If you were obedient to God you would be obedient to me. If you were following God you would be listening to me."

Rose spoke quietly. "I follow his Word and I follow his Holy Spirit in my heart before I follow you."

He nodded. "I see how it is. You have grown wild without a rider and a bit in your mouth. I blame myself. I will take more care with my next bride. My true bride." He placed his black broad-brimmed hat on his head. "It is clearly not God's will we be together. I was mistaken."

"Juerg, don't say that. Pray with me."

"No."

"Please stay and pray with me."

"I will never pray with you again. You are a stranger to me. A sister in the Lord who sits far from me when we gather for Sunday worship." He put his hand on the door. "It is your own flesh that is doing this, Rose Lantz. Your own pride. Not the Lord God. Once or twice I have seen this spirit in you. I thought it would vanish as you became a woman and honored God with your life. But it has not." His eyes went hard. "The English will come for you. Not just Lydia Beiler. You will see. They will come for you. I will not defend you. There will be no one to defend you. Your end will be worse than hers."

Volume 5

The Trial

"*Rosa?*"

"Ja, Papa?"

"Is est Zeit."

She lingered over the Bible in her room. It was open to the rose she had pressed with her friend Lydia months before. Her finger was on the text from Lamentations they had chosen together as a sign of their commitment to one another. Some of the red from the petals had stained the words and paper.

It is of the Lord's mercies that we are not consumed because his compassions fail not. They are new every morning. Great is thy faithfulness.

"The rose is quite dry, Lydia," she whispered. "Yet it is still full of color and carries all its delicate lines and its shape. Our hearts are right. Our faith is true. The Lord will prevail today."

Her mother remained at the farm with her younger brothers. Seated beside her father, Rose kept her eyes straight ahead as the wagon moved slowly through the streets of Lancaster under a dark December sky. A stream of horses and carts were all around them, some traveling in their direction, others moving against them. They went past the jail to the courthouse. Like the jail, it was simply a home that had been transformed into a place for the judges to sit and dispense justice. A large crowd spilled out into the road at the courthouse and her father had to move quite a ways down the block before he could find a place to park.

"There is Juerg." Her father pointed with his bearded chin. "I take it he is not attending the trial."

Rose glanced at the tall thin man on the other side of the street. He was entering a general store that had not closed for the trial—she noticed that the Peachtree shop just down from it had a sign on its door. Juerg saw her and turned away, closing the door behind him as he went inside.

As you wish, Juerg. I cried enough tears over you when you walked out on me last week. Once we were to be husband and wife. Now we will be strangers to each other.

"Let me help you down." Her father extended his hand after parking the wagon. "How are your knees today?"

"They are good, Papa."

"Why didn't you bring your staff?"

"It looks like a weapon. I didn't want people to think about me in that way."

He smiled. "Always turning things over in your head, *mein Rosa*."

A young man came running up to them. "Pastor Johannes. The lawyer is waiting for your daughter. *Guten Morgen, Rosa.*"

"*Guten Morgen, Samuel.*"

"The other pastors and Jakob Ammann have a seat for you, sir. But they wish to pray with Rose before she joins Mr. Frankling at the front."

"*Danke.* Let us walk together."

Rose slipped her arm through her father's. Men and women turned to stare at her as they made their way from the wagon to the courthouse. Some were Quakers, some were people from their church, others were the *Englisch* who lived in town or who had driven in from their farms. The Quakers removed their hats for her and inclined their heads and the followers of Jakob Ammann nodded and greeted her and her father and Samuel in German.

"I'm sorry, no, there isn't any more room inside. No, not even to stand, it's packed, you must wait outside. You can go to an open window and listen, yes, yes, and look inside, but you cannot come in, thank you, no."

A constable or deputy was standing at the crowded doorway and turning people away. The sheriff popped his head out to look at the lineup, spotted Rose and her father, and beckoned to them, asking people to step aside, clearing a path the two of them could take right to the door, faces frowning or crisscrossed with lines of anger as they went to the head of the line.

"She is part of the trial," the sheriff explained in a loud voice. "I must ask thee to make way for her and her father. Yes, part of the trial, thou must give her room, thank thee, we cannot begin without her."

Rose and her father followed him inside.

"Miss Lantz," the sheriff greeted her, tight-lipped.
"Sheriff What-God-Will," she replied.

People stood by the wall at the back of the courtroom and along both sides of the room. Every seat was taken. Talk was constant, rising and falling like wind gusting through a forest, now strong, now soft. The sound dropped away for several long seconds the moment Rose set foot in the room with the sheriff. Feeling hundreds of eyes on her she was about to look at the floor but thought of Lydia.

Ignoring the countless stares, she peered over the heads to the front where three judges sat at a long table with books and papers, dressed in long black robes with Geneva tabs like preachers. Lydia sat in a chair next to them, as white as the tabs at the judges' throats, black shawl over her hair.

"Lydia," she said quietly, willing her friend to see her.

Lydia was staring at her hands that were clenched in her lap. Suddenly she raised her head and the friends' eyes met. Neither spoke or smiled but Rose saw the plea and responded with a prayer. Then Jakob Ammann was talking to her.

"How are you, my daughter?" he asked.

"I am trusting God, *Opa.* Still none of us know if I will permitted to speak up on Lydia's behalf."

"Well, you are trusting God and God knows. Come. We will pray quickly with you, yes, right here where we stand."

Her father, the other two pastors, and Jakob Ammann, hats off, stood in a circle about her while necks craned to get a better look at what they were doing. The prayers were short but heartfelt. A peace went through

Rose's arms and chest and mind. Then her father guided her to the front where Obadiah Frankling waited at a small table facing the judges, tapping a pencil and swinging his leg. He got up quickly as soon as he saw her and pulled back a chair for her.

"How are you?" he asked, tapping his pencil on the tabletop again after they were both seated.

"Much better after the moment of prayer I just had with my church leaders."

"Good. I hope you said a prayer for me as well as for yourself and Miss Lydia."

"We did, sir."

"Thank you, thank you." He pointed to the judges with his pencil. "Judge Hallowell, of course, from here in Lancaster. The round one is Blackwell. The other one Meriwether Cook. Both from outside the county."

Blackwell reminded Rose of a stout keg of nails, the kind she saw in general stores. Cook seemed half asleep and at complete peace with the world and the noise and restlessness of the courtroom. Her heart dropped—Judge Nails looked like a hard man and Judge Cook a lazy and indifferent man. What sort of trial was her friend going to get?

Lord, please, have pity. Stir their hearts towards righteousness.

"And that man is the prosecutor. You may have seen him around town. Stephen Shearling."

Rose did not recognize him but the sight of Shearling made her heart drop still further. He was long and tall and everything about him sharp and angular and tightly strung—he reminded her of a bow and arrows, the bow bent back, the arrows ready to fire. He was talking to

Mr. and Mrs. Peachtree, his eyes black and darting, his fingers playing with the sheets of paper in his hand, narrow and thin like knife blades.

Lord, do not let him have his way. You are the righteous judge. See to it that your ways overcome the schemes of man.

Staring ahead at the three judges she felt her peace leaking out of her body and out of her soul. Dozens of images and Bible verses went through her head. The faces of her father and mother. The crowded street. Sheriff What-God-Will's frosty countenance. Juerg turning his back on her and walking into the store.

Ethan.

I have not seen you once since Juerg deserted me. Do you know about that? Do you care? Where were your soups and ointments? Why did you not come and help me milk our herd? It is like you have fallen into an old well and disappeared into the bowels of the earth. Will you not come? Will you not help us? Will you not look me in the eye and tell me I am doing the right thing and that it will turn out all right? Or have you gone back to the forests and far away from the madness of man? Oh, how could I blame you if you have? I wish you had taken me with you. But no, my place is here, by Lydia's side. I thought you said that was your place too. Didn't you promise us that?

"Hear ye, hear ye, this court is now in session." The sheriff stood at the front.

"God's righteousness will prevail on this day of his grace, Thursday, December 2nd, in the year of our Lord, 1728. Reverend Cotton shall pray."

A minister in a black robe without any collar stood

up from where he sat in the audience and began to drone in a thick voice. Rose squirmed in her chair.

German seemed a much livelier language for divine entreaty than English and she soon had trouble paying attention.

I need your strength, God, yes. But I need Ethan's too. Where is he?

"Mr. Shearling, are you ready?" asked Judge Hallowell.

"I am, your honor."

"Mr. Frankling?"

"Yes, your honor." He whispered to Rose so softly she could barely hear his words: "It means nothing at all unless you can provide testimony. It will be over in less than an hour and Lydia's fate sealed."

Judge Hallowell leaned forward, folding his hands on the table. "Pray proceed, Mr. Shearling and may God's will be done."

"Yes, your honor, amen." Shearling was on his feet, holding a sheaf of papers. "Judge Hallowell. Judge Blackwell. Judge Cook. Miss Lydia Beiler sits in the seat of the accused for good reason. She is accused of witchcraft and I will present many witnesses who can testify to her crime."

"Yes, yes, we did not think we were here for a church lunch." Hallowell scowled. "Pray proceed."

People laughed, breaking a tension that had felt to Rose like someone was stacking bricks against her back and shoulders.

Mortified, his face scarlet, Shearling tripped over his words. "Yes—yes—I wish to call—well, I will not call them but I have their testimonies—right here—in my hand—I shall read them to the court—"

"What?" Blackwell's roar made Rose snap up her head. "What, sir? Your witnesses will not appear?"

"Your honor, yes, many of them will appear, but these first few feel quite awkward about making a public statement and I thought—I thought—"

"You *thought*?" barked Blackwell, beard bristling along with his thick dark eyebrows.

Eyes still half closed, continuing to lean back is if on the verge of sleep, Judge Cook spoke quietly. "It is one of the hallmarks of English law that the accused has the right to face their accusers, Mr. Shearling."

"A number of my witnesses—well, they find it difficult, your honor."

"Difficult? Do they, sir?" Cook smiled. "Imagine how difficult it is for the accused to sit there and face you and a hundred of her neighbors and townsfolk. Think on that a moment. I cannot speak for my honorable colleagues here but I for one cannot preside over a trial, especially one where the charges are so serious as to possibly result in the accused's execution, where those who testify against her shall not stand up in court and be seen. No, sir, I must step down if that is the case."

"They will testify!" Blackwell smacked a fist on the table. "Body and soul, they will testify! Or their testimonies will not be heard!"

Hallowell nodded. "Pray put down your papers, Mr. Shearling, and call your first witness. I am in agreement with my esteemed colleagues. A witness that is not present is no longer a witness."

"But—"

"You have had five minutes of our time, sir, and nothing at all has happened. Call your first witness. I presume at least one of them has not been conjured away by the accused, hm?"

Again the laughter. Again Shearling's blood-red face. Rose felt a little sorry for him but not sorry enough to be grateful he had lost some of his razor-edged composure.

"I will need five minutes," protested Shearling. "Five minutes to rearrange my affairs, Judge Hallowell."

"You have had your five minutes, sir. Soon it will be ten. Who was the first person you were going to ask to stand before us?"

"Why, William Goodman, but he thought—"

"There is altogether too much thinking in your lawyering," growled Blackwell. "Action, sir, might be a good idea at this point. In twenty-three days it will be Christmas morning. I fear we may still be sitting here."

During the fresh burst of laughter Shearling gestured with wild hand movements to a small man sitting at the very back of the room. The man shook his head but finally his neighbors nudged him to his feet and he walked unhappily down the aisle between the rows of chairs.

"Mr. Goodman, face the judges just here." William Goodman stood beside Shearling's table, only six feet from Rose's left shoulder. "Now please tell them what you saw on the night of October 31st of this year."

"What?" Goodman was pale. "What do you mean?"

Shearling closed his eyes. Rose saw his lips moving as if he were counting. "Mr. Goodman." Shearling's voice was almost a whisper. "Did you see the accused, Miss Lydia Beiler, on the night of October 31st around midnight?"

"I did but it wasn't her."

Shearling's eyes sprang open. "It wasn't her?"

"No. She had turned into a bat." He looked at the judges. "And the bat flew away."

Laughter rippled through the audience yet again. Hallowell banged his gavel. "Silence."

Cook smiled. "Did you see the bat's face, Mr. Goodman?"

"I did."

"What sort of face was it?"

"A bat's one. With beady little eyes and big sharp ears." Once again the laughter. Once again the gavel.

For the first time since she had entered the courtroom, Rose saw Judge Cook move. He leaned across the table in front of him to peer at Lydia.

"Hmm." Cook sat back. "It may be I am losing my sight but beady eyes and large sharp ears does not appear to fit the description of the accused."

Even Lydia smiled as chuckles passed through the audience. Rose thought Judge Hallowell would wield his gavel but looking at him she saw he had his head down and was struggling to keep from laughing himself.

"You did not see the accused?" asked Blackwell.

"No, sir, I saw the bat."

"Then how do you know it was her?"

"Why, she had been on the road five minutes before and there was no one else so when I saw the bat I knew it had to be her, your honor."

"Did you?" Blackwell waved a huge hand. "Thank you, Mr. Goodman, we will take particular care to keep your testimony in mind when it comes to passing judgment on Miss Beiler. Please return to your seat. Mr. Shearling, what do you have for us now? A black cat?"

Shearling made a face, Rose thought, as if he had been kicked by a horse in the pit of the stomach.

Why, he was going to have someone testify about that very thing.

Shearling picked up a scrap of paper. "Why, uh, I ask—I ask—Mr. Samson Trueblood to come forward and provide testimony." He turned around and looked over the audience. "Mr. Trueblood? Sir? Will you step up here, please?"

Rose recognized the witness as one of the Lancaster blacksmiths. A husky man unafraid to voice his opinion at his forge, her father had told her, Trueblood marched to the front, cap in hand, and faced the judges.

Shearling appeared to have regained his composure. "Please tell the magistrates what happened at your forge, Mr. Trueblood, on the night of October 21st."

Trueblood spoke boldly. "I seen my anvil, my great heavy anvil, lifted six foot off the ground and dropped on my head."

"How could this be?" prompted Shearling. "Black magic, what else?"

"How was it possible for you to escape injury?"

Trueblood shrugged one shoulder. "For a big man I'm quick on my feet, Mr. Shearling."

"What else did you see that night?"

"I seen her."

"Who?"

Trueblood pointed at Lydia.

"Where was she?"

The blacksmith gave a jerk of his head. "Hoverin'."

"Hovering? How?"

"Howsever witches do it. She was leering down at me and I knew she had tried to kill me with the anvil."

"How could you tell it was her in the dark?"

"Why, I had a lantern with me, of course."

Shearling nodded. "The light made her face quite clear?"

"Oh, it was her, all right. No other woman looks like that."

"How do you mean?"

Trueblood suddenly flared up and pointed at Lydia a second time. "No woman has looks like that! No woman has beauty like that! It's not natural! It was her! She's a witch!"

Hallowell pounded with his gavel as the courtroom erupted.

"Mr. Trueblood." Judge Cook had one hand on the table and the other on the side of his chair. "Are we to believe Miss Lydia Beiler is a witch because she is comely?"

"Comely and bewitching. A beauty as dark as that long hair of hers she keeps pinned up by day!"

"Why, sir, if being comely was the strongest mark of being a witch we should have to hang half the women in Lancaster County." Cook looked at the audience and smiled. "And all the women in this courtroom."

Laughter moved through the room.

"It ain't just that." Trueblood's face was red and black like coals at his forge. "People have lost good healthy cows. Days of milking have gone bad in the can. Folks have had their children turn sick in front of their eyes. Crops ruined. And every time people have seen those unnatural eyes. Every time they've seen hair like a flock o' ravens." He began to plead. "Judge Cook, they hear her screechin' when the deed is done. They hear her howling with glee when the worst things happen. You've got to save us from her. Only you can do it. Almighty God's put the power in your hands."

Cook listened to him and finally nodded his head slightly.

"Thank you, Mr. Trueblood," said Hallowell. "Power or not, I think we'd just as soon hear what happened from the witnesses themselves regarding cows and cans of milk." He glanced sharply at Shearling. "No hearsay. No testimony at second hand."

"I'm sorry, your honor. Mr. Trueblood is understandably upset."

"Yes, well, I'm sure Miss Beiler is upset with a man shouting at her in my courtroom but I do not hear her screeching and howling in return. No more of this, sir. I will not have you prejudice my trial."

"Nor I," rumbled Blackwell.

"No hearsay. No loss of temper." Hallowell glanced at Obadiah Frankling. "You may have wished to raise some concerns about these matters and other points of law, Mr. Frankling. Are you satisfied that I have dealt with any possible legal grievances of yours?"

"Yes, your honor."

"Thank you, Mr. Trueblood. Pray return to your seat."

Frankling leaned over and whispered in Rose's ear. "It goes well for us, Miss Lantz. Both witnesses thus far have done little to advance the credibility of their testimonies."

She whispered back. "I suspect the testimonies that Shearling had committed to paper were stronger."

"Perhaps. But he cannot use them."

As if Shearling had overheard the whispered remarks exchanged by Rose and Obadiah Frankling he stared at them, paused, then bent over his table, scribbling on a piece of paper. Folding it in half he handed it to a man sitting behind him, saying something Rose could not hear.

"Mr. Shearling, are you prepared to call your next witness?" asked Hallowell.

Shearling straightened his suit coat. "I am, your honor. I will bring forward those who can speak personally to the events mentioned by Mr. Trueblood."

"Pray do so."

For the next hour Rose and the court watched a steady stream of witnesses go to the front, both men and women, and testify about having seen a crow that was Lydia Beiler perch on their roof when they brought their milk from the barn fresh and only to discover it had gone sour once they placed it in the cold room; having seen her turn into a black cat followed by a mist moments before a fire destroyed their hay; having seen her ride a broomstick across the face of a full moon, black hair half a mile in length streaming out behind her; having seen her walk past their farm minutes before their chickens died, their child caught a fever and collapsed, mold was discovered on a barley crop harvested only hours before, roasts to feed ten people for five days turned black in the pan and had to be thrown out.

Finally Judge Hallowell scratched his cheek. "I think that is adequate, Mr. Shearling, unless you have testimony about her turning into smoke and going up the chimney. Are you prepared to conclude your case against Miss Beiler?"

"A final witness, if I may."

"A final witness? And who is that?"

"Mrs. Abigail Peachtree."

Frankling spoke softly, "So Adam's mother. I think she had written her testimony down and now Shearling has persuaded her to come forward."

"Will this be very bad for Lydia?"

"Shearling is trying to gain sympathy from the judges. A mother's tears. The murder of her son by witchcraft. It's impossible for me to say how the three of them will respond but, yes, it could go hard for us."

Mrs. Peachtree already had a handkerchief to her eyes. "I did not believe in witches until I lost my son. But I know it was witchcraft that took his life."

"How do you know that?" asked Hallowell gently.

"He warned me that a young woman was bewitching him but I did not believe him. I thought it was just a young man's fancy."

"What young woman?"

"Miss Lydia Beiler."

"What did he tell you she had done?"

"She would come to our store and cast spells on him, he said. Smile in the most disarming way. It would put a fever on him. He tried to mind his business but she always went up and down the aisles until she found him and once she did she would put the evil eye on him so that he could scarcely think. She would ask him questions that made no sense just to keep him by her side so she could spin her charms. Once she touched her fingers to his cheek and put her lips to his. It nearly drove him mad."

Lydia shot to her feet, her face crimson. "That's a lie!"

Hallowell banged his gavel. "Sit down!"

"I never touched him, I never laid eyes on him, I certainly never put my lips on his!"

"The accused will remain silent and in her seat! Mr. Frankling!"

Frankling jumped up. "Let her finish her testimony, Miss Beiler. It is the law."

"Then the law is a pack of lies!"

Frankling quickly went to her side. "You must sit down," Rose heard him say. "This does us no good."

"Her son was a liar and so is she!" Lydia hissed. "Who do you think made eyes at who?"

"Nevertheless you must refrain from speaking or there will be nothing I or Rose Lantz can do to save you," he said so quietly Rose could hardly make him out. "Nothing. This trial will be over. Do you understand?"

Lydia's fists were clenched and she continued to glare at Mrs. Peachtree, who looked down and dabbed at her eyes with the handkerchief.

"Please, Miss Beiler," pleaded Frankling. "Think of your family. Think of your friends."

She looked at Rose. Rose did not smile but once again spoke through her eyes. Lydia relaxed her fists and sat down in her chair.

"Thank you, Mr. Frankling. Pray proceed, Mrs. Peachtree."

Mrs. Peachtree blew her nose and looked at the judges in a broken and forlorn way, appearing to sag where she stood. "Why, as I've said, your honor, she had him spellbound but I did not take the matter seriously when he complained. I should have barred her and her family from the store. Their whole strange church, I should have locked the door on them."

A murmuring swept the courtroom and was gone. Hallowell lifted his gavel but silence had already returned.

"How did this bad business end?" asked Blackwell in his deep voice.

"He could not sleep. He could not eat. I feared he might waste away. The doctor said there was nothing wrong with him fresh air and exercise could not cure. So his father and I encouraged him to ride. Practically ordered him to ride though he told us he felt too weak." She began to weep, the tears pouring over her face. "Oh, what did we do? We made him get on that horse, though he was afraid to do so, he said he had dreamed she would cause the horse to pitch him. And that is what happened, his mare from birth, a gentle soul named Holly, she threw him onto a great mound of rocks and bricks. She, who would scarcely bite at a fly, she reared up and hurled him down. I was scarcely a hundred feet away." She looked from one judge to another. "As I ran to him Lydia Beiler put her face in my mind and spoke."

The courtroom was weighted with silence. Rose felt she could not move her arms or legs or turn her head.

"What did she say, Mrs. Peachtree?" asked Hallowell.

"She said—she said she had killed him because he had not returned her love. And that she would kill anyone who did not honor her. That she would use her powers to destroy all of Lancaster County if people continued to reject her and her powers."

"Liar!" Lydia was on her feet again.

"She called herself The Witch Of Great Darkness, a darkness she would bring to the whole colony of Pennsylvania."

"No!"

"That she met with the devil in the woods and that he would make her his bride."

"You're the witch!" Lydia was shouting. "God will send you to hell for the corruption and deceit you are spinning here today! He knows the truth even if others do not and he is the true judge, Abigail Peachtree! Aren't you afraid of him who has the power to cast soul and body into a fire that never stops burning?"

Hallowell did not demand she sit down or stop shouting. He turned in his chair and examined her eyes and face. Rose had never seen the color in her friend's eyes so bright as if lit by a blue fire behind them, nor her cheeks so red as if all the blood in her body had come together in one place. Her hair had unraveled from under her shawl and it was blacker than night and the gleam in it like the sharp light of a winter star. She was beautiful but frightening. Rose felt herself shrinking from the sight of a friend all ablaze as if firewood had been stacked at her feet and ignited.

"Do you deny every one of her accusations, Miss Beiler?" asked Hallowell.

"I do. I do, sir."

"You did none of these things? Nothing to her son?"

"Never."

"You did not cause the horse to rear or stumble?"

"No, sir, no."

Hallowell turned his attention to Mrs. Peachtree. "You may sit down, thank you."

Now it was Mrs. Peachtree's face that took on color. "I am not finished, your honor."

"You are. Indeed you are. What you have shared is sufficient."

"But she—"

Hallowell's eyes became flint. "You have said enough to send this woman to the gallows or the fires. Pray return to your seat, Mrs. Peachtree."

She bowed her head and walked back down the aisle. Hallowell wrote something on a piece of paper and handed it to Blackwell, who read it, shook his head, and passed it to Cook.

"You may also sit down, Miss Beiler," Hallowell said without looking at her.

Her face had gone as pale as ice and she took her seat quietly. "You as well, Mr. Shearling."

Shearling was going to say something, stopped, and did as he had been told.

Hallowell folded his hands on the tabletop and turned his attention to Obadiah Frankling. "Sir, I am considering whether or not to permit you a witness to Miss Beiler's character. It is unusual."

"Unusual?" Blackwell glowered at Frankling and Rose. "It is unheard of!"

"Not exactly unheard of, my honorable colleague." Cook smiled. "The role of defense and witnesses for the defense has been developing in our Mother Country."

"We are not the Mother Country, God bless her. We must forge our own destiny."

"Yes, well that is what we are trying to do here. The charges are grievous, the punishment severe, the accusations extraordinary, and the denials of the accused unflinching. I have seen many who deny their guilt in court and all present immediately recognize it to be false. Can you say that is the case here, sir? Her protestations of innocence have the ring of truth."

Blackwell shook his shaggy head. "We move too fast if we allow a character witness for the defense."

Cook continued to lean back, one hand on the table, the other gripping the side of his chair. "The law is not stagnant, sir, it is not a swamp. It is an ever-flowing stream surging ahead to greater displays of justice. I move we permit the defense a witness."

Hallowell nodded. "I concur."

Blackwell looked from Cook to Hallowell. "I see I am in the minority position. But I shall raise this with the governor when I am next in Philadelphia."

Cook smiled. "A good thought. So will I. We must see this right afforded all those accused of capital crimes in the Commonwealth of Pennsylvania."

"Hmm," grumbled Blackwell, lowering his head.

Hallowell beckoned to Frankling. "Come, sir, let us have your witness."

Frankling stood quickly and helped Rose to her feet. "God has favored us. Stand and face the judges and answer their questions."

All along Rose had been hoping for the chance to declare her friend's innocence. Now that the opportunity had come her way she felt awkward and uncertain. She walked to the table where the judges sat and stopped.

"What is your name?" asked Hallowell.

"Rose Lantz, sir."

"You dwell in Lancaster?"

"On a farm nearby."

"Have you known the accused a long time?"

"Since we were children, sir."

Hallowell nodded. "Pray tell us about the accused. What do you make of the charges brought against her? Do they hold any water as far as you are concerned?"

Rose could not think of anything to say. There was a pricking at the back of her neck and she lifted a hand to rub it, turning her head as she did so. Ethan Daniels stood by the door, a head taller than anyone else, leaning on his rifle, its stock to the floor. For a moment their eyes held. She wanted to ask him how long he had been there, how he had got in, if he had faith that she could find the words that might save her friend's life. Was there a smile? Did she see his head nod ever so slightly, eyes gray and soft but still strong and never moving from her own?

"Miss Lantz?" Hallowell coughed into his hand. "Pray direct your attention to the three of us, if you please."

She turned back to the judges. "Thank you for this opportunity, sirs. I realize it is not commonplace to permit a character witness."

Blackwell mumbled something she could not hear. Hallowell had his hands folded on the table and was watching her closely. Cook remained in his half-awake position but she knew now he was far from asleep.

Lord, be with me. Ethan, are you praying?

She maintained eye contact with the judges, holding her head erect. "I find the testimony against Lydia

Beiler astonishing. This is someone who loves God, who prays with me, who tells me what parts of the Bible she has read, who sings with such grace and beauty when we gather for a service."

"Behold, the devil can masquerade as an angel of light to win us to our harm, Miss Lantz," responded Hallowell.

"No, sir, not to the point of bowing the knee to Christ, not to the point of speaking his name with love and devotion, not to the point of praising him and obeying him in all things. The devil does not do any of that, indeed, he and his minions cannot. How is it possible for her to adore the Word of God? How can she go to Jesus Christ on bended knees, hands clasped, and declare him Savior and Lord? How can she exalt him as King of Kings? Do any of you honestly believe she is able to worship our Redeemer with heart, mind, soul, and strength and practice witchcraft? There is no fellowship of light with darkness. She is either one or the other, she cannot be both. If you spent as much time with her as I do you would know she is a child of God, not a child of Satan."

Hallowell tapped his fingers on a thick black Bible. "What of her rage and shouting, Miss Lantz? Do you think her outbursts this morning exhibit the godly temperament of a godly woman?"

"We all lose our tempers at one time or another, sir. Is that the mark of a witch? What shall we do with Jesus cleansing the Temple if that is the case? What shall we do with his anger when he confronts the priests and declares them a brood of vipers?" She looked at Judge Blackwell. "How should you react, sir, if a woman called you a murderer and a devil and the heart of all darkness? Would you sit there and smile and nod your head in peace?"

Blackwell barked a rough laugh. "I should think not!"

"It is the same for Lydia. She is sweet. She much prefers light to darkness, an even temper to one out of control. But you must consider her circumstances. Look at the place her neighbors have put her in. No wonder she has reacted as she has done."

Blackwell nodded his large head.

"You are learned men and wise men," Rose went on, the words coming to her mind swiftly now. "Surely you do not take these accusations seriously that have been leveled at my friend? Surely we have not returned to the dark days of the Massachusetts colony where anyone could say anything, even young girls, and they were believed? Do you think she turned into a bat, Judge Hallowell? Or flew a broomstick across the night sky, Judge Blackwell? Or dropped an anvil on a blacksmith's head, Judge Cook? Is this 1692, sirs? Didn't the whole Massachusetts colony repent of their misdeeds? Were not men and women put to death who should rather have been left alive to live out their days and bless their townsmen and country? Wasn't the wickedness in Salem the wickedness of those who made accusations rather than any wickedness on the part of those accused?"

"Still." Judge Cook opened his eyes. "Real witches have real powers." Surprising the judges and herself Rose stepped to the table and snatched up Judge Hallowell's black Bible in her hand. "Where is it written, sirs? Where is it written that followers of Satan turn into cats or bats or ride brooms? Where is it written that they hover about at forges or fly about as crows and ravens? Why it was ravens that brought food to Elijah in the wilderness. And where are we taught that the devil's great purpose on earth is to turn cows' milk sour so that humans cannot drink it? Have such ideas come from the mind of God or the corrupt thoughts of man?"

She placed the Bible back on the table with a thump.

"Where is the deception in the courtroom this morning, learned sirs?" she demanded. "Does it lie with the accused? Or does it not rather lie with those who point the finger and cry witch and then spout nonsense about brooms and bats and milk cans and ravens, things the Bible has never taught and has never told us to consider marks of evil? Doesn't the Word of God instead teach us not to bear false witness, that the Lord detests it, as well as detesting those who stir up strife among neighbors? Which are the true marks of wickedness in the courthouse this morning?"

Both Judge Cook's eyes were wide open. "Do you say so?"

Rose felt heat all through her face. "I have been taught since I was a very young girl to heed the Bible, sir. Not to shrink it or make it less. But also not to go beyond what it declares and call that good and holy."

Hallowell steepled his fingers under his chin. "What do you make of Abigail Peachtree's testimony, Miss Lantz? What do you make of her son's murder?"

"I am sorry for his death, sir. I am sorry for the grief it has brought into Mr. and Mrs. Peachtree's home. But have you proven it to be murder, sir? Wasn't Adam Peachtree simply thrown by his mare? I am not unfamiliar with the ways of horses. None of us in this courtroom are. A fly can bite them, a wasp sting, a sudden hand movement or sharp noise startle them into flight. Horses do not need witches to make them act dangerously or lash out with their hooves despite being gently handled."

"Why may not a witch cast spells to injure a man who refuses to be her lover?" Blackwell's eyes on her were large and dark. "*Hell hath no fury like a woman scorned.*"

"Sir, you did not know Adam Peachtree, nor did you, Judge Cook. But Judge Hallowell did." She fixed her eyes on Hallowell. "Look at Lydia Beiler, sir. Look at her beauty. Look at her grace. Now, with all due respect to the Peachtrees and their son, consider the looks and the manners of Adam Peachtree, may he rest in peace. Why should a beauty such as she cast a spell to win the love of such a dreary young man as he?"

Judge Cook sat erect. "What?"

"May God forgive me but it is so. Would you not think her casting a love spell on Adam Peachtree to be a very odd and strange and nonsensical thing, Judge Hallowell?"

Hallowell went back to tapping his fingers on his Bible once again. "What do you make of Abigail Peachtree's testimony then? Why has she declared it?"

"Grief, sir. And the belief that since others found Lydia's beauty unnatural, and considered her a witch because of it, that perhaps she really was a witch and had an inclination to hurt her son."

"Why should she think that?"

Rose paused. Then decided to speak her thoughts.

"She does not like the church Lydia Beiler and I belong to. She is not happy with those who walk with Jakob Ammann. Abigail Peachtree despises our language, our clothing, our customs, our way of worship, our use of homes to gather in rather than church buildings. I fear she has little use for us. So perhaps today is a way of getting back at us by attacking one of our own."

Judge Cook was still sitting up straight in his chair. "How do you know she thinks these things?"

"Because she has told me these things, sir. Often she has questioned me when I purchased items at her store. Often she sought to argue with me and dissuade me from remaining with my church." She took a breath and looked down. "She said we were a sect from hell and ought to be burned at the stake just as we were in Europe."

The silence that fell on the room was dark and thick and impenetrable. "I see," was all Judge Cook said in response.

Hallowell began to write on a sheet of paper. "Thank you, Miss Lantz. Do you have anything further you should like to say to us on Miss Beiler's behalf?"

"Only to reassert that she is a godly woman who loves Jesus Christ, good sirs. And that this is not 1692 and not Salem. Do us honor in Lancaster today. Do God honor."

"Thank you, Miss Lantz. You can be sure we shall endeavor to do that very thing. Pray take your seat."

Rose sat back at her table next to Obadiah Frankling. He patted her arm and whispered something but she felt far away and in a different place. She watched the judges conferring with one another, Hallowell whispering, Blackwell muttering, Cook remonstrating with both of them. Her mind was empty of words so she let the feelings in her heart be her prayers. Once she looked at Lydia, who returned the look with such love and hope Rose struggled not to cry.

"Quiet in the court." Sheriff What-God-Will stood facing the room. "The judges will render their verdict. The accused will stand."

Lydia stood alone, her face pale and rigid. The three judges got to their feet.

"We have heard the testimonies," said Judge Hallowell. "We have weighed the evidence. All of us concur. Before man and God, we find the accused not guilty of the crime of witchcraft and not guilty of the crime of murder. The prisoner is free to go. Sheriff, see to it that Miss Beiler is escorted to her carriage and that any items of hers remaining at the jailhouse are returned to her. We believe God's will has been done."

Rose rushed to her friend and embraced her. The room exploded with shouts and cries and clapping. But she also heard curses as she and Lydia hugged each other tightly. The judges exited by a side door and ignored the commotion.

"Thank God, thank God, thank God." Rose kissed her friend on the forehead and cheek. "We're blessed. You're free. We can go back to our quilt and all our wonderful times together."

"Thank God and thank you," Lydia responded, tears on her cheeks. "Thank you so much for everything you said, oh, such strong and important things you said."

Lydia's parents were suddenly there and Jakob Ammann and many of the people from the church, the women taking Lydia in their arms, the men nodding and smiling and praising God in German. Rose stepped back to watch and saw the sheriff waiting with three of his deputies.

"I should like to take Miss Beiler to her carriage now, if you please," he said. "There is a mood to some in the crowd I do not like. Let us see her safely away."

"Very well." Jakob Ammann took Lydia's hand. "We shall have a service of praise and Thanksgiving this Sunday at your home. The Lord has delivered you from the lions' den and we will give him honor."

"Yes, Grandfather."

"Meanwhile you should be with your family and rest and gain back your strength. You have been through a terrible ordeal. Yet God will use it to deepen your faith. It is what our people went through all too many times in the old country."

The deputies cleared a path. Rose trailed behind Lydia and her family and the church members. On either side of them people made way, some with good will, others with reluctance, others in a kind of stiff fury. At the door a man drew alongside her.

"You did well."

His face was only inches from hers.

"Ethan." She had meant to say Mr. Daniels. "Thank you for being here."

"Your words made the difference. I believe they would have found her guilty without them." His gray eyes smiled along with his lips. "I am only sorry your back was turned. I should like to have seen the fire in your eyes when you took up the Bible in your hand and spoke with so much strength and courage."

She glanced down. "I'm sure there was no fire."

His fingers gently lifted her chin. His touch sent a shock through her body.

Their eyes came together.

"I have feelings for you, Rose Lantz. Take care. Many people are not happy with what you have done today."

She gazed back at him, hot and cold rushing through her in waves. "I—I don't know what you mean."

"About my feelings or about the people?" He brushed at a strand of hair that fell across her cheek. "I will come by. I only ask you to take care just as you would take care if you were in the forest with me and well aware of its beauties and dangers."

He was gone.

Rose walked down the street and climbed into the wagon next to her father. "How are you?" he asked.

"I felt great joy when they set Lydia at liberty. But all around me as I walked from the courtroom I felt great anger."

"Many still believe she is a witch. So they think she should not have been set free. They blame our church."

"And me?"

Her father guided their wagon out into a road busy with carts and carriages as people left the courthouse. "It will pass, my daughter. With the *Englisch*, these things always pass."

Over supper her brothers and mother wanted to know everything. She said very little, taking small morsels of food, letting her father do most of the talking. She did not like it when he praised her, feeling God was responsible for the good that been done, not her, but she had no desire to argue about the matter. Her elation was spent. She found herself worrying about what the townspeople might do next.

Would they still harass Lydia whenever she went walking, call her names, throw mud and stones? Would there ever be peace for her so long as she remained in Lancaster County or was a day coming when the Beiler family must move from the region? And not only the Beiler family but the whole church?

"Rose, eat, what is the matter, it is a good day, praise the Lord, let us see a smile on your face."

Rose managed a weak smile. "Oh, Mama, of course I am glad Lydia is free. I just feel so tired and spent."

"Of course, my dear, of course, such a day for you, so much was riding on your shoulders. I don't want you to catch something. Go to bed early. We will clean up. No, please go up to your room and lie down. You will feel much stronger in the morning. Pray to God and you will have peace."

Rose went to her room, undressed, and put on her flannel nightgown. After brushing out her long brown hair she slipped under the covers. Thought. Prayed. Saw Lydia's face, the face of each judge, the sharp features of the prosecutor.

I will come by.

"Ethan," she whispered. "I wish I could see you tonight. Oh, I wish you could hold me. I feel so lost. But how can I ask you to do that? How can I even dream about it?" She put her fingers to her chin. "I wish you would do that again, lift up my face, only this time end it with a kiss. Do you truly think well of me? Do you truly have feelings for me? What shall we do? You are a man of the forests and hills and I am a woman of the church."

She had just begun to drift off when she heard the rapid hoof beats of several horses.

"Lantz! Johannes Lantz!"

She sat up in bed. It was the sheriff's voice.

He has come to arrest me. Fists pounded on the door. "What? What?" Her father.

She listened in the dark as the door creaked open. "Mr. Lantz. Will thou use a gun?" The sheriff.

"What do you mean?"

"They waited until all the judges had left town. Now there is a mob. They are on the march. It is only a few miles to the farms here."

"What? They are after Lydia Beiler again?"

"They are after thy daughter. They blame her for what happened in court today. In ten minutes they will be at this house. Will thou use a gun?"

"On people? Never. Never."

Rose jumped out of bed, feeling only a small pinch of pain in her knees, threw a thick housecoat over her flannel nightgown, and raced from her bedroom and down the stairs. The sheriff held a lantern and so did her father. The December air was chill and she could see the sheriff's breath in the open doorway. He looked up at her as she descended the steps from her room.

"I am sorry, Miss Lantz. They gathered by the Peachtree store after the verdict and I dispersed them from there. But hours later they formed again. Now they are coming with pitchforks and hoes and scythes. They are bent on mischief."

One of his deputies called out. "I can see the torches on the main road. Men on horseback and men on foot."

The sheriff and her father rushed out to see for themselves and Rose followed. The torches were like sparks rising and falling in the night. It did not seem real to her just as the courtroom had not felt real before the judges pronounced their verdict.

"What are they going to do?" she asked.

The sheriff turned his head. "Thou must stay indoors with thy mother and brothers."

"I will not."

"They are a hundred or more. I cannot protect thee. There are only six of us."

"Seven."

Ethan walked towards them from the direction of the barn, a rifle in his hands, and a rifle on his back.

"Do thou mean to stand with us?" asked the sheriff.

"I do."

"Then I deputize thee in the name of the king."

"As you wish."

"Ethan." She stared at him in the light of the lanterns. "You should not be here. You should not put yourself in danger. It is not your fight."

"Not my fight?" His warm smile. "Has a law come to us from London or Philadelphia now that a man may not lay down his life for the woman he loves?"

Volume 6

The Kiss

Not my fight? Has a law come to us from London or Philadelphia now that a man may not lay down his life for the woman he loves?

Rose stood rooted to the spot. His words stunned her.

Her father had run inside to speak with her mother and brothers.

Sheriff What-God-Will was talking to his deputies and telling them where to stand as the mob approached. Her and Ethan were alone in a swirl of light from a lantern placed near her feet.

"Ethan. How can you say that?"

"Why, it's the easiest thing in the world. Look at you. Your hair is golden brown and shining in the light. Unbound and flowing all down your back. Your eyes are like gemstones." He picked up the lantern and held it closer to her face. "Rose Lantz, you are the most beautiful woman I have ever seen in my life. These people marching upon your house are not going to take you from me."

She could not tell if her face was warm from the lantern or his words. "How can you talk that way when you don't even know me?"

"I think I know a few things about you. I know what I saw in that courtroom. If you didn't keep me at arm's length I'd know a lot more. What are you afraid of?"

"I'm not afraid."

He set down the lantern and his rifle.

"Don't you have any feelings to spare for a wild frontiersman like me?" His fingers were under her chin again. Fire shot through her body from head to foot. "None at all?"

She could hardly get his name out. "Ethan—"

He took her in his arms, pulling her up against himself with strength she had never felt from Juerg or any man, the scent of deerskin and trees and earth filling her head as his lips came down on hers. She felt like she was burning as his kiss covered her mouth. Grasping one of his arms her fingertips pressed into the hard muscle under his shirt while her other hand, at first trying to push him away, seized onto the equally hard muscle of his back and shoulders as if he were saving her from the rapids. His kiss did not stop and flames ate at her heart and lungs and stomach until she surrendered and put both arms around his neck and kissed back with a wildness and passion she would never have thought were inside her. Soon she was leading the way, making his mouth move where she wanted it, making his kisses come harder or softer depending on how she held him, pressing down on his lips with so much force she knew she had taken most of his breath from him but she didn't care, she just wanted more of him and more of him.

Finally she pulled away so she could speak his name. "Ethan." His lips moved over her throat and long hair and over her eyes.

"I'm here."

"Ethan. I love you. But I don't know what to do."

He smiled and framed her small face with his large hands as gently as if he were holding a baby or a kitten. "Just keep doing what you're doing. You're pretty good at it."

"Ethan, I don't—"

"Shh." He kissed her lips. "I've loved you for weeks. Months. We'll make it work. We'll figure it out as we go."

"How?"

"With one more kiss. After that I guess we'd better get ready for your house guests."

Behind them her mother and father were placing lamps and candles in all the ground floor windows, not even bothering to glance outside they were in such a panic. In front of them the sheriff was barking orders and deputies were crouching behind rain barrels or wagons and checking the priming on their flintlocks. In the lane leading up to the farmhouse men were shouting and chanting, shaking pitchforks and raising torches, while others reined back their frightened horses, causing them to rear. But for Rose Lantz there was the only the smell of Ethan Daniels on her hands and face, the feeling of his body under her fingers as she ran them over his back, the strength and tenderness that poured over her from his kisses to her lips and throat and neck, kisses so warm and sweet she could not get enough. The way he loved her made her feel as if she had been deprived of affection all her life, that she was starved and thirsty, and that she had to make up for all she had never had in the two or three minutes left to them before the mob broke upon the farmyard. She pulled Ethan to herself one last time, putting everything she had into her kisses and the arms that wound about him more and more tightly, grasping the long knot of his hair that fell down the middle of his back, heat all over her and within her and through her, and the heat of his own body and breath and mouth igniting her like flint sparking against steel.

Oh, dear God, he is so beautiful. What shall I do? What will I tell Mother and Father, what will I say to our people and to Jakob Ammann? But I cannot go back now, I cannot. I adore him.

They ended their kiss, their breath coming in short bits and pieces.

"Well," he said as they both took in air and held on to each other, his hands caressing her back and shoulders and the long soft hair that flickered in the lamplight. "I could do this all night. But then your father might shoot me instead of the rioters."

She ran his hands over his face again and again. "Do you truly care for me? Truly?"

"I love you, Rose. In a few moments you will find out how much." He gently stepped away from her arms and unslung the rifle from his back. "Were you ever taught to shoot or to hunt?"

"No."

"Do you think you could point this rifle at a man and pull the trigger if you had to?"

"What?" She stared at him in the mixture of dark and light the lantern gave them. The kissing had made her eyes flash and color rise to her cheeks so that it looked as if she were a foot taller. "No. No. Never."

"They don't know that. I expect you can hold it in your hands if nothing else." He placed it in her grasp. "Mind your fingers. It's primed and ready to shoot. You only need to cock back the flint."

He stole a final kiss and disappeared into the shadows. Rose was left standing by the lantern with a rifle taller than she was and her mind whirling. She saw the sheriff's perpetual frown directed at her, saw the torches and axe handles and the snarls on the faces swarming towards the house, heard the yells and cries, but it did not move her in the least. Every part of her body was tingling, her fingertips, her toes, even the roots of her hair. She had never felt more excited and more alive and more full of God and love in her life. At any moment she expected she might throw her head back, shake her long hair looser than it already was, shout out to Jesus in German, and laugh and sing and raise her arms as high as she could. The yellow flame furled and unfurled and flashed brightly in the lantern by her feet and she knew it was the same way with her heart.

"That'll do, Mr. Finch!" The sheriff leveled his musket at the men leading the mob. "Thou has had thy march to the Lantz farm to express thy disagreement with the verdict today and now ye can turn around and march back."

"We're not going anywhere!" a heavy man bellowed. "Not until justice has been done!"

"It has been done, Tom Finch. Three judges delivered the same verdict in the king's name. The accused was declared not guilty and set free. Thou hast made a riot but rioters are not the king's magistrates and they do not administer the law. Go back to thy homes and thy beds before the governor sends troops."

"Troops?" Finch laughed. "You'll not get redcoats from Philadelphia to Lancaster in a week." He was holding a torch in one hand and a pikestaff in the other. "Give us the woman and we'll be on our way."

"Thou shall not leave with any woman from this farmstead."

"We'll leave with the young woman who lied today and twisted the judges' hearts around her pretty fingers. We'll leave with her or we'll burn the house down around her ears."

"I and my deputies stand between thee and the lady."

Finch laughed again. "There are but six of you. How many of us can you kill before we knock you down and sweep over you, ha? Stand back, sheriff, or you will lose your life for no good reason. God is on our side and he urges us to do what must be done."

"That's odd, Tom Finch. I'm fairly certain God told me he was on my side and that I was on his." Ethan stepped out from the darkness by the barn, long rifle cradled in his arms. "I'd hate for you to be misled."

Finch stared at Ethan. "You. What are you doing here?"

"You'd protect your wife, wouldn't you, Tom Finch? I am here to see that my own bride comes to no harm."

"Your own bride? Rose Lantz?"

"Look at her in the lantern light. Doesn't my bride's beauty strike home even with a rough sort like yourself?"

"Bride! Why, she's the devil's bride!"

"Take care, Tom Finch. Most men will not abide such words directed at the woman they love."

"You love her? The devil's mistress?"

"I say again, take care." Ethan cocked the hammer that held the flint in its jaws. Finch took a step backwards. "She is not of the devil. Look at her. Even a blind man can see that so fair a face and so fair a creature is of heaven."

"You have only one shot!" yelled a skinny man with a musket behind Finch. "One shot and you're through!"

"That's true, Bill Seward. But I swear I shall get my shot off before you get off yours and that I shall put it right between your eyes. The sheriff and his men will kill another six. And Rose Lantz a seventh."

There was a silence. Rose watched the white puffs of breath and the smoke unwinding from the flames of the torches.

"And then we'll have her and burn her," Finch finally said, his voice less bold than before.

Ethan slowly pointed the rifle in his direction. "You will not have her, Tom Finch, for you'll be dead and in hell."

"In hell!"

"Where else do murderers go? For murder is what you propose to do here. You do not act under the king's law or God's law but your own law. And for that you will burn long before Rose Lantz does. Will you risk it?"

Tom Finch did not reply.

The skinny man pushed his way forward. "You can't stop us all! Once you have fired your guns, what will you do then?"

"Why, turn to my tomahawk and skinning knives, Bill Seward. And while I am at work with those the sheriff and his men can reload and fire a second volley. More than a dozen of you will be dead by then."

Ethan loosened one of the long skinning knives in his belt so that the torchlight flashed off its blade. "Have you ever been skinned alive, Bill Seward? I suppose not for if you had you'd be under a gravestone now. The Iroquois taught me the technique. It's fast. I suppose I could relieve three or four of you of your flesh while the sheriff and deputies shot the rest of the leaders. Shall we begin?"

Ethan jerked up his rifle sharply. Tom Finch and Bill Seward and two or three dozen other men at the front of the mob cried out and threw themselves to the ground. But Ethan was pointing at someone else.

"Ben Shepherd! I see you have the idea of throwing your torch onto the roof of the house! Bring your arm down! Bring it down by my count of three or I will shoot you through the heart!"

Rose saw the man, fifty yards away, arm bent back, obvious now that the others in front of him were flat in the dirt.

The man shot a glance at Ethan and the barrel of his Lancaster County long rifle. "You can't hit me in the heart from there."

"What do you think, Tom Finch?" asked Ethan, not

lowering his rifle. "Can I make the shot? You were at the last turkey shoot."

"Ben!" called Finch as he lay sprawled on his stomach. "He can put a bullet wherever he wants from two hundred and fifty yards!"

"You're all cowed by him!" snarled Ben Shepherd. "Daniels won't do a thing! He's all bluff! It would be murder if he shot me!"

"What do you think, sheriff?" asked Ethan. "Would it be murder if I put a bullet in Ben Shepherd for trying to set this home ablaze with children inside?"

The sheriff's musket was on Shepherd too. "This is an armed rebellion. These men have risen up against the divine authority of the king. There would be no murder charge placed on those who suppressed the rebellion. On the contrary, Ethan Daniels, ye should be hailed as a hero and the king's man in Philadelphia and London. So pray go ahead and shoot."

"One, two, three," counted Ethan.

With a glare, Ben Shepherd put his arm down. "Drop the torch," said Ethan.

"What?" responded Shepherd.

"Drop it on the ground and stamp it out. Then go. You can be the first to head back to town."

Shepherd looked at Ethan a moment and at the muzzle of the rifle.

He let the torch fall and bore down on it with his boots, orange sparks flying. Once it was out he turned and walked along the lane to the main road.

Sheriff What-God-Will gestured with his musket. "The rest of ye can follow him. Go now and there'll be no charges laid in the morning. Stay and the governor will hang ye. Come back tomorrow or the day after and ye will hang for that too."

"In case you wish to risk it," Ethan spoke up, "I plan to be here all night."

"And two of my deputies will be here after breakfast," warned the sheriff. "Take my words to heart. The governor will press charges. Revolt never goes over well with those in authority. Thou will lose thy life. Go home to thy families and in the morning go about thy business as good citizens. Christmas will be with us in a few weeks. Prepare for that if thou have time on thy hands. I say to thee again, go."

The leaders picked themselves off the ground and headed back to the main road as Ben Shepherd had done. Slowly the rest of the men turned and followed, several casting spiteful glances at Ethan and the sheriff. One by one torches were extinguished so that after a few minutes the crowd was dark and silent as it moved along the road to Lancaster.

"D'ye think any will come back?" the sheriff asked Ethan.

"Now and then you have a reckless one."

"Aye." The sheriff clapped a hand to Ethan's shoulder. "Thou'll be all right then?"

"I just need some coffee."

What-God-Will turned to Mr. Lantz, who had been standing in front of the door with a Bible in his hand. "Pastor Johannes? Can ye spare some coffee for the man here? He'll be thy watchman for what's left of the night."

"*Ja, ja.* Of course." He nodded his head at the sheriff and Ethan. "*Danke.* God used you both this night. No blood was shed. I am grateful for your protection of my daughter and my family. Perhaps all of your men would like coffee. It is cold."

What-God-Will glanced about at his deputies. "Aye. I think we could all do with some."

"Come in, yes, come in, warm up, our kitchen is warm."

"Thank thee. We shall do that."

The sheriff and his men trooped into the house, shutting the door behind them. Ethan talked to several of their horses where they were tethered at the side of the house and ran his hand over their necks. Then he walked across the farmyard to where Rose still stood, rifle in her small hands and lantern at her feet.

"You have no shoes on," he said. "There wasn't time."

"You're not cold? You only have a housecoat on."

"I'm not feeling the frost, no."

"You don't look afraid either." Gently he placed his fingers under her chin again. "I'm proud of you."

"I didn't do anything."

He smiled. "You didn't run and scream and hide."

"But I wasn't brave like you."

"Yes, you were." He ran his hand over the side of her face and took up lengths of her hair in his hand. "I didn't tell you how soft your skin is and how soft your hair. It's like the purest water moving in secret through the heart of the forest."

She put her hand on his as he touched her cheek. "You saved my life."

"Thank the sheriff for that."

"I shall thank him and his men. But they didn't stop Tom Finch and Bill Seward." She brought his face closer to hers and kissed him on the lips. She had no thought of stopping. Finally she put her fingers on his mouth. "I love you, Ethan."

"I'm blessed."

"I still don't know what to do about it." She pushed his hair back from his forehead. "Do you?"

"Yes."

Rose smiled with her eyes and lips. "Always so sure of yourself."

"I'm sure of how I feel about you. I'm not going to let go of that."

"Will you come in for coffee?"

"I won't."

"Where will you be?"

"I'll roam. In five minutes I'll be in the barn to get warmed up."

"I'll bring the coffee to you." She ran her hand over his chest, feeling the soft texture of the deerskin and the strength of his muscles underneath. "Ethan?"

"Yes."

"Are you really mine? Do you truly love me?"

He put his lips to her forehead. "Come to the barn with the coffee and we'll see."

Ten minutes later Rose left the house wearing a long winter coat, hair pinned up under a white shawl, holding a steaming mug of coffee in her hand. She could not see Ethan anywhere so she went straight to the barn. Several cows lifted their heads and stared at her. She wandered past the stalls and back to the barn door but she could not find him.

Cautiously stepping into the darker shadows in one

corner she whispered, "Ethan? You are not hiding on me, are you?"

One arm swept around Rose and scooped her up until she was standing on her toes as Ethan buried his face in her neck. She gasped. A moment later his lips were on her mouth and she had no breath at all. Waves of heat and light went through her as his strength held her close. Finally he pulled back a few inches.

"What happened to your hair?" he asked.

"My mother happened to my hair."

He reached a hand under her shawl but she seized it with a laugh. "No, you don't. It would be too much work to fix it up again before I returned to the house."

"I work quickly."

"Oh, I know that, Ethan Daniels. In love and in war you move like the wind. But I only have ten minutes. Mother is watching me like a hawk."

"Why is that?"

She made a face. "Oh, I don't know. Do you think it might have been the kissing? Or you calling me your bride?"

"I meant to speak to you about that."

She smiled and ran a finger over his lips. "Yes? Was that your proposal? Is that how a frontiersman does it?"

"I can do better than that."

"Hush. Not today. So much has happened I can't think straight. The trial, having to give testimony, Lydia being set free, the mob. And then you."

"Me?"

"You had a key in your pocket. You inserted it in the lock of my heart and turned it. Out sprang feelings I've never had. I don't even recognize myself anymore.

I can't believe how I kissed you. I've never kissed anyone in my life like that. What have you done to me? I should give myself a new name and put on different clothes and ask Mama to dye my hair."

"Don't do that. I love Rose Lantz exactly the way she looks right now—golden brown hair, golden green eyes, lips like rose petals."

"Stop it." She playfully swatted his arm. "I'm serious. Since you kissed me I haven't been Rose Lantz anymore."

"It was Rose Lantz who set the court on fire with her words and saved her friend's life. It was Rose Lantz who ran out into the night and stood before a howling mob without fear in her eyes. It was Rose Lantz who held me and kissed me like a thunderstorm gripping my body and crashing all over my face and lips. That's the woman I want and that's the woman I have in my arms right now."

"No, I—"

"For years you hid under that shawl because it's part of your religion. You thought you also had to hide the fire of your spirit and keep your head down to hide the fire in your eyes. You thought you had no beauty and that God wanted you to cover up what womanhood you might have under cloaks and wraps and a downcast face. But in court you stood erect. And when you kissed me you struck flame to my tinder. You think I have never held a woman before or admired those I took into my arms? You don't think I feel the difference when I look at you or hold you? You don't think you did something to me tonight?"

He gripped her face tightly with both hands. "I am

on fire from head to foot. No woman has ever done to me what you did to me an hour ago. I am burning up. And it is Rose Lantz who has done it. All your life you have played the mouse. But you are no mouse. You are a cougar, a panther, a mountain lion, one of the great cats I see west of here, free, strong, rippling with power and moving with dignity and grace, sheer beauty and magnificence, tawny and golden-eyed and courageous. You are everything I want and admire in one person. Thank God you are also a woman."

He kissed her quickly. "Your head is spinning. Yes, it was a day like no other for you. You don't want to hear my proposal because I move too fast, it is too much, the day and night are already full. But you will hear it anyways. I love you, you excite me like no one and nothing else, your worth cannot be measured in mountains or rivers or herds of deer or anything I treasure. I would die for you. But instead I will live for you. Be my bride. Be my woman. I will cherish you forever and you will always be by my side. You will have a love I give only to you and share with no one else. I will cool you like a mountain's waters and warm you like sun filling up a meadow. Come to my heart. Please come. You are my rose. You are my lady."

Rose's mouth was half open. She looked in his gray eyes and saw the storm there as well as the tenderness.

He means every word.

"Oh, Ethan." She dropped the mug and put both arms around him and pulled him to her, cradling his head at her neck and shoulder. "I wanted the day to stop so I could catch up with myself. Now I don't want it to end. I pray to God it will never end."

"Speak the word and it *will* never end. I swear it."

"Ethan." She tugged his head free so she could look at him again. Tears cut down her face. She laughed and smiled and cried at the same time. "Yes, yes, yes, yes."

His kisses again, fiery, soft, strong, gentle, penetrating, powerful, overwhelming her and a lifetime of defenses and precautions, breaking every wall down and every high tower, opening up her heart, opening up her soul, giving her a liberty in God, a liberty to love, a liberty to leap like a deer.

I run in the path of your commands for you have set my heart free.

She touched her fingers to his mouth and he kissed them. "I must go," she said.

"I know."

"I'm afraid I've dropped your coffee."

"I don't need it. You're better than coffee."

"Shh."

"No coffee I've ever drunk has made me as warm and full as you."

"Now you're being silly."

"Stay with me."

"I can't. You know I can't."

He kissed her down the side of her face, pressing his lips against her temple, her ear, her neck and shoulder, her rich brown hair that he had tugged loose with his fingers. "I will say hello to you before I leave in the morning."

She leaned her head back and closed her eyes. "Will you?"

"You'll come to milk the cows, won't you?"

"Yes."

"So I will give you a milking kiss before I go back to my cabin."

She smiled, eyes still closed, as he continued to move his lips from her ear to her throat to the long silky strands of her hair. "What have you done with the pins?"

"They are in my hand."

"I will need them."

"I know."

"You may have your milking kiss, Long Hunter, but I will have you. You shall not be returning to your cabin."

"No?"

"No. Mother has prepared a spare bedroom for you. She will not hear of you going back to your cabin alone."

"She trusts me in your house? Putting the cat with the bird?"

Rose laughed. "The way you describe me perhaps I am the cat and you are the bird." She surprised herself by biting him gently on the chin. "It is her way of saying thank you. She knows there is something up between us and I doubt she is comfortable with it. But she also knows you saved our lives last night. So until things settle down you are sleeping and eating in our house. Father and the boys are going to bring your dapple gray over here as well as a few items of clothing, whatever they find."

"When was all this established?"

"While the coffee was brewing. You don't have a say in such matters."

He smiled. "I surrender freely. I will be close to you day and night and that pleases me."

"It pleases me as well, my love." She opened her

eyes and gazed at him. "I feel so strange saying that. Is it true? Has God brought us together? Are we lovers?"

"Yes."

"Am I to be your bride? Will you take me to your home and to your bed?"

"I will."

"I don't see how it can all happen. I don't see how my parents or my church will accept it."

"Let God figure that out. Just be true to the love you feel for me and be true to the woman he has set you free to be." He ran his thumbs back and forth slowly over her eyebrows and eyelids. "No more of the mouse. Not after today and tonight. Stand erect. Eyes up and eyes clear. Only as much clothing as you need and no more. Let your smiles be full and your whole demeanor radiant."

"I'll try."

"And I'll help."

"I must go. Really, I must. Mother will swoop down upon us."

He continued to kiss her as she pinned her hair back up. She made no attempt to stop him, she loved the feeling of his lips on her face and neck and skin. When she was done they held each other more tightly than they had before and she placed her mouth over his, loving him as long as she dared, putting all her desire and all her hopes and prayers into her kiss. Then she pulled away and hurried across the farmyard to the house. At the door she turned and looked back at him, knowing his eyes were on her, pursed her lips, and blew him a kiss, something she had never done in her life.

Who are you, Rose Lantz? Who, in heaven's name, have you become?

At five in the morning she returned to do the milking, not feeling tired in body or mind or heart. Once again he was hiding and surprised her, once again they kissed as if it would be their last opportunity for a hundred years. Her father popped in to say several deputies had arrived and found his daughter and Ethan busily milking the herd. He spoke with them a few minutes, stroking his beard, said breakfast would be ready in half an hour, and left.

"Where are the deputies?" she called after him.

"At the front door."

As soon as he had gone Rose splashed milk over Ethan's face and ran to the other side of the barn. She let him catch her and they began to kiss all over again, her lips taking up the taste of his lips as well as the sweetness of the fresh milk. When they went in for breakfast she had to fight the urge to hold his hand. The deputies joined her and Ethan and her family at the table and after everyone had eaten Mrs. Lantz showed Ethan to his room, just down the hall from the kitchen.

"It's very kind of you," said Ethan.

"Never mind. You have done a great deal of good. You should not be alone in troubled times. When you wake up there will be a hot supper for you."

Ethan leaned his two rifles against the wall near his bed. "Thank you."

All day as Rose helped in the kitchen she wanted to tiptoe down the hall and peek in at his door. Finally she gave in and did it, even though her mother was at the stove making a kettle of venison stew. Soon her mother was peering in over her shoulder.

"He looks like a boy, Mama," she whispered.

"Hm. Some boy. His feet hang out over the end of the bed and his arms look like they are made of iron."

"He is gentle as a lamb."

"Ja?" She took her daughter's hand. "Slow down, my girl. Catch your breath. Bring everything to God in prayer."

"I do, Mother."

"Good. So Jakob Ammann is coming to share our meal this evening. He wishes to speak with you and Ethan."

For the first time after hours and hours of happiness Rose felt like a stone had lodged in her chest. "Yes. All right."

"He will come early. Before Ethan is up. He told Father there are matters he must raise with the family alone."

The stone grew heavier and took on sharper edges. "Yes, Mama."

Jakob Ammann arrived in the afternoon in the company of Pastor Ulrich and Pastor Philip. Mrs. Lantz poured coffee and Mr. Lantz joined the men at the kitchen table. When Rose came in from hanging the washing and giving the deputies fresh cookies and cups of coffee they asked her to sit down with them.

"A hard day yesterday, daughter," Jakob said to Rose as he sipped his coffee from a blue mug.

"Yes, Grandfather."

"You were tested as our people were tested in Switzerland and Germany. I praise God you acquitted yourself well."

"The Lord was with me."

"Yes. But it was required of you to respond to his

work on your heart." He wrapped his fingers around the warm mug. "The winter chill is in the air today. As it was last night."

Rose nodded.

"A night as difficult as the day. But again no different than Europe. A mob. Only this time the officers of the law defended us instead of persecuting us."

"We thanked the sheriff and his men."

"Of course. I met two of the deputies outside. I was telling your father and mother they will not need to be here long. The governor was sent a note by special rider. He is sending a company of troops to Lancaster. They will be stationed here for a year or more until the sheriff is satisfied the witch hunt is over."

"A company. Where will they put them all?"

"Judge Hallowell had an acreage he sold to the town when it grew past its old boundaries. There was a barn that was never torn down. The town planners simply built around it, *ja*?" He put his coffee to his lips. "It is sturdy. Good workmanship and materials. Two floors. So the carpenters are putting up walls to make rooms for the soldiers and a kitchen as well. Four men to a room. Officers have private quarters. Some of our own people are busy today with this task. If you go into Lancaster you hear the saws and hammers. I praise God."

"When will the troops arrive, *Opa*?"

"They are not marching but coming in wagons. We expect them Monday."

"*Gute.* So then the sheriff and his deputies will be free."

"Yes. And your night watchman as well."

Rose felt ice move into her blood. She did not respond but dropped her eyes.

"Do not misunderstand me, daughter. I am well aware of what your young man has done. He has been God's instrument to deliver your family from evil. Sheriff What-God-Will was quite blunt in expressing his opinion of last night's affair with the rioters. He told me that without Ethan Daniels' boldness he is certain the mob would have rushed the house and overwhelmed himself and his deputies. But the rioters feared Mr. Daniels' prowess with his Lancaster County rifles. And with his tomahawk and knife. It is not our way, daughter, but so God sometimes uses the sword to deal with lawlessness and unrighteousness. I do not fault him. No one should fault him."

Rose kept her eyes down. *"Danke, Opa."*

"So. You have feelings for this young man, my daughter?"

"Yes, Grandfather."

"And he for you?"

"Yes, Grandfather."

"Please do not be afraid. Raise your eyes. Come. Look at me." Hesitantly, Rose lifted her head.

"I was once a young man too, my dear. I was enraptured with my young bride—her spirit, yes, her faith, but, oh, I thanked God for her eyes, I thanked God for her beauty." He smiled and ran his fingers through his untrimmed white beard. "Do my words surprise you?"

"I suppose they do."

"So I was not born a hundred years old. It's true that once I was twenty."

The men at the table laughed. Rose saw that even her mother, busy at the sink, let her face open with a smile.

Jakob reached across the table for Rose's hand and she gave it to him.

"I have something to tell you. A good thing. Your parents do not know, the pastors do not know. Only my wife knows. All right?"

Rose waited. She knew she looked tense and worried but could not change that.

"For months young Ethan Daniels has been visiting with me at my house in the evenings."

A shock went through Rose. *"Vas?"*

"Visit is perhaps too mild a word. He has asked me to teach him about our faith. He has asked for baptism."

Rose's mother spun around from the sink and stared at Jakob Ammann, almost dropping a cup in her hand. Her father and the other pastors were equally startled, their eyes opening wide and full.

"So there are many rough edges to hone but our Lord is the Master Carpenter. Ethan proceeds well. More time is needed but he comes along very well." Jakob smiled at Rose with as much warmth as she had ever seen. "He admitted that at first he came to me with an eye to winning your hand even though you were still betrothed to Juerg. Later it grew into a true interest in understanding our way of life, our path in Christ Jesus our Lord. Our talks continue. We pray together and study the Scriptures. Does this amaze you?"

"Yes, Grandfather."

"But perhaps also delight you?"

Rose smiled for the first time. "I confess it seems too good to be true."

"Even now you are not sure, hm? It was a secret between us. But at the courthouse yesterday I asked him if you did not deserve to know. You have been so brave yet so alone. I told him the two of you would be free to court just as our people courted in Switzerland and court here in America. He seemed to like that idea a great deal."

Everyone smiled and Rose felt the blush beginning at her neck. "So when he wakes I have a request as your father in the Lord." He squeezed Rose's hand. "Go on a buggy ride. Go on a wagon ride. That is what we do. It is a very good thing." It was rare for him to chuckle but Rose and everyone in the kitchen heard him. "No need to always court in the barn. Give the milk cows some peace, *ja*?"

Even her parents laughed but Rose's face flamed.

Jakob nodded. "My poor Rose. You expected something else, did you not? You thought I would come and tell you a relationship with Ethan Daniels was impossible. But now God has given you the delight of your heart. So sometimes he surprises us in such a way." He consulted his pocket watch. "He should rise now. Let him speak with us and pray. By then we will all be hungry and will break bread together. Then the buggy ride." His eyes were bright. "Go, wake him. Open the door and call to him. If he sleeps the sleep of the dead, give his shoulder a good shake with the Swiss hand. Go, my daughter, go. You have found favor in the eyes of the Lord and all his people."

Rose looked at her father and mother. Both smiled and nodded.

Her face still crimson she got up and went down the

hall and opened his door. There he lay, completely trusting them, fast asleep, his unbound hair a wave of dark brown across the pillow. It felt to her as if she slept too and had dreamed everything Jakob Ammann said. She waited but Ethan did not disappear and neither did the strong beating of her own heart.

Oh, how I should love to cradle you. How I should love to wake you with a kiss.

"Ethan," she said softly. He did not stir.

"Ethan," she said a little more loudly. Nothing.

Taking a breath she walked into the room and up to his bed. "Ethan."

When there was still no response she bent over him and gently shook his bare shoulder. "Ethan. You must wake up."

He continued to sleep.

She bent lower and put her mouth by his ear. "Ethan. Can you hear me? Wake up." Then she decided to dare it and whispered, *"Please wake up, my darling. I so much want a kiss."*

An arm immediately shot up around her shoulders and pulled her down sharply.

"Ethan!" she whispered frantically. *"No, no, don't! The door is open and everyone is in the kitchen!"*

His lips covered hers with a rich warmth and a taste of the coffee and bread and jam he had taken before the night before. She tried to push him away, bracing both hands against his chest, but he was too strong. His kiss grew warmer and warmer and finally she gave up, letting his arm bring her to her knees beside his bed, running her hands through his long thick hair, returning the kiss with a heat and a strength of her own.

"Now that is the way to wake up in the morning," he murmured finally. "I keep saying to myself, a kiss from Rose Lantz, that is far better than any rooster crow."

She giggled but clapped a hand over her mouth. "Hush, hush," she said through her fingers. "They are just down the hall at the kitchen table."

"Who is?"

"My father, my mother, the pastors, Jakob Ammann."

"Ah, well, that's all right then."

"All right? The pastors and Jakob are the spiritual leaders of my church. And they can hear everything."

"No, they can't."

"Yes, they can."

"It doesn't matter," Ethan responded, kissing her again.

She pushed away. "What do you mean, it doesn't matter? Of course it matters."

"He promised me one kiss. He had fallen in love with a Swiss girl too and he promised me my one kiss of a Swiss girl when I woke up. *If she is willing it is little enough for all you have done.* Are you willing?"

"What?"

"It's true."

"It's not."

"It is." He drew her head back down and kissed her shawl and the hair pinned up underneath. "Didn't he send you in here to wake me?"

"Yes."

"Didn't he tell you to do what you must to wake me? To come in and shake my shoulder if I didn't respond to your call from the doorway?"

She stared at him. "Yes."

"You see? It was a conspiracy."

He kissed her cheek and neck and she said, "I can't believe it."

"You didn't think the old man had it in him, did you?"

"No. And you speaking with him about baptism and Mother making a bed up for you under our roof and you and your rifle and tomahawk and the men with the pitchforks and muskets turning away, no, really, all of this is beyond me."

"Not to mention I asked you to marry me. But that is a small thing."

"Oh, you are crazy. The whole day is crazy. My life is crazy."

"One more kiss."

"No, but you have had your one kiss."

"No, no, no. One Swiss kiss is worth a dozen kisses in America."

"You are as crazy as the day is crazy." She pushed away with all her might and stood up. Straightening her shawl and hair, she said, "I must get back out to the kitchen."

He smiled. "All right."

"Please get dressed and join us."

"All right. Then what?"

"Then, well, then, you may take me on a buggy ride."

"Suits me. I know a good place we can go on a buggy ride."

"*Ja?* And where is that?"

"The Kissing Bridge."

Heat blazed up from her neck. "Oh, Ethan, I wish you would stop doing that to me."

"Doing what?"

"The blushing, the blushing, always the blushing." She tugged down on her dress and went to the door. "You will not be long, will you?"

"Not if a buggy ride to the Kissing Bridge is involved."

She closed the door and closed her eyes, leaning against it.

How does he do this to me? How does he always do this to me?

She put both hands to her cheeks and looked down the hallway to the kitchen where everyone was waiting for her.

I am burning up. I cannot go back to them in this state.

Adjusting several loose hairpins she walked quickly along the hallway in the opposite direction. Picking up a large basket she darted out a side door and went to bring in the washing. The afternoon was cool and bright. The deputies saw her and doffed their hats. She nodded and began tugging shirts and pants and dresses free of the clothesline.

Lord, I am glad you do not tell us much. Because if you had told me when I woke up the morning of the trial all of these things would happen in the space of a day and a half even you I would not have believed.

When she returned to the house with her basket of laundry all of them were sitting at the table together and laughing, the pastors, Jakob Ammann, her mother and father, her younger brothers, and Ethan. As she folded the clothing away she even heard Ethan use a few German phrases that were spoken well and enunciated properly. By the time she finally sat down at the table between her father and mother she felt like a stranger. The others dug into the stew and fresh bread while she pecked at her bowl with her spoon.

What else has been kept from me? What other things do people know about Ethan that I do not?

Her mind elsewhere she did not dress for the chill of sunset. She climbed up to sit on the driver's seat of a carriage the family hardly ever used. Her father had hitched it to their black mare Gretta. Ethan flicked the traces and they left the farmyard, moving quickly down the lane to the main road.

"You're quiet," he said.

"I like to be quiet."

"Are you all right?"

"I'm perfectly fine, thank you."

"I'm not sure you've dressed warmly enough."

"I certainly know to dress for winter, Ethan Daniels."

He did not reply or speak again. After a few minutes he steered Gretta off the roadway to a narrow track that meandered through barren oak trees to his cabin.

"What are we doing here?" asked Rose. "I have no intention of stepping down and lingering at your living quarters."

Ethan smiled. "I don't want you to."

"You don't?"

"No."

"Then why have you brought me to this place?"

"I need to get something. One moment."

Ethan stepped down and went inside. He was not long. When he returned he was wearing an animal skin coat with the fur side out. In his arms he carried what looked to Rose like a large brown fur blanket.

Climbing up he draped it over her. It carried a whiff of wood smoke. The shivers she had been trying to hide from Ethan immediately disappeared.

Gratefully she sank her face into the curly fur. "Oh, Ethan, how is it you can get me out of my sour moods so quickly?"

"No woman can be happy who is chilled to the bone."

"What animal is this?"

"You have never seen it. The animal lives far to the west. It's huge and has horns. Different tribes have different names for it: *eeVnii, Bi Shee, Buskwa Moostoos, ta Tanka, hotowa'e.* I traded several fine knives for this skin and another."

"How could you bring this back on foot?"

"I went back and forth by rivers and lakes. You've seen the *kenu* or *canoe* the tribes use?"

"Only once."

"That is how I was able to move so far west so swiftly. Still I was gone a year and wintered there."

"Wintered there?" Rose looked at his coat. "What are you wearing?"

"*Wapiti.* They have antlers but are much larger than a deer. Good eating, warm fur, magnificent to see. The males have a long wailing cry that stirs my blood."

"I wish you would tell me stories about your journeys."

"Is that what you desire?"

"Very much."

Ethan swung back up onto the driver's seat next to her. He cupped his face in her hands. "Taking instruction from your leader Jakob Ammann was not meant to hurt you. Learning German in secret was not done to exclude you. These things were supposed to be a pleasant surprise, Rose, they were not intended to make you feel unimportant."

"I'm not sure why I feel so lost." She dropped her eyes, fingering the *wapiti* fur on his chest. "I'm sorry for acting out of sorts when the Lord has given me so much to be grateful for."

He kissed her slowly on the lips, still holding her face in his hands.

"Thank you for loving me," she said.

His eyes were only inches from hers. "When I started to call on Mr. Ammann you had no use for me. What good would telling you have done?"

"No, I—"

"A wild man who lives in the woods. Runs around like a beast. Why, when you stumbled upon my cabin where I was chopping wood that afternoon you fled like a deer from a hunter."

Her face crimsoned. "Please don't say those things. I didn't know any better."

"I'm sorry. I seem to be making many mistakes. Everything I'm doing is hurting you."

She continued to twist the fur in her fingers. "You aren't hurting me. When I saw you that day you had removed your shirt. So I ran because I was—I was attracted to you—to how you looked—so strong—so perfect—I didn't want any of those feelings—I ran because I was frightened of how I felt—and you."

"Are you still afraid of me?"

She laughed, still looking down, watching her fingers toy with the *wapiti* coat. "Of course not. I feel safe when you are around. Safer than I have ever felt in my life."

"And I am happy. So happy I thank God more than I ever have in my life."

"You do not."

"I do."

She finally looked up. "How can you say that? A man who has traveled where hardly any have ever been? A man who has seen marvels? Who puts a fur around me of an animal none of us in Pennsylvania have heard of?"

"Well, there was always this greater marvel at home. Hidden under a shawl. Eyes cast to the ground. I saw her beauty, an exceptional beauty, because I have been trained by my wanderings to find it in the most unlikely places. I knew what you thought of me. I did not think we would ever come together. I did not think the day would come when you would like me let alone love me. But I decided to try and win your hand anyways. Should I thank the witch hunt for that?"

She ran a finger over his nose and mouth like a child playing with a strange face. "Is that over, do you think?"

"Once the redcoats arrive they will keep the peace."

"But is it over?"

"People are capable of great goodness and great wickedness. Even the same person is capable of both. I won't be letting down my guard. But I believe the winter will be quiet."

"Then what?"

"Shh. Then I will marry you."

"Ethan—"

"Jesus said he would never leave us or forsake us,

didn't he? His spirit is in me and neither will I." He took both her hands and wrapped his large fingers over them. *"Danke Gott fur diese Frau. Ich danke Ihnen fur ihre Schonheit, fur ihre Geist, fur ihre Gebete, fur ihre Liebe. Liefern sie vom Bosen und gewahren ihren Frieden. Durch useren Herrn Jesus Christus."*

Tears glinted in her eyes. "Ethan!"

"So to pray for you in German is a good surprise?"

She threw her arms around his neck. "You thank God for my beauty, my spirit, my prayers, and my love? You don't mean it."

"Of course I mean it. You know I mean it." He kissed her eyes, one after the other. "And he *will* deliver you from evil. And he *will* certainly grant you peace. *Amen*, Swiss girl?"

"Ethan—"

"Amen?"

She leaned her head against his. *"Ja, mein schonner Mann. Amen."* Now her hands found his neck and shoulders and the long rope of hair that fell down the middle of his back. "Ethan—"

"What are you going to argue with me about now?"

She kissed his cheek and nuzzled his throat and put her lips gently to his ear. "Can we please go to the bridge? *Bitte?*" she whispered.

Volume 7

A Rose In Winter

"Oh, I can't! It's too hard!"

"Come on! Just try another step!"

Rose stumbled on her snowshoes and grabbed on to a tree to keep herself upright.

"This is crazy!" she laughed. "I'll never be the Tuscarora scout you are!"

Ethan reached out a hand to her, standing on his snowshoes about fifty feet away. "You'll be the pride of the Iroquois Confederacy. You just need to remember to walk differently. Lift your leg up high each time you take a step. Step up and then forward."

"I can't."

"Of course you can. Up and forward."

Rose let go of the tree trunk and lifted her leg in her long dark dress and the deer coat he had given her, planting her foot firmly in the thick white snow. She lifted her other leg just as high or higher and set it down next to the other. To her surprise, she did not pitch forward on her face, something that had already happened twice.

"Look at that!" Ethan grinned. "She walks!"

"Ha ha. We'll see how you do in the kitchen, Ethan Daniels."

"If we ever get to one, I'll show you a few things, Miss Lantz."

"Will you?" Rose continued to make her way towards him. "You may get your opportunity sooner than you think, my boastful man. Then you will be put in your place."

Her movement was rapid as she became more adept at raising her leg high and putting her foot down squarely on top of the snow. Hair still pinned up under a white cap she had purchased from a Quaker woman, she made her way through the trees to Ethan, both of them smiling at each other. When she reached him he took her in his arms and kissed her on the cheek.

"Your cheeks are redder than rose hips," he said. "Someone help me. You get more beautiful every day."

"Oh, hush. Hasn't Jakob Ammann taught you about modesty?"

"He didn't say it applied to your God-given beauty."

"Please don't say that." Her face turned more crimson. "You make me blush and it isn't true."

"Oh, yes, it's true. You want me to lie? You want me to say God had no part in your birth or the bloodline in your parents or how he put it all together in your face and figure?"

"Ethan—"

"What would Jakob Ammann say about lying?"

Rose brushed his hair out of his eyes. "You always

have these perfect answers. What am I supposed to say?"

"Just be the person you were born to be, Rose. Be the beauty God created." His hand touched her cheek. "Look at your eyes. Look at your eyebrows—they're like fine gold. Look at how white your teeth are. Someone help me. Can I last even another minute without being married to you?"

"Who is it you expect to help you?"

"God. A Quaker. Anyone who can save me from your beauty and charms."

"So do you want to be saved, Ethan Daniels?"

He pulled her closer to his chest and the *wapiti* coat he was wearing. "I guess not."

She ran her hands over the soft fur. "I certainly don't."

Her eyes were liquid gold and green and underneath the color of earth. He tilted her chin with his fingers and her beautiful eyes closed in anticipation of a kiss when a shout rang through the forest.

"Kommen auf Sie zwie! Warten wir!"

Rose pulled back from Ethan quickly.

"It's my father!" Rose put her hands to her cap and her hair. "What is he doing here?"

Ethan took a good look at the sleigh that had stopped at the edge of the trees. "He's not alone. Your mother and brothers are with him."

"Kommen auf Sie zwei Turteltauben! Genugend Zeit fur die spatere!"

Rose made a face. *"Lovebirds! Plenty of time for that later!* We hardly ever get time alone."

"Well, they're watching and waiting. This is a good

time to show them we have not just been standing around kissing."

"Kissing? Who has been kissing? All I've been doing is falling face forward in the snow! But of course Mama and Papa show up the moment I am about to enjoy myself!"

Ethan looked at her in astonishment and laughed. "You really are a keg of gunpowder when someone lights your fuse, aren't you?"

The tip of her nose was bright red and her eyes shot sparks. "I don't recall anyone mentioning a sleigh ride this morning at breakfast. The trouble is that farmers in the winter have too much time on their hands."

"Well, let's make the best of it. Come. We'll head towards them. They'll enjoy the sight. I'm sure no one in your family has used snowshoes before."

Rose muttered something but began to lift her leg high before placing the snowshoe down. Step by step she walked beside Ethan, never tripping or losing her balance, until both emerged from the forest. Nathan, the oldest of her brothers at twelve, gaped at her. So did Hans, the younger of the two, only eight years old. Envy was scribbled across both their faces and was easy enough for Rose to read. Her annoyance vanished instantly and she smiled at them.

"Hello, you two," she said. "Is this something you would like to try? I was pretending to be a Tuscarora brave."

"You are very good at this!" exclaimed Nathan. "You are going along as swiftly and smoothly as Long Hunter."

Nathan and Hans never called Ethan by his Christian name. Long Hunter was far more fun and dramatic.

Rose laughed. "It is not a contest. And I'm sure Long Hunter here could go like the wind if he needed to. I am just happy I am not lying face down in the snow anymore."

"Oh." Wrinkles deepened on her mother's face. "Are you hurt?"

"Sure, my pride is hurt but Jakob Ammann would say that was a good thing, wouldn't he? Anyways, I am not falling so much now for which I praise God." Rose put a hand on the wooden side of the sleigh. "This is the first time you've had it out all winter, Papa."

Her father nodded. "It was past time we had a ride together. It is 1729 and we are halfway through January already. Can you pull those off and join us?"

"Of course."

Her and Ethan sat beside the sleigh and removed their snowshoes. The two black horses snorted and swung their heads. Rose handed her snowshoes to Nathan and Ethan gave his pair to Hans. Then Ethan jumped into the hay in the back and helped Rose up.

Her mother glanced back at them. "Are you two settled?"

"Ja, Mama, danke."

"Are you cold?"

Rose shook her head and smiled, putting an arm through one of Ethan's and leaning into him with a hug. "With this coat I have on? And this furry man beside me? It is like a summer's day."

Her mother scrutinized her coat. "Yes, I noticed the coat. Deer? From Ethan?"

"Yes, Mama. A Christmas present, he says."

"And the mittens also?"

"Deer hide, yes, Mama. My hands are very warm, much warmer than the woolen gloves I knitted for myself."

Her mother nodded. Then she smiled at Ethan with her biggest smile. "Thank you for taking such good care of our daughter."

"It is a pleasure, Mrs. Lantz. She means all the world to me."

"All the world?"

He nodded. "Probably more than that."

"Such an expression."

He grinned and shrugged. "I don't know what better way to get my point across. Look at her. The winter sun and the sharp cold make her shine like the fields of snow around us. I have to squint to look at her."

Rose laughed and playfully swatted his hand. "Will you stop it?"

"It's true. You are as bright as a snowflake."

"A snowflake?"

"I can't think of a better word to describe you."

She laughed again. "You see, Mama. What can I do with him? If I take him out in public he embarrasses me. He has too much book learning and is always saying such crazy things about me."

Her mother nodded, saying nothing, and turned to face the front of the sleigh again. But inside she was filled with delight. Someone who had not seen her Rose for three or four months would blink and look twice—"And who is this? Who do we have here?" Where was the girl who always had her head down? Who never looked a stranger in the eye? Who was quiet as a mouse? Her cheeks were red as freshly picked apples and her eyes flashed silver and gold. The beautiful straight teeth God had given her were always breaking out in a smile. Her laughter rang through the house.

"So sometimes love does these wonderful things to us, thank God," she murmured.

"Ah?" Her husband raised his eyebrows. "What's that, my dear?"

"Nothing. Let us be on our way."

He shook the reins and the horses started forward.

Rose snuggled next to Ethan and took in the silver white fields of snow that blazed in the sunlight. Spray from the sleigh's runners sprinkled her face and she caught some on the tip of her tongue. The rich and pleasant scent of Ethan's *wapiti* furs and his own wonderful rugged scent that she knew so well came into her body with each breath she took. For a moment she closed her eyes.

I have never been happier in my life. I have never been so grateful in my life. It is like another birth. Thank you, my Friend. Thank you, my God.

"Rose." Ethan was whispering in her ear. He took the opportunity to gently brush a loose lock of her coffee brown hair with his lips and her whole body reacted as if he had pricked her with a pin. "Do you dare me? No one is looking."

The simple touch of his lips had made her take in an extra breath and part her lips. "Dare you to do what?"

"The boys are caught up with the snowshoes, trying to tie their boots into them. Your mother and father are staring straight ahead. There are no houses nearby."

"So?"

His lips were over hers in an instant, the potent scent of his furs and body and the long hair tied at the back of his head overwhelming her. She did not even care if her mother should glance back or one of her brothers look up. Ethan came down on her with more and more strength, yet the kiss remained sweet and tender and warm, so warm it spread from her mouth to her throat and down into her chest and stomach. She found herself praying as he kissed her, thanking God again, asking that he never be taken from her, that the kiss last longer and longer, that the snow from the sleigh runners continue to shower their faces and cheeks, and turn into small drops of water that would run down their necks and under the collars of their coats. A tiny moan escaped from her and she drew a hand out of her deer mitt and grasped the long strand of his hair, tugging on it as if she were ringing a bell, yanking back so hard in a sharp moment of pleasure and joy that his whole body suddenly tightened, but she did not care, she knew he was strong enough to handle her love. When the kiss ended she pulled lungfuls of air into herself and leaned her head against the *wapiti* fur on his chest.

"Oh, how I love you." Her breath came in small quick pants. "The Lord knows how much I love you. It is too good to be true."

"No, it's too good not to be true." He pressed his lips against her forehead and against the hair gathered up under her Quaker cap. "Something like this a man could not even imagine so it must be real. Who would be able to think up beauty like yours out of thin air? Who could dream up such kisses? Your scent is like lemons and warm bread and chocolate and coffee—what person could mix together a recipe like that? No, you have to be real and everything that goes with you has to be real too. A rich imagination does not explain how incredible you are. God has done it, here you are, and you make me as warm as a wood fire."

"Don't exaggerate."

"I never exaggerate. I state what is so." His lips found hers again. "You have exceptional flavor today. I wonder what it is?"

"The coffee and cream and cake you fed me at my house before we strapped on the snowshoes."

"Is that it? Are you sure you don't naturally taste this way?"

She laughed into his fur. "How could I?"

"Well, you are Swiss and the Swiss are famous for their chocolate."

"How silly you are today."

"Still no one is looking." His kiss was sudden and strong. "Mm. Yes. Swiss chocolate."

"You are crazy."

"With a hint of the rose hips you chewed and swallowed."

"No." She pushed on his chest. "Go away."

"I'm not going anywhere. I hope your father keeps this up until it's dark."

"Why?"

"Ah, then we are truly hidden from everyone's eyes."

"Oh, you say that, but you would soon get hungry and cold."

"I have no appetite for food. And it is impossible to get cold when you are in my arms. It cannot happen."

Before she could reply his kisses were sparks along her neck and throat and darts of fire on her mouth that made her open her lips and take his beauty into herself again. She felt she could lose consciousness as the sleigh swayed and leaped and his lips found every part of her face and every loose strand of her hair and sweetened everything he touched.

"I cherish you," he whispered.

Once more his mouth was over hers and her hand that was free of its mitten slipped up into his sleeve and grasped the hard muscles of his arm and the broad strength of his shoulder. His kiss grew longer and fiercer and flames seemed to be running back and forth just underneath the surface of her skin. She opened her mouth to gasp and he took the opportunity to hug her more tightly and kiss her with even more force. She flicked her wrist so that her other deer mitt fell off and put this hand under his coat and up over the shirt on his back, digging her strong fingers into the muscle she knew was there and that she adored.

What a beautiful lover you have given me, Lord. How you have blessed me inside and out. This is like reading the Song of Songs. It is like some sort of love story from the Bible. Thank you that I have lived to see this day. Thank you that you have decreed I should have Ethan Daniels. Oh, how many other women among our people would want to be in his arms right now. How many Quaker women and English women would want to be in his arms right now. But it is I who am here and I enjoy this gift of yours so much.

Now she rested her head against his chest again. Now his arm was snug around her back and shoulders.

Now the sun was setting in a long line of red flames. Now her brothers complained they wanted to try out the snowshoes they had tied to their boots. Now her mother finally turned her head and glanced back.

"Aren't you boys hungry?" she asked.

"No," replied Nathan.

"No." Hans lifted a foot to show his mother the snowshoe with its long tail. "We want to be Iroquois."

"You can try them out by our house. How about you, Ethan? Aren't you hungry?"

"I haven't thought about it much, Mrs. Lantz. Any time that is good for you and your husband is good for me."

"Ja?" She looked at her daughter. "Your cheeks are red from the cold. How are you feeling?"

"Perfect."

"What? Not chilled at all?"

"I am like a pot of coffee over the fire."

"Huh." Her mother faced forward again. "Well, your father is turning around now. But it will be a half hour before we reach the farm. It will be dark."

Rose smiled into Ethan's *wapiti* fur. "I'm fine with that, Mama."

The entire winter went that way and it seemed to Rose she changed every time she glanced in the mirror. What had happened to her hair? What had happened to her lips? What had happened to the color of her skin? Even to her critical eye everything about her appeared to have taken on a new luster as if someone had polished her inside and out to achieve a new sort of brilliance. Whenever Lydia and she sat down in the parlor to work on the rose quilt her friend always mentioned the changes in Rose's appearance.

"So yesterday you looked like a basket of October apples. Today you are like a bowl of dark red cherries. What will you turn into tomorrow, sister? Peaches? Pears? How about a handful of purple plums?"

"Oh, Lydia, I am not like any of those things."

"Yes, you are. Perhaps Ethan Daniels is casting spells on you."

Rose smiled and worked her needle. "It's not spells, Lydia. It's blessings."

In the middle of February Ethan took Rose to meet Samuel Dressler, a man with a bald head like a brown acorn. He sat at his workbench wearing a long smudged apron and a pair of gold-rimmed spectacles, smiling warmly as she approached him from the doorway.

"So this is the young lady who has stolen our brave Long Hunter's heart when no Huron warrior could do it with a knife." The voice was deeper than the man looked and more resonant than she had expected. "You do my humble shop an honor."

Rose lowered her eyes. "Thank you, sir."

Samuel turned to Ethan. "She is far more beautiful than you described."

Ethan grinned. "If I'd told you how extraordinary she really was I'd have had to use language you would have dismissed with a wave of your hand." Ethan imitated Samuel Dressler's sweet, rolling voice. *"Poetry, Long Hunter, the sheer poetry of a romantic frontiersman. Hold your breath for one minute and start again and tell me only what is true about her. As you hold one of my rifles at its point of balance before you aim and fire so you must hold your thoughts and balance your imagination."*

The old man's smile broadened. "So I might have. But now there is no need as I see God's creation for myself. Just as I see a grove of spruce trees on a sunny slope or a cardinal lovely and red on a twig crisp with snow."

Rose felt her cheeks flame.

Samuel removed his glasses. "I understand you have a birthday coming up, young lady."

"Did Ethan tell you that?"

"He did indeed. Congratulations."

"My birthday is not until the 25th but I thank you."

"Ah ha. Come with me." Samuel got up from his stool and walked to a corner of his shop where there was a rack of rifles. "I am not the only one making long rifles in Lancaster County but I am one of the most careful when it comes to drying the wood and making the barrels straight and the locks sure." He hummed a tune to himself that Rose recognized instantly as the German hymn *Schonster Herr Jesu* which she had heard in Switzerland as a child. As he ran his hand over the rifles on the rack the words came out under his breath.

Schönster Herr Jesu Herrscher aller Herren
Gottes und Mariä Sohn Dich will ich lieben Dich
will ich ehren Meiner Seelen Freud und Wonn

To her surprise, she heard Ethan sing for the first time in her life. He picked up the tune, which she knew was from an old Silesian folk song, and sung his own English translation of the words Samuel had used.

Beautiful Savior King of Creation
Son of God and Son of Man Truly I'd love thee
Truly I'd serve thee
Light of my soul, my joy, my crown

Not only was Ethan bursting into song the only surprise of the moment. The other was the pleasantness of his singing voice—full, strong, rich, falling easily on the ears like a good warm wind stirring the thick green branches of tall pines. She knew her mouth had opened and that it stayed open as she watched him complete the verse.

He smiled. "It's a good thing there are no flies in winter, Miss Lantz, or one would surely find a home at the back of your throat."

"I do not hear you sing like that when you attend our worship services as our guest in Christ."

"I do not know your songs yet."

Samuel coughed into a handkerchief as smudged as his apron. "This is very good maple, see the curl in it? A German silver lock. The barrel forged true by Herman Schlick at his smithy. I cut the rifling in the barrel myself." He brought the firearm down from the rack. Light from one of the many windows in the shop brought out the sharp, dark striping in the wood. "Forty-five caliber. I have cast some round shot for it and procured a mold for the owner so he can make more of his own."

"Why, the wood is beautiful." Rose traced her fingers over the smooth stock. "Surely not even Ethan's rifles are as lovely as this one."

"Possibly not, even though I made them." Samuel

smiled and extended the firearm to her. "May I wish you a very happy and blessed birthday?"

Rose stared at the old man and the rifle. *"Vas?"*

"This was built for you specifically. Long Hunter was quite accurate as to your height and weight. You should be very comfortable with it. Please go out into the woods behind my shop here and test fire it. Mind there are no people about."

Rose's mouth was open again. "Me? Fire this?"

"In the Old Country many of the women hunted meat for their children if the husband was dead or injured. You are of proper build and proportion and have a lively eye. I believe you will shoot straight as an arrow."

"But my church—"

"Your father and mother know about this. So does Jakob Ammann. In fact he stopped by to watch me as I worked on it several times."

"Jakob Ammann?"

The woods were empty behind the shop. Ethan pointed to a round plate of iron fastened to an oak trunk. The tree's limbs were bare and gray.

"You will need to ring that to make Samuel happy. He will be listening for it."

"Ethan, that is almost two hundred yards away."

"It is."

"How can I hit such a small object so far from me? Especially when I have never fired a rifle before?"

"Well, perhaps you will not strike it on the first try. You do not have to do that. But with practice you will ring the iron like a church bell. I am sure of it."

"Sure of it, are you?" Rose held the rifle in her hands,

its rich striped wood glowing in the morning sun. "I do not even know how to load one of these."

"Here." Ethan unslung two powder horns from his chest, one small and one large. "The small horn has the small powder. That's how you remember. The small powder, the fine powder, it goes into the small pan on the lock. Go ahead, sprinkle some in. Pull back the lock first, about halfway. That's right. Not too much powder. A thimbleful."

Awkwardly, unsure of herself or how to move her hands, Rose did what Ethan asked.

"Good. Now the big horn for the big powder. This goes down the barrel and sends the lead shot to its target. Two hundred yards will need a decent amount of powder. You'll have to get used to measuring it in your hand. Cover your palm with it. A bit more. Good. Cup your hand like a funnel and send it down. Stamp the butt end of the stock on the ground to settle the powder. Now a patch of cloth." He gave her a small white square of cotton. "I cut this from a sheet of bed linen. You can use your old dresses, I expect. Place it over the muzzle. Center it. Now the bullet." Ethan gave her a small round ball. "Press that down into the cloth, right into the middle and into the barrel. Use your thumb. Get it right in there. How tight is it?"

"A little tight. Not so much I can't get the ball into the barrel."

"Good. I don't want it so tight you can't move the bullet easily. That makes it difficult to reload if you're in a hurry to get off a second shot."

"Why would I be in a hurry to get off a second shot?"

Ethan did not respond to her question. "Take the rod

out from underneath the barrel. It's good and strong and you use it to seat the bullet and patch on the powder charge. Keep the rifle butt on the ground. You've seen your father and the men do this countless times. Thrust the bullet right down the barrel with the rod until you can't go any farther. One smooth stroke is best. Perfect. Now place the rod back under the barrel and you're ready to shoot."

He stood behind her and reached his arms around Rose to show her how to fit the butt of the rifle stock into her shoulder. "The barrel is heavy. You can't hold it on the target for minutes at a time to get your aim right because even with good muscles it will begin to dip and sway."

"I don't have good muscles. I'm not a man."

"You are a farm girl and you have all you need to get started. The more you shoot the more you'll develop what you require to hold a rifle steady. For now just bring the barrel up on the target, hold it there for no more than the count of three, line up the front blade sight with the fork in the back sight, maybe aim a bit low—we don't know if the rifle will shoot high or low and we may have to file down the front sight a bit—then squeeze the trigger, don't jerk it. Hold rock steady while the flint shaves metal off the frizzen and hot sparks ignite the small powder in the pan and send a flame through a hole into the barrel. It only takes a one count and then the main charge goes off and your shot is cutting through the air. So you must hold steady between the fire in the pan and the fire in the barrel or else your bullet will go astray."

"It is too complicated. I'm not going to be any good at this, Ethan."

"You have a sharp eye and strong arms."

"I do not have strong arms."

"I have felt them around my back, my lady. I know."

Once again that morning Rose's face flamed. "Even when we're shooting rifles you do this to me."

"Are you ready?"

"I don't want to disappoint you, my love."

"You won't. Are you ready?"

"Yes."

"Cock the flint all the way towards yourself. Good. You must remember that once you cock back the flint the rifle will fire when you squeeze the trigger, so be careful. Only aim at what you wish to shoot from this moment on."

"Well, I want to shoot the metal plate."

"Take a look at it. See where it is. Now lift the rifle to your shoulder, tuck it in firmly there, put the sights on the target, go ahead, line them up, very good, now count one-two-three, breathe out, squeeze the trigger, hold steady for the fire in the pan and the fire in the barrel, hold steady, Beauty."

His new nickname for her, which thankfully he only used when no one else was present, distracted Rose for a moment. But the barrel was up, the sights were on the distant metal plate which looked no bigger than her thumbnail, she counted one-two-three as if she were a little girl about to jump into a pond for a swim, squeezed the trigger, heard the click as the jaw that held the flint sprang forward, saw the flash as the powder in the pan lit up, waited a heartbeat, her rifle still lined up on the plate, the barrel not falling away or wavering, then the roar and the smoke and the jolt to her shoulder and, to her shock, a moment later, the loud chime as lead hit iron.

Ethan whooped. "First shot, first time! I'll be! Amazing!" He turned his head and hollered, "Samuel! First shot!"

The old man poked his head out a window at the back of the shop. "I see that. And I hear that. Well done, Miss Lantz, well done, indeed. Though what with all the praises Ethan has sung about you I shouldn't be surprised."

Rose looked at Ethan through the quick drift of smoke. His smile was so large, his eyes so bright, and his pride in her so evident she bit her lip and did not know what to say or do. He kissed her on the forehead.

"What an incredible woman you are," he said. "What a gift from God."

"Please don't think too much of me, Ethan. Don't put me on a pedestal. I'm very ordinary, really."

"If a summer's day complete with sunlight and heat and robins and a thunderstorm followed up by a rainbow is ordinary, well, then, I guess you are right, Rose Lantz, you are a very ordinary woman." He put his arms around her and kissed her on the lips. "But it's an ordinary I'll praise God for the rest of my life because, in truth, it is utterly extraordinary."

A week later he was in the kitchen at her house. They cleaned the fish the two of them and the boys had caught through a hole in the ice in the creek. After that he showed her how to stuff them with a concoction he fried up in a pan and then roll the fillets in a mixture of flour, salt, peppercorns, and dried herbs he brought from his cabin. The day after it was Rose's turn and she led the way in pie baking, putting together one out of dried apple slices and brown sugar that she called *snitz pie* and another out of meat and vegetables. On both days there were fast and furious flour fights between Rose and Ethan that her mother squawked about which left the two of them white from head to foot. There was also a snowball fight in the farmyard, Rose and Hans and Nathan taking on Ethan, the end of the fight finding Rose pinned on her back getting her face washed with snow.

"Enough, Ethan, enough!" she spluttered and laughed. "My face is freezing off!"

"Not nearly enough. Your cheeks are just getting that nice bright color I love. Rosy red Rose."

"Stop it!"

"No, not until I get the exact color I want."

She wrestled him with all her might and then collapsed back in the snow, laughing even harder. "Oh, it's pointless, you're too strong. Help, Hans! Help, Nathan! The wild man from the woods has me trapped! Help, help!"

The boys pounced on Ethan's back, shoving handfuls of snow down his neck.

On her birthday Ethan gave her one of his three horses to ride, a sorrel named Sugarcane, while he rode a gelding with a cream-colored body and black tail and mane he called Moonlight. She had never sat on a full-grown horse before, only a pony, and had never done anything bareback. By the time the ride through the forest and fields was over her legs ached from gripping the flanks of Sugarcane as tightly as Ethan had taught her. Standing on the snowy ground by his log cabin her legs quivered beneath her long dress and long deer coat. He put his arm around her.

"Your muscles will get used to it," he said. "Just like with the arm muscles and the rifle. Your legs will strengthen."

"Yes, well, I do not want to wind up looking like an ox when you are through making a Mohican brave out of me."

Ethan threw back his head and the loose mane of his hair, laughing. "Small chance of you looking like an ox, Beauty. You get more entrancing each day. Twenty winters and you are more ravishing than the winter before or the winter before that."

"How do you know what I looked like the winters before? We've only known one another six months."

"I always had my eyes on you. I've told you that before."

She smiled as he kissed her cheek. "You have. I'm never sure if you're just making that up."

"No lies, Beauty." He took her hand. "The horses are fine here for now. Time for some coffee and a bit of bread and bacon."

Rose hung back, tugging against his grip. "Ethan, I can't go into your cabin, not the two of us alone. Think of the gossip and what people would say. You know better than that."

"I don't know what I know when I'm around you. My head is always spinning."

"Don't be silly. Walk me back to my own house and we can have coffee there."

"Coffee there? What? All alone? Just the two of us? Think of the damage to your reputation."

"Ethan, what on earth are you going on about? My parents are there. My brothers are there. For all I know Jakob Ammann has dropped over for a slice of dried apple pie, *snitz* and a chat."

"Well, that would be remarkable. I know he is an exceptional man but I have never seen Jakob Ammann in two places at once."

She narrowed her eyes at him. "What are you talking about? Why are you acting so crazy?"

"I'm just looking out for you. I can't take you to an empty farmhouse."

She repeated his words, still staring at him. *"An empty farmhouse."*

"What else could it be when the party is here?"

Rose felt more confused the more he talked and a spurt of anger shot up in her chest. "Ethan Daniels, you are being so irritating. Will you please stop playing games and walk me to my parents' house?"

"I won't."

Her eyebrows slashed downwards. "You won't? Fine. I will walk through the woods by myself."

"You won't."

"What do you mean I won't?" She flared. "Just watch me."

Anger cutting lines all over her face she started into the trees. She had not taken two steps before Ethan scooped her up in his arms and took her towards the door.

"Put me down!" Rose kicked and squirmed in his arms. "Ethan Daniels! PUT ME DOWN!"

Jakob Ammann swung open the cabin door and looked out, smiling. "So and what is all the shouting about?"

"Grandfather!" A flush darted over Rose's face. "I'm—I'm—"

"She is so excited." Ethan carried Rose into the cabin, her arms and legs and feet still. "I have never seen her so excited."

"Good, good. That is how it should be. We are only twenty the one time."

Ethan's cabin was full of people. Rose's parents, her brothers, the pastors and their families, Lydia and her family, all the church members and their families, there were even Quakers and some English. She stared at them as Ethan continued to hold her. She could not understand how they could fit in his small cabin or when they had done it or where their horses and buggies were.

"Happy birthday!"

"Happy birthday, Rose!"

"Bless you!"

"Christ be with you all the days of your life!"

Jakob Ammann raised his hands. "There will much time for well wishes and the joy of the Lord. But let us begin this time of fellowship and praise with a prayer for our dear daughter and sister in Christ."

Heads were bowed and Ethan gently placed Rose on her feet. She smiled sheepishly, looking as contrite as a wayward puppy, and put her hand in his. There were the prayers and after the prayers the Scripture passages and after those a few games with the children followed by kettles of hot food and pots of coffee and slices of chocolate cake. Once the day was over Ethan walked her back to her farm through the woods and snow, half moon shining on the white, the trees like tall dark men who guarded pathways left by deer and fox and hare. Far from his cabin and her farmhouse, Ethan sang another verse from the hymn he had startled Rose with the day Samuel Dressler gave her the rifle.

Fair is the sunshine Fair is the moonlight
Bright the sparkling stars on high Jesus shines brighter
Jesus shines purer
Than all the angels in the sky

She felt such peace and contentment she sat with her mother and father by the fire in the parlor after Ethan had left, her Bible open in her lap, the red rose placed there by her and Lydia still marking the page of their covenant. For an hour or more she read through the Psalms, her heart filling up with the words and with God's Spirit as creek water filled its bed and ran free in the spring rains. They prayed a few minutes together and then stood up to get ready for bed. Rose had just started up the staircase when there was fast and hard knocking on the door. Her mother looked at her father and frowned.

"At this hour?" she asked.

He shrugged and went to the door with a lantern. The knocking started up again. *"Ja, ja,"* he said loudly. "I am coming."

He opened the door and Pastor Philip stood there, the hat removed from his bald head, fresh snowflakes in his thick brown beard. Rose glanced at him and the tiny bits of white falling silently in the dark.

"I am sorry to disturb your household." Pastor Philip's face was as pale as bone. "Jakob Ammann has asked that you join us at Ethan Daniels' cabin."

"Why, what is the problem?"

"When Ethan returned to his cabin tonight, after we had all left, two or three dozen men attacked him with sticks and clubs and ax handles."

Rose gripped the bannister with her hand as if she meant to break it in two. "What?"

Pastor Philip looked at her with his deep, dark eyes, black hat in his hands. "He fought back. But there were so many. The sheriff got wind of it and arrived on horseback with his deputies and scattered the mob. Several were captured. Still, it was not in time."

Her mind and chest iced over like the pond behind the barn. It did not even seem to her she was speaking but that her mother, standing beside her father, had opened her mouth.

"What has happened, Pastor Philip?" Rose demanded in a voice that cracked. "Speak plainly. Have Ethan's wounds been bandaged? Has he been taken to the doctor in town?"

Pastor Philip could not look into her face anymore and dropped his eyes. "*Es tut mir leid.* I am sorry, my dear girl, so sorry. Ethan is dead."

Volume 8

Resurrection

Rose did not even know how she got from the staircase to the front door or when she grasped the pastor's arms with her hands, gripping him so tightly he winced.

"Were you there when he died? Did you see him die?"

"He stopped breathing. That is when Jakob Ammann asked that I come to your family."

Rose flew through the open door, yanking her shawl from its peg. "Rose! Wait!" It was her mother's voice. "You cannot raise the dead!" Rose ran across the farmyard and into the fields beyond the barn. "Rose! We will take the buggy! Rose!"

Rose floundered in the snowdrifts, fell headlong, got up, fell again, felt the lash of a branch against her cheek, scrambled to her feet a second time, found a well-used deer path in the moonlight and made her way over its thick ice, kept one hand over her face as she darted through the woods and pine boughs, spotted the lights of Ethan's cabin, saw a soldier raise his musket and cock his flint as she hurtled into the open, half-running, half-staggering.

"Stop! Who goes there?" The soldier saw it was a woman with blood running down her cheek and did not lower his weapon. "What do you want? What is your business here?"

She practically ran over him. "The man in this cabin is the man I am to marry! We are betrothed!"

She swept past six men bound hand and foot, sitting in the snow with more red-coated soldiers standing over them, muskets raised as she burst upon them.

"Shoot me if you must!" she cried. "I am going in!"

She shoved against the door with both her hands and almost tore it off its two leather hinges.

"Ma'am!" a soldier shouted behind her.

The sheriff was inside, his deputies, the captain of the redcoats, and Pastor Ulrich. All of them snapped their heads towards the doorway, startled at her violent arrival in their midst. She saw Jakob Ammann bent over a body in the small bedroom off to one side. There was another man, hair and beard white, holding a tiny feather to the body's nose. Jakob turned his head at the sound of the crashing door and her rapid steps. His eyes and face were sharp.

"My daughter—" he began.

"Is it true?" demanded Rose, rushing to his side, gasping for air from her hard run. "He cannot be dead—he cannot."

The white-haired man glanced up with a scowl. "Who are you? What are you doing here? Be quiet!"

She was about to retort when Jakob Ammann laid

a hand on her arm. "Daughter. This is a doctor from town. Schwartz. We must have quiet."

"He—"

"Shh. Ethan's breath has stopped and started, stopped and started. If you will do anything, pray. His life is in God's hands and it is balanced on the edge of a knife."

She looked at Ethan's handsome face, streaked with blood. The doctor continued to hold the feather to Ethan's nostrils. Her throat tightened and a burning started up in her eyes. She knelt on the other side of the bed, held his limp hand to her cheek, and whispered, *"I love you, oh, I love you, please, you must stay, I need you so much, my love, you must stay."*

She began to pray silently, the words forming in her mind.

"It trembles." The doctor's voice was low and cautious. "It trembles ever so slightly."

Rose kept her eyes open, watching. She saw Jakob bow his head and could see that his lips were moving.

"All right." The doctor stood up slowly. "Who knows? It is a back and forth battle. He must be kept warm and his room quiet. Any jarring of his body would finish him for good." He glanced at Jakob. "Will the soldiers remain on guard?"

Jakob nodded. "That is what the captain gave me to understand."

"I cannot imagine any of those who did this plan to return tonight. They will expect they have killed him. If the captured men talk the others in the mob will go into hiding knowing they will face the stocks or worse." He put the feather on a small table and looked at Rose.

"Who are you? Is it common practice for you to enter homes by breaking down the doors?"

"I had been told he was dead."

"So he was dead. So he has been dead two or three times. So he may die again once and for all. How does smashing doors help?"

"They are betrothed, Dr. Schwartz." Jakob spoke up. He got to his feet. "She was to be his bride."

Some of the hard lines left the doctor's face. "Ah." He wiped his hands on a cloth. "Will you remain with him?" he asked her.

"Yes."

"All night?"

"Yes."

"Even if others seek to remove you?"

The doctor and Jakob Ammann saw Rose's eyes spark green fire.

"No one shall remove me," she snarled. "I will not let them. God will not let them."

Both men were shocked by the change that came over her features. Then they dropped their heads to hide their smiles.

"The lioness guards her mate," murmured Jakob. "May the Lord's will be done."

The doctor drew Jakob to one side. "Who is she?"

"One of our pastor's daughters."

"I have seen her before."

"She gave testimony on her friend's behalf at the witch trial."

The doctor nodded. "Ah. I remember now. She was fierce there as well."

"She has that inside her, yes."

"We are both old men and our prime is past. But it is astonishing how striking this woman is when such anger comes upon her. The colors in her face and eyes. I have seen few women more lovely in this county."

Jakob nodded. "She is one of our Lord's rare birds, it is true. No one who has seen her face and been drawn in by her eyes and taken the measure of her soul forgets her."

"You speak of her like a father with a godly pride in his daughter."

"I do see her as my daughter, yes, I have always seen her that way, my Rose." Jakob's face suddenly creased with hard dark lines. "Will he live?" he asked in a voice so low he was certain Rose could not hear him.

The doctor's voice was even lower. "Personally I cannot see it. We have lost him so many times. The blows to his head were vicious. But who knows? Who knows?"

Rose's parents and brothers rushed through the front door. "Rose!" her mother cried out.

Jakob Ammann went to them immediately. "My friends, I ask you to calm yourselves. Rose is here with Ethan. He is barely alive. We must have quiet."

"Alive?"

"He has been dead and alive many times over the past hour."

Rose's mother entered the bedroom and looked at the tear-streaked face of her daughter.

"Your cheek is cut," she said to Rose.

"Never mind my little cut. Look at his."

"*Ja*. I see."

"Can you warm some water on his stove and bring me a cloth and basin? I want to clean him up."

Her mother hesitated. In her mind the thought formed, *Why bother?* She did not speak it. But Rose saw the words in her mother's eyes.

"He is going to live, Mama. I have prayed and he is going to live."

"Rose, we pray, yes, always and for everything. But what we will is not often what God wills."

"Please, Mama, a soft cloth and a basin of warm water."

Her mother nodded. "Very well, my girl."

Some water had already been heated for coffee and she poured it into a wooden basin and brought it to Rose along with a blue cloth. Her daughter soaked the cloth, wrung it out, and gently dabbed at the dried blood on Ethan's face. By the time she was finished the grim look of his features was gone. She untied his hair and ran her fingers through the long strands and arranged it on the pillow under his head. In minutes he looked more like a boy sleeping deeply than a man hovering between life and death.

Her mother knelt and put her arm around Rose. "So we will see what the Lord will do."

Rose leaned her head against her mother. "Thank you, Mama."

"You have all but knocked a hole in the roof with your faith and lowered him down to rest at Jesus' feet." She stroked Rose's hair. "I suppose you intend to stay by his side through the night?"

"Yes, Mama."

"And the soldiers are staying?"

"Yes."

"It would be best if we could move him back to our

house. But I can see he is too weak for that." She kissed her daughter on the head and stood up. "Father will take the boys home. I shall remain with you here."

"No, Mama, it will wear you out."

"Wear me out? The evil men do wears me out. Working to repair the damage they inflict does not. I will brew fresh coffee and bake some biscuits. Then I will make up a chair to sleep in. When it is daylight you can rest and I will watch over him. Once you are up again I will see to our own household. Father will need to leave me a horse and buggy." She put her hands on her hips and looked down at Rose, who sat on the floor by Ethan. "So we will make it work as long as we must. Others will help. Here and at our house. I know you shall wish to remain in the cabin here."

Rose ran her hand rhythmically over Ethan's forehead. "Don't you think he is breathing better?"

"What was he breathing like before?"

"You could not even see his chest rise."

Her mother watched Ethan's shallow breathing a few moments and nodded. "I can see the rise and fall. So if you could not see it before, *ja*, it has improved."

She went out to Jakob Ammann and her husband. "She will stay here until he is on his feet. That is what she says, it is what she will do."

"Ja," her husband responded, his face tired, knowing it was what Rose would say.

"And you will remain with her?" asked Jakob.

"Of course."

"Our ladies will come in the morning."

"I know."

"I think the Quaker women too will come. And some of the English."

She nodded. "That will help. Rose will not leave this place until Ethan is back on his feet. That is what she believes and that is what will happen for her. If the Almighty has other plans he can argue with her. I don't have the strength."

A smile came and went over Jakob's face. "It is sometimes such defiant prayers the Lord hears. Let us see. Meanwhile we ourselves shall pray around the clock as we set our hands to our daily tasks."

The mother's face remained pale and crossed with sharp lines. "It will be safe here?"

"There will be soldiers and deputies in the forest and around the house. Until he can be moved."

"Moved?" She raised her eyes to heaven. "Ethan will have to walk out of here on his own two legs. She will demand nothing less."

All night Rose watched Ethan's face and never felt sleep pull at her eyelids or lean on her shoulders. At one point she glanced around his bedroom, spotted a Bible, got up, brought it back, and began to read softly out loud to him, her mother sleeping in a chair nearby. The Bible was in English but she read Psalm 23 in German.

Ein Psalm Davids.

Der Herr ist mein Hirte, mir wird nichts mangeln.

Er weidet mich auf grüner Aue und führet mich zum frischen Wasser.

Er erquicket meine Seele, er führet mich auf rechter Straße um seines Namens willen.

Und ob ich schon wanderte im finstern Tal, fürchte ich kein Unglück. Denn du bist bei mir, dein Stecken und dein Stab trösten mich.

Du bereitest vor mir einen Tisch im Angesicht meiner Feinde. Du salbest mein Haupt mit Öl und schenkest mir voll ein.

Gutes und Barmherzigkeit werden mir folgen mein Leben lang, und ich werde bleiben im Hause des Herrn immerdar.

At dawn her mother got up and busied herself, getting her daughter something to eat and then making her curl up in the large chair she had made into a bed with blankets, a quilt, and pillows.

"So he even has this quilt from one of our own people," she murmured as she tucked it around her daughter.

"Whose?" Rose asked.

"Just sleep."

"I'm not tired."

"If you don't sleep now you will not be able to watch over him tonight, my dear."

"How is his breathing?"

Her mother stopped fluffing a pillow and took a long look. "Still his chest is moving. No need to use the feather to find out."

Rose fought sleep several times but eventually drifted off, dreaming all kinds of things in all kinds of colors, images that vanished from her mind forever the moment she woke. One of Ethan's candles was lit. She sat straight up as soon as she realized where she was and what had happened. Her mother was sitting quietly on the other side of the bed. Several women from the church were standing at her shoulder and praying. They all had their eyes closed. Rose craned her neck. She could see the rise and fall of Ethan's chest under his blankets and even hear his breathing. Encouraged, she slipped out from under her quilt and sheets and stood over him, thanking God silently that he was still alive.

"My Rose. You are up?"

She smiled at her mother. "Thank you for keeping an eye on Ethan, Mama. Did he say anything?"

"Say anything?" Her mother got to her feet. "I am going home to see how they are getting on. I will sleep there tonight. Myself or one of our ladies will be here in the morning."

"Thank you."

"Soldiers are all around the house. There is an officer in charge. And a sergeant." Her mother hugged her. "So there is also a stew I made of venison from his smokehouse."

"Venison? That is just like Ethan."

"Well, it is my own recipe and my mother's mother before me. I hope you will like it as much as you like his."

"Of course I will."

"Hm. God be with you, my daughter."

"And with you and Father and the boys."

Rose sat by the bed with a bowl of the stew and deliberately held it close to Ethan's nose so that steam curled up and into his nostrils.

Who knows what God will use? Sometimes it is the most ordinary things. Didn't he heal people with mud plasters or by rinsing with water or by means of his own spit?

To her surprise, Lydia showed up later in the evening, the rose quilt bundled in her arms. Rose got up from her chair at the bedside and they embraced and kissed one another on the cheek.

"How is he?" Lydia asked in a whisper.

"He hangs on, I thank God."

"I am so sorry, Rose, so sorry."

"Papa tells me the sheriff and army captain have captured the ringleaders and that they are in the public stocks."

"It's true. The English children pelt them with snowballs. Our people and the Quakers chase them off but no one can be there all the time. If Ethan dies they will hang the men."

"No." Rose's tone was soft but sharp. "He will not die."

Lydia held her tongue. "As you say." She handed her friend the quilt. "I thought you might like to work on this while you are sitting through the nights. I have brought you a bag of thread and needles and cloth as well."

"*Danke, Lydia.* I think we could lay it over him and you could sew one side and I the other and it would not bother him."

"Oh, I—" Lydia struggled with her words. "Father is waiting in the buggy—I am not—I am not staying—"

"Not staying? Are you busy tonight? Tomorrow night then?"

"No, no, not tomorrow." She looked away. "Not any

night. I—I have been through a great deal already, Rose. The arrest and trial were very hard on me."

"Of course I know that."

"I can't risk going through that again. I can't spend time with you."

"But why not?"

"They will see us together. They will accuse me again. I will go to jail and court a second time when they take you."

Rose stared. "When they take me? What are you talking about?"

"They will, Rose, they will. God help you but they still scheme even with their leaders under arrest. English friends have told me money was raised on behalf of the Peachtree family and a man was sent for from England. They say he is coming in the spring."

"What man?"

"Why, a special man with special authority from the crown. They call him a witch finder."

"A witch finder? I have never heard of such a thing."

"They expect him in the spring or sooner. He is supposed to be an expert on ferreting out witches and all who work with them. His arrest powers go beyond those of the governor." She looked down at the floor. "I'm sorry. I can't be seen with you. Mother and Father insist on this. I thought it only right you have the quilt. I argued with them over bringing it here."

Rose gripped the quilt tightly. "I don't know what to say."

"We shall pray for you. You will always be uppermost in my thoughts. But for now we must be apart." She raised her eyes. "Perhaps by summer all this evil will be done with and we can go back to a normal life, Rose, and begin another quilt together."

"Yes, yes, I would like that."

"I must go. God bless you."

"Thank you, Lydia. God bless you as well."

Lydia was out the door. Rose caught a glimpse of her father and a buggy and a horse in the light of the torches soldiers had ringed the cabin with. Then the door fell shut.

The army captain was standing by the wood stove. "I can bring you coffee, Miss Lantz. And a slice of the meat pie some Quaker women brought this afternoon."

"Thank you, captain. I would like that. My—my stew has gone quite cold—"

She went into the bedroom and slumped in her chair by the bed. The officer in his redcoat brought the coffee and meat pie and took away the bowl of half-eaten stew.

"I will reheat it," he said.

"I think the meat pie will be enough, sir, thank you."

"Well, I will let it sit in the warming oven in case you change your mind."

Rose ate and prayed and sat quietly looking at Ethan. Around midnight she carefully spread the rose quilt over him and began to sew at one corner. She kept at it for days. When she slept by day her mother and other ladies from the church worked on it and some Quaker women and English women too. They did not tell her but she knew just by looking when she woke up each evening. She did not mind. It was a quilt for Jakob Ammann. The more women in the community who worked on it the better.

"Did the doctor come while I slept?" she would always ask her mother.

"Yes," her mother would reply.

"What does he say?"

"Ethan is much the same as he was yesterday."

One evening Jakob Ammann and the pastors, including her father, came to bless her and to pray for Ethan. When they had done and were preparing to leave she asked them about rumors of a man being brought from England by people in the town.

Jakob removed his hat. "So news of this has come to you?"

"Lydia Beiler mentioned it."

"I did not wish to have your spirit troubled by this. It may only be talk. This man may never set foot in the colonies."

"Lydia thought it was certain."

"It is by no means certain. I have spoken with the sheriff."

"He is called a witch finder."

Jakob hesitated. "Yes, my daughter. That is his job."

"Are they after me, Grandfather?"

"They do not know who they are after. But cattle still die from time to time. Children take ill. Men claim to see strange things by the light of the moon. No witch was caught and executed last fall so now people look for a man who has been successful in his witch hunts many times before."

She looked at her father. "Papa, if this witch finder comes all the way from across the sea I cannot believe he will be satisfied if he does not put someone behind bars. Nor will the townsfolk who pay him."

Her father nodded, his eyes dark.

"There seems to be so much anger," she went on, "that I do not think anyone will satisfied unless some-one is hung or burned at the stake."

Jakob let out a long breath. "That is so. But again I remind you we do not believe enough money was raised to bring the man over. The governor would not request his presence so the English have to bring him on their own shilling and in gold. To my knowledge this has not been done. I ask you not to fret."

"They are after me, Grandfather."

"As I said a moment ago, they are not sure who they are after."

"They attacked Ethan because they were afraid of him and because they knew he would defend me."

"You have a company of his majesty's troops around you, child."

"If the witch finder has authority over them who will protect me if he orders the soldiers to step aside?"

"The sheriff and his deputies, his constables."

"If he can order the redcoats to lay down their arms he can order the sheriff and his men to do the same."

Jakob put his hat back on his head. "We have prayed for you this night. Hold to that. The Lord is your Master and he is the Master of thrones and powers and witch finders as well. We will return tomorrow."

Rose would wash up in the pantry each evening after she woke. It had a door she could close and she took a basin of hot water in with her. She tried to approach

Ethan's bedside with faith and optimism once she was ready but the sight of his hollow face, the flesh melting away from his cheekbones, eventually worked its way through her defenses and when she was alone she would cry silently, the tears pouring over the skin of her face and onto her hands folded in her lap. The crying could come at any time—while she was sewing, while she ate, when she turned the pages of Ethan's Bible and read out loud to him, as she prayed.

I don't know how long I can keep on if you don't do something. I don't know how long he can keep on. How can Ethan live without food or water? How can I live seeing him waste away day after day? I cannot do anything to help him, I cannot do anything at all. You are God, you know how he defended me when I was threatened, you know what he did for me when my legs were so badly hurt I could hardly stand—was it all for nothing? No love, no future, no marriage, no children? Nothing? And this is all you can do? You are God and this is all you can do? Leave me here to watch him die?

She fell asleep one night. She knew as she dreamed that she was asleep and ought to be awake to keep an eye on Ethan but she could not pull herself free and wake up. A man spoke her voice over and over until she grew angry in her dreams and snapped at him. A hand shook her more and more roughly but she was submerged in deep blues and greens and could only try to push back with her own hands, neither of which would work properly, and fight to open her eyes, eyes that would not respond.

"Miss Lantz. Miss Lantz. Please."

"I can't," she mumbled.

"Miss Lantz."

"I told you, I can't. I'm too far away."

"Miss Lantz!"

"Stop it. Go away. Don't yell at me. *Sie haben schlechte Menschen!*"

It was her own shout that woke her up.

A man's face was close to her own.

"What is it?" she demanded, startled, unsure of where she was or what was going on.

"Miss Lantz. He is asking for you."

"Who? Who is asking for me?"

She saw the candle burning, the man's red uniform, a Bible on top of a bookcase. Suddenly she turned her head and looked at the bed. A broken smile was on Ethan's sunken face and his eyes were open and black and held some of the gleam from the candle flame.

"Rose—Rose—could I have some water?"

She put her hand to her mouth. *"Mein Gott im Himmel."*

"Could I—have—some water—*bitte*?"

"Here." The soldier beside her gave her a ladle of water. She saw his stripes.

"Danke, sergeant."

She had not shaken off the effects of her deep sleep. Holding the ladle towards him she spilled half of it on the rose quilt.

"Oh, no, I'm sorry!" She tried to hold the ladle more steadily. "I'm so sorry!"

Ethan put a hand weakly on hers. "Never mind—before I drink—I need something else—from you—"

She continued to hold the ladle towards him, her

hand shaking. "What? What do you want? I have the water here."

He pushed aside the ladle. "Kiss me—Rose—a kiss first—please—more than anything—I want you in my arms—"

"No, but you need the water—"

The broken smile again. "I cannot be—in heaven—because here you are—arguing with me—just like on earth—" He tried to lift his head but could not. "What I need—most of all—is not water—or food—I need you—"

She did not know what to do with the ladle. The sergeant saw this and took it gently from her hand.

"I will be just outside the door," he said. "I shall fetch a cup."

Rose put her hand to Ethan's bearded face and thin cheeks and lowered her mouth slowly onto his. His lips were dry and he scarcely had breath in him so she kissed him lightly and tried to draw away but a sudden strength in a hand that gripped her arm tugged her back.

"What are you doing, Ethan?"

"A bit—longer—please—"

"Don't be foolish."

"One more—and where is—your beautiful soft hair?"

"My hair is up under my cap where it belongs." A laugh bubbled out of her chest and throat she could not stop. "This is crazy. You are supposed to be dead and you want to kiss my hair?"

"It is—what dead men—do best—" His lopsided smile.

"Kiss hair?"

"Kiss—beautiful—women—they are in love with—"

She rolled her eyes and shook her head so that long golden brown strands of hair fell loose. "Don't tell anyone how I brought you back from the dead by unpinning a lock of my hair."

"Dead men—tell no tales—"

He pressed her hair to his face and lips and managed to get one arm around her. Then he kissed her mouth again. Finally he sank back against his pillow.

"I am sorry—I am such a wagon wreck—"

Now it began to become real to her and tears were darting down her cheeks. "Do you think I care, Ethan Daniels? I can't believe it, oh, I can't believe it." She hugged him. "My love, I thank God for you, I thank God with all of my being."

"You look wonderful—you smell wonderful—you're perfect—"

"Ethan, I am far from perfect."

"Stop—arguing—for once—a dead man who comes back to life—knows something—you don't—"

She smiled, still crying. "Oh, yes? And what is that?"

"What is worth—living for—and dying for—"

"Oh, Ethan, you make me want to kiss you all night and you don't have the strength."

"Yes—I do—give me a few minutes—"

"You don't. *Sie verruckter Mann. You crazy man.*"

She turned to face the doorway. The sergeant stood there with a cup in his hand.

"Thank you." He came into the bedroom and she took the cup. Then she smiled at him. "But isn't it a miracle? Isn't it something from heaven?"

He smiled back. "It is, right enough. I have seen men

recover from wounds on the battlefield I knew for certain were fatal. It was impossible for them to live. Yet there they were the next day, breathing, taking in water and some broth, a grin on their face. I can only lay it at the feet of God Almighty."

"I agree with you." She put one hand behind Ethan's head and with the other put the cup to his lips. "Slowly, my love, slowly."

"Shall I draw off some broth for you, Miss Lantz?" asked the sergeant.

She glanced at him. "You have soup?"

"The lads and I made some from hambones we brought from the barracks in town. It's thin stuff but hot and tasty."

"Sergeant, that would be exactly the thing, please bring me a bowlful if you have any to spare."

"It's a big round kettle of soup we have. Enough for a small army. One moment."

She heard him go to the front door. He opened it and leaned out.

"Corporal. Tell the others. The man's made it. He's pulled through."

"God's truth, sergeant?"

"Aye. Let them know. I'll put some of the soup into him. A good Grenadiers' soup will have him on his feet in no time and then it's out of the woods and back to town."

"Amen to that."

Rose smiled and tipped the cup carefully as Ethan sipped the water.

"Amen to that," she said quietly. "Yes and forever, amen to that."

* * *

Her mother dropped the armful of towels she was carrying when she arrived in the morning—Ethan was sitting up in bed holding her daughter's hand. She rushed to their sides, hugging both, laughing, praising God, taking a handkerchief from the pocket in her dress and wiping her eyes and cheeks, running to the front door and calling to the women who were arriving with hot meals and preserves of peaches and plums, waving her arms and using such a loud voice Rose put a hand to her mouth to hold back her laughter. One woman swung her buggy around and went to tell Jakob Ammann and the pastors who followed her back, adding their praise and well wishes to that of the women who had gathered in the cabin. Rose was afraid to go to sleep, afraid something might happen to Ethan while she was unconscious, afraid she might wake up and realize she had imagined everything and that he was still at death's door. But finally she drifted off, gripping his hand tightly. When she woke in the evening it was to find him shaved, his hair and body washed, his face shining, and her mother twisting his hair into one long thick braid that fell down the middle of his back.

"Mama!"

Her mother and Ethan looked at her and smiled.

"It's good to see you awake," said Ethan in his normal voice. "How goes it with you?"

"Good evening, my girl." Her mother continued to braid Ethan's hair. "You slept longer than usual."

"What on earth are you doing?" asked Rose.

"So what does it look like to you, my dear? Fixing your almost husband's hair for him."

"When have you ever done such a thing?"

"We must all do whatever we can to help Ethan get back on his feet."

Ethan's smile was full and his teeth strong and white. "I feel like a new man, Rose. I am more than ready for you now."

Her mother snorted and kept braiding. Red burst instantly over Rose's face.

Ethan winked. "Not much has changed while I've been away."

After a few days of food and water the doctor and Jakob Ammann helped Ethan walk out, climb into a buggy, and take the short ride to the Lantz farmstead. He was placed in the room he had slept in before and his horses were brought over as well. Soon he was taking meals at the table with Rose and her parents and brothers. Then he was walking with Rose through the melting snow of March and getting onto Delaware and riding the stallion through the fields of water and mud and greening grass.

Such a miracle, Lord. Thank you for blessing me. Thank you for giving Ethan and myself a second life.

She continued to worry that his strength would fail, that he might injure himself trying to do too much too soon, that he would fall asleep one night and not wake up. But any fears she hung on to as the weeks passed were dispelled one afternoon when they were walking through the woods and she was taking care not to step into one of the many pools of snowmelt. Noticing how careful she was being, Ethan bent down and splashed her with mud and water, covering her face and dress with a few quick flips of his hand. She was so startled, and the water was so ice cold, she just looked at him in shock, her mouth wide, her eyes wider, trying to find the words to shout at him. Before she could get them out he picked her up and carried her to a birch tree that had sprouted bright green leaves, pinning her up against it with hands that were both firm and gentle. He removed the Quaker cap from her head and began to kiss her hair and neck and throat, moving his lips slowly and lovingly over her skin, his hands keeping her against the tree, his warmth and strength pressing against her until she finally gave in and threw her arms around his back and returned his kisses, putting her mouth to his, pulling him closer and closer, feeling the muscles of his body again, the smooth rock of his arms, the sweetness of his breath, the scent of wood smoke and earth and pine filling her up, his love making the fear and darkness in her burst like a dam so that all kinds of goodness and light and hope flooded her from head to toe. Somehow, she never knew how, her hair was down and unraveling to her waist and his kisses were harder and fiercer and burned with so much heat and warmth the chill of the spring day never touched her, his hands running over and through her hair, kissing it, burying his face in it, finding his way to her shoulders and neck again, his lips tender against every part of her face he could find, and then his voice, his perfect voice, the voice of her man, the man she had almost lost, the man God had given back to her just as he had given the world back warmth and green grass and red-breasted robins and high-flying swallows.

"I love you, Rose, I love you, I'm on fire and you're more beautiful than seeing the sun."

His love and his healing preoccupied her as March greened into April. Her fears about a new witch hunt and a dark witch finder coming for her across the cold sea faded with the vanishing snows and ice. She prayed about it, read Bible verses that put heart in her, and thought about the threat less and less. But it returned in a rush like a great hurry of wind that stirred up old leaves and dust and she thanked God that Ethan and his fierce love were with her that day. She did not see it coming. There was only the impossibly tall and impossibly gaunt man, with caved in cheeks and a tall black hat like a church steeple, who stopped them on the street in Lancaster, bowed, and swept the hat from his head.

"I believe I am speaking with Miss Rose Lantz and her beau, Mr. Ethan Daniels?"

"Yes, sir," responded Ethan.

"Allow me to introduce myself. Archibald Kendall, by appointment of his majesty the king, just arrived from Boston where I left my good ship *Cynthia Fellowes* and made my way by coach to Lancaster County and your fair town."

"Very good. I hope you enjoy the spring weather, Mr. Kendall."

"Oh, I will, Mr. Daniels, I will. I see so much clearer in the bright light April affords us."

"I'm glad to hear it. Please excuse us."

"Often the witches emerge from their cottages in spring and perform their rituals in the forests and by the marshes. Unhidden by walls and roofs they are easier to apprehend and bring to justice for the good of all mankind. For that is my employment, nay, my calling from God, Mr. Daniels. To rid the world of sorcerers and all who practice witchcraft and defile the face of heaven."

Rose's stomach tightened. But Ethan's grip on her hand was tighter.

"There are no witches here, Mr. Kendall," Ethan said, meeting the man's black gaze with steady gray eyes.

"Oh, I beg to differ, sir. There are always witches. From what I understand you have a number of them hereabouts. Perhaps one great queen of witches who has gone undetected for some time. But no more." He laid a long finger to the side of his nose. "I will find her and cleanse the land."

"Will you? Are you certain of that?"

"Quite certain. I have never failed yet. Lancashire in England is free and full of the Spirit of the Lord today due to my humble ministrations, I thank God."

"Well, I still think you took a long journey for no good purpose, Mr. Kendall. The land here is free and flourishing and God blesses us richly. Perhaps you need to go farther west. Or north. Or perhaps you need to return to Boston and get back on your ship before she sails for London."

"And leave my work undone, Mr. Daniels?"

"You have no work here, sir."

"Oh, I do, sir. Closer to hand than you think, sir."

Cold seized Rose as the man's voice darkened. But Ethan put his arm around her shoulder, something she had asked him not to do in public, and the warmth of his body warmed away the fear she felt just as the strength in his arm gave her back some of her own strength.

"Mr. Kendall."

Ethan's voice had changed just as Kendall's had. She glanced at his face. His eyes were not the soft gray she knew. They had gone the color of stone she had only seen once or twice.

"I'm not the man to play games with, Archibald Kendall. If you wish to speak to me, speak plainly. I know who you are. You murder innocent people and call it God. You will not work your black magic here."

Kendall's face seemed to gather to a sharp point. "Are you threatening me, Mr. Daniels?"

"I am. You seem to think people want to save their own skins and that you will always get what you want when you press charges against some poor soul. That no one will dare raise their voice against you for fear of losing their life. Let me speak the plain speech you seem incapable of. Miss Lantz means more to me than my own life. Or yours. I will not hesitate to give my life for hers. Or to take your life away from you to preserve her own. Before God I will not hesitate."

"You do not know who I am or you would bite your tongue."

"I know who you are. The witch finder they have paid for with blood money. The man who will not leave Lancaster unless he leaves a string of corpses hanging from the gibbet. You have been skulking about for three days gathering the nonsense and hearsay and spite you call evidence. You have been gathering it against Miss Lantz. It will not work, Archibald Kendall. I stand between you and her. So get back in your coach and return to Boston Harbor before you find yourself here permanently and under a grave marker."

"Ethan!"

Rose could not believe the words he was speaking.

Kendall had turned the color of a spring storm. "I tried to come in peace."

"No, you didn't. You came in deceit."

"I came in righteousness and in the name of the Lord."

"You came in the name of the devil. And I'll fight you like I would fight the devil." As Rose watched, aghast at the change that had come over Ethan, he seemed to grow another five inches and turn to rock. "You'll not put a torch to her. You'll not put a noose around her neck. If you try I shall send you to hell."

Kendall's eyes were flat and dead. Rose was stupefied by the change that had come over both of the men.

"How do you intend to do that, Daniels?"

"It shouldn't be hard. You came from the pit. The way back will be easy for you to find."

Kendall put his hat back on his head. "You are a fool, Daniels."

"I am not a fool, witch finder. I am dangerous. I will not warn you a second time. Beware how you tread."

"I expected more of you, sir. I confess to being disappointed at your rough spirit. But then they say you are a woodsman who lives on roots and berries and dresses in animal skins."

"Lay a hand on Rose Lantz and you will get more than you expected, witch finder. A great deal more."

"The day I will come, I will come. You will not stop me."

Ethan's eyes had gone as black as Kendall's. "Yes, I

will. For the first time in your life you will be stopped dead."

Kendall marched away with long violent strides.

Rose gripped Ethan's arm with both her hands. "What are you doing? What in heaven's name has gotten into you?"

The stone had not gone from his eyes. "The war has come. If they think they will take you from me they had better go back to the table and go over their plans. No one takes you from me. What God has joined together no one breaks asunder. No one."

The sweep of love and fire in his eyes overwhelmed her.

No one can love me this much.

Heat seemed to pour off him. "I knew he was here. I did not tell you. Everyone in the church will know before the day is out. He has people ready to swear they saw you do the same things they swore they saw Lydia Beiler do. They will use your black cat Nitz against you. They will use the testimony you gave in court against you—the witch who charmed the judges and cast a spell over their decision so it would favor her friend. They will even use the fact I am came back from the dead against you. Who else could reverse death but a witch?"

"God healed you!" exclaimed Rose, frightened again.

"They will believe what they wish to believe."

"Ethan—"

He turned to her, face granite. "He has come for blood, Rose. Like his kind always come. All the fear and superstition has gathered together a second time, just as it did at Salem, and formed a thunderhead worse than the first one that burst over Lydia Beiler. I am going to watch you like a hawk. Never leave your side. They will not jail you. They will not try you. They will not put you to death."

"You're scaring me."

"I want you to be afraid enough to pray hard and work even harder to stay clear of town and the English until this is over."

"Over? When will this be over?"

"It will be over once God takes Archibald Kendall's life."

"Then it is not for you to do, Ethan, only him."

"For he is the minister of God to thee for good. But if thou do that which is evil, be afraid. For he beareth not the sword in vain. For he is a minister of God. A revenger to execute wrath upon him that doeth evil."

"Paul is talking about the legal authorities. Not everyone can apply that teaching to themselves as they wish. Not even you."

"In the absence of legal authority that honors God then God himself appoints those who bear the responsibility to see justice done."

"Please don't keep on this way. I feel like I hardly know you."

"You know me all right. You have just never seen me at war."

"Even with the mob at our house you did not act like this."

"The mob was just a group of misguided men with their tempers up. Kendall is cold and heartless and knows exactly who he wants to kill and how he intends to do it."

"You exaggerate."

He shook his head. "No."

"We have the sheriff. We have our own Judge Hallowell."

"He will dismiss them. Perhaps he already has. Have you seen What-God-Will on the streets?"

"Why, he can't just do that. There is the company of soldiers, the Grenadiers."

"They will do his bidding."

"Oh, stop, listen to yourself. You are making the same arguments I made to Jakob Ammann. I only half-believed them. We have laws."

He gripped her arms tightly above the elbow. "There is no law now. Kendall is the law. Anyone who resists him he will swat aside. Anyone who will not follow in his footsteps he will jail. As soon as I heard a man was to be brought from England I began to make enquiries, yes, while I was healing, yes, while I was loving you. Because I knew, just like your friend Lydia knows, just like all the Quakers and English and the followers of Jakob Ammann know, that there is only one person the witch hunters want, just one."

"Please don't talk this way anymore, Ethan. I can't bear it."

"I know who this man is. I know his history. I know how many people he has killed. I know the kind of danger you are in."

"Ethan, please."

He led her into an alley between two buildings and took her behind a high stack of barrels where no one could see them.

"Rose." Suddenly his eyes were like the soft gray feathers of a sparrow. "You need to understand how serious this is. People are still found guilty at witches' trials. People are still put to death. But that is why you also need to understand why I am going to be strong for you, as strong as I can possibly be. I was careless when I approached the cabin that night the men attacked. I saw my horses were restless but I ignored the signs. It will never happen again. And I will never let happen to you what Kendall has done to scores of others. He has torn families apart, Rose. Taken daughters from their mothers, sons from their fathers, wives from their husbands. He has no mercy for this is how people who believe they need to be ruthless for the sake of Christ act—they become less like Christ than anyone else on earth."

"I don't like the hardness I see in you."

"It's a hardness that shields you, not one that harms you, Rose. I am a stone in the sling of David and I am heading right for the giant's head." His fingers gently lifted her chin in the way he liked to do. "Rose, love is more than soft clouds and sunny days and pink flowers. It is fire. It is wind. It is power. It comes from God and it is unstoppable. It is stronger than death. That is the love that is all around you now. The love the witch finder has to face. The love he fears, the love all darkness fears with him."

The kiss came with the fire and heat and power of his words. If she had thought their first kiss was something, the kiss he gave her the night the mob assaulted her house, it did not hold a candle to this one, a kiss like scorching flame that defied all wickedness and all hate and all hell. She did not know what to do with her hands, did not even know what to do with her lips, he took her so far, so high, and into an ecstasy and liberty so intense that she knew she could never return. It was as if their bodies melted together and their skin fused, as if great tongues of flame leaped through their souls and into the air all around them, burning, cutting, piercing, and blessing. The fire came from his mouth and stabbed her throat the moment he put it there, pricked her shoulder, went like a knife into her own mouth and lips, made her cry out and arch her head back, dropped red hot coals into her blood. He had picked her off the ground and his kisses were on her fingers and hands, on her arms, in her hair, painful sparks that started dozens of new fires of their own throughout her body and mind and heart so that she struggled for air, unable to do anything more than take it all in, unable to kiss back, or tighten her arms across his back, his love like great sheets of lightning that tore into her again and again, leaving her helpless and practically lifeless. His lips came to hers again and ignited whatever was left in her so that her hands finally found their way to the manhood of his arms and shoulders and the long braid of hair her own mother had twisted together so many times. Desperately she pulled and wrenched and dug with her fingers and nails until she had torn it loose and could grab handfuls of his hair and hang on for dear life as the fire kept burning over her and setting everything ablaze.

Oh, marry me, marry me, take me away and marry me, please, oh, Lord, help me, I can't take this kind of love without turning into streams of smoke, without turning into a forest fire that consumes every tree and every blade of grass in its path. There will be noth-

ing left of me for him to hold in his arms or take to his wedding bed if you let him keep on loving me like this. I am dying, Lord, I am dying, but, oh, Lord, please don't listen to me, I want to keep on dying, don't listen to me, please, please, I don't want him to stop, don't ever let him stop.

She clung to him in the alley as if she had just drowned and he had pulled her from the water. No matter how she tried she could not get her breath. Her fingernails bit into the strength of his back.

"A few more inches and your hair will be well past your waist," he said quietly, nuzzling her ear with his lips.

"What?" She could hardly get the word out.

"Your hair is growing out more and more. I love that."

"What?"

"You're the most beautiful woman. There's so much to you it'll take a lifetime to get to know it all. Do you have a lifetime to spare for me?"

"Oh, Ethan, no wonder I don't understand you half the time, you say such crazy things."

"Love isn't crazy."

"No? Your love is."

"Then God's love is crazy too because I learned it all from him."

"From him? Really?"

"Would you like me to start with the Song of Songs?"

"Hush. Maybe after we're married."

"Maybe?"

"We're not married yet. Who knows what could happen between now and then?"

"I thought I'd kissed that fear out of you."

"You did. Almost."

"I guess I'll have to try again."

She laughed and pushed a hand against his chest. "Not yet. Give me a minute."

"It's the best I can do to lay your ghosts to rest."

"You could pray."

"My kisses are my prayers."

"Oh, Ethan, you're impossible. It's like trying to rein in a tornado or a hurricane."

"And the wind is about to blow again."

She put her lips to his. "Make sure I get a chance to love you this time, yes?"

"Rose—"

"Yes?"

"All right. I'll try and leave you some room, Mrs. Daniels."

"I'm not Mrs. Daniels yet."

"Soon."

"You don't know."

"I do know."

"Ethan, aren't you afraid of anything?" she asked, planting soft, short kisses on his mouth.

"I fear God. I kneel to him."

"And that's all?"

"That's enough."

"Can you really protect me from all the witch hunts in the world? All the witch finders?"

"Love is bigger than all the witch trials. Light cuts through the dark like a strong knife in a frontiersman's hand. The witch hunters are the ones who need to be afraid. Not me. Not you. Never you."

"Why do you love me so much?"

He smiled. "I told you. You're perfect."

"I am not perfect, Ethan Daniels."

"You're perfect for me."

"Do you mean it?"

"What do you think?"

She had meant to control the situation this time but he caught her off guard and robbed her quickly of her breath, her thoughts, her strength, and all her plans. The flames swarmed over her eyes and face and arms. She let go and let him take her again, glad the barrels were stacked high on both sides of them, glad the day was ending, glad the sun was setting, glad the good dark of silver stars and silver moon was coming in over them like a river, glad she was in his arms, glad his lips were on her mouth and the skin of her neck, glad they were in love, glad for the God who had pieced it all together for her like a quilt and raised Ethan Daniels from the dead.

The next day Jakob Ammann and the pastors joined her father and her at the farmhouse.

"The peace of Christ be with you," Jakob said as he entered the house, removing his hat.

Pastor Philip and Pastor Ulrich followed him in, raindrops on their shoulders. They came to the kitchen table and sat, smiling their thanks as Mrs. Lantz poured each of them a cup of coffee. They asked after Rose and she came in from the laundry room and took a chair next to her father.

"And where is the young man?" asked Jakob. "Has he moved back to his cabin?"

"He will not return to the cabin," Rose's father said.

"No? Why is that? Hasn't his strength returned?"

"He fears for Rose's safety. He wants to remain close until the witch finder has left."

"Ah." Jakob sipped at his coffee. "We have come to pray about all of that. Pray and talk." He put down the cup. "Where is he?"

"He scouts the woods."

"Hmm." Jakob tugged at his untrimmed beard. "He thinks that is necessary?"

"Grandfather." Rose sat up straighter in her chair. "We met the man Archibald Kendall yesterday in town."

"Yes? How did that come about?"

"He walked up to us and introduced himself. He said he was here to find witches. Especially the queen of witches."

Jakob's eyes narrowed. "Queen of witches. He used this phrase?"

"Yes, Grandfather. It was not a pleasant meeting. Ethan took exception at Archibald Kendall's remarks. He felt the man was pointing his finger at me."

"Was he?"

Rose looked at the tabletop. *"Ja."*

Jakob drummed his fingers against the side of his coffee cup. "Did he threaten you?"

"Yes. And Ethan threatened him back."

"What?"

"He said the witch hunters would never take me away from him. That he would protect me with his life. He and Mr. Kendall did not part on good terms."

Jakob nodded. "I don't suppose I would expect Ethan Daniels to say anything else. Now that he is healthy we will begin our talks together again but, to tell you the truth, I don't know what I could say to a man who is in love with a woman God has given him, not when that woman is threatened. I would ask him not to take life in her defense. I would ask that there be no violence whatsoever. But I could never tell him not to try and save her. Not after what you both have been through already. No." He smiled at Rose's mother, who stood nearby, and she came and refilled his coffee.

"Can we count on Judge Hallowell to render a just decision if it should come to trial?" asked Pastor Philip.

Pastor Ulrich snorted. "You have not heard, huh? He has been sent away."

Everyone looked at him.

Ulrich nodded. "*Ja, ja.* I was picking up feed in town earlier and that was the news. Hallowell did the last witch trial so he is not fit to do the next. He has been ordered to Philadelphia for the time being."

"Vas?" Jakob stared at Ulrich. "Already he has left the county?"

"Ja, ja."

"So this witch finder is preparing for a trial so quickly. Who will be his judge?"

"He declares himself the judge."

"How can he declare such a thing?"

Ulrich shrugged and folded his arms over his chest. "He says the king."

"Someone must challenge him."

Ulrich picked up his coffee. He tasted it and put it back down without drinking it. "He has papers from the governor. The soldiers are with him. That is what everyone says."

"What do you hear of the sheriff and his deputies?"

"They are not to be involved in apprehending any suspects the witch finder lays charges against."

"Why not?"

"They defended a suspected witch from arrest last year."

"What?" Rose's father made fists. "When the mob came against this house? They now call that the lawful arrest of a suspect?"

"Let us be calm, Pastor Johannes." Jakob Ammann leaned back in his chair and looked at the ceiling. "*Ja, ja.* It is time to pray. So much makes no sense. God sees all this better than we do. The news is troubling and strange. But how troubling was the news that came to Noah that he must build his ark? To Joseph that he must take Mary to Bethlehem when she was with child? Let us take this witch finder and all his schemes to the Almighty."

Ethan came through the front door half-dragging a man with him.

Jakob got to his feet. "What is this?"

"Stand there," Ethan said to the man who had a short red beard, pushing him against the wall.

"Ethan Daniels, I ask you to explain this."

"The man was spying on the farm from the woods, Jakob Ammann."

"How do you know he was not just walking through?"

Ethan tossed a pistol that the older man just managed to catch.

"He had two of those loaded and primed."

"I am under orders from the king," the red bearded man growled. "If I don't return soon they will send in the Grenadiers."

"What were you doing in the woods?" asked Jakob.

"Searching for signs of witchcraft."

"Did you find any signs of this kind?"

"That is for the ears of the prosecutor and judge, not for you, old man."

Jakob held up his hand for he could see Ethan's face darkening at the man's tone and words. "We are about to pray. You will join us. Then we shall take you back into town. I wish to discover for myself all the changes that are going on in Lancaster."

"I don't need to pray with you, old man." The bearded man glared at Rose. "Or her."

Ethan shoved him towards the table. "We all need prayer, brother."

The man sat with them, refusing to bow his head. Rose thought his face looked like a snarl of bad rope. She kept an eye on him while the men at the table closed their eyes. She wasn't the only one. Ethan's head was bent but he was looking at the man while the praying went on and the man knew it.

Once the praying was done her father and the pastors and Jakob Ammann drove into town with the red-bearded man. Ethan stayed behind. He kept the pistols. Rose returned to the laundry and her mother began to knead dough for bread. Ethan spent some time with the boys and then went out to the barn to make sure all the cows had been milked. It was several hours before the pastors and Jakob returned. Rose was helping her mother place loaves in the oven when the door opened and they came in, their faces pale. Behind them were several soldiers in red.

Mrs. Lantz wiped her hands on a towel. “What is this?”

The men removed their hats as the soldiers filled the kitchen, muskets in their hands. Rose recognized the sergeant as the one who had given her water the night Ethan came back to life. He recognized her too and almost smiled but then turned his eyes away.

“My dear Rose.” Jakob seemed to search for the words he wanted. “You must be strong again.”

The sergeant unrolled a stiff sheet of paper. *“Charges are laid against Rose Lantz on suspicion of witchcraft. She is placed under house arrest. His Majesty’s Grenadiers will be quartered in the home to ensure she remains on the property. The trial will commence at this location three days hence. By special appointment of his majesty the king Archibald Kendall will preside as prosecutor and judge. There will be no lawyer for the defense. There will be no witnesses for the defense. The decision of Archibald Kendall regarding the charges laid against Rose Lantz will be final. By order of King George II. By order of the governor of the Commonwealth of Pennsylvania.”*

Rose stood facing the sergeant. “Is this how you pay me the visit you promised, sergeant?”

He would not look her in the eyes. “A soldier follows orders.”

“Do you believe I am a witch?”

“What I believe is of no concern here.”

“You were there when Ethan Daniels recovered. You saw me sitting at his bedside night after night. Did I speak incantations? Converse with the devil? Draw my own blood?”

The sergeant did not respond. He found a spot on the wall behind her head and fixed his eyes there.

Rose approached him. "Why, I was not even awake when Mr. Daniels regained consciousness. It was you who shook me and told me. For all we know you were the one who cast a spell over him to raise him from the dead."

The sergeant's face whitened quickly. "I did no such thing."

"Neither did I. And you know it. Yet I stand condemned and you are free. Is this what a British soldier fights for?" She looked at the soldiers. "Is this how you defend your loved ones back home? By taking away my liberty and my life at the order of one demented man?"

"That's enough!" barked the sergeant. "I have six Grenadiers with me. They require a place to lay their bedding. In addition you must provide hot meals at regular intervals. We will not trouble you long. The trial is set for Monday next. Once it is done our duty is also done. Now, show the soldiers to your spare rooms, if you will, and direct me to a room of my own as well."

Rose felt a black fire rising in her instead of a cold fear. She was about to open her mouth to speak again when Ethan made his way past the soldiers and took her hand.

"Say no more to them." His voice was low. "They don't hear you. Speak your heart on Monday."

Her eyes were dark. "What makes you think anyone will hear me on Monday?"

"They'll hear. Kendall is not the only one who can command regiments."

"What do you mean?"

But Ethan had turned to face the sergeant and his men.

"I trust you will treat my betrothed with every courtesy and all due respect, sergeant," he said.

"Naturally."

"And all who abide under this roof."

"Of course."

Ethan smiled and half-bowed. "Thank you. It is good to know that soldiers who fight for the liberty of British citizens understand how to conduct themselves when they are quartered with those same citizens whose liberty they have taken away."

The sergeant's face flushed crimson.

Mrs. Lantz stumbled over her words. "I—well, I was not expecting you, sergeant. It will take a few minutes to prepare rooms for your men."

"We will wait, ma'am."

Ethan half-bowed again. "My room is quite ready. Let me offer it to you, sergeant, sergeant, I'm sorry, I don't know your name."

"Gunn."

"Well, Sergeant Gunn, I only need to remove a few items and it's yours."

"Thank you," grunted the sergeant.

"It's the least I can do. You were the men who guarded me from suffering a second attack from a mob." Like Rose he glanced at the soldiers behind the sergeant. "Though today your assignment is less honorable, is it not?"

There was no sound in the house.

Jakob laid a hand on Ethan's arm. "That will do, young man. Understandably we are all upset but if the soldiers have their duty, well, then, we have ours, and it is to bring the peace of Christ into this situation."

Ethan nodded. "Yes, sir."

"Show the sergeant to your room. Then we can all help Mrs. Lantz find quarters for the others."

Rose squeezed Ethan's hand. "Where will you stay?"

"The barn." He grinned. "If you will visit me there."

She smiled. "If I'm allowed to go to the barn I'll be there."

His eyes were the soft sparrow gray. "I will see you through safely to the other side of the river."

"Yes?" She twisted her fingers around his.

"I told you," he whispered. "What God has brought together no one breaks asunder."

"Long Hunter must bunk with us!"

Rose's brother Nathan came swiftly down the stairs and ran to where Ethan stood with Rose and Jakob Ammann. His younger brother, Hans, remained standing at the top of the staircase, taking in everything, his eyes wide at the sight of redcoats assembled in his kitchen. Rose was holding one of Ethan's hands and Nathan seized the other.

"Come on," Nathan said. "I will show you. There is a third bunk."

Ethan let go of Rose's hand and mussed Nathan's dark hair. "Thank you, sir. I accept. So long as it is all right with your mother and father."

Nathan looked to where his father stood near the Grenadiers. "Please, Papa?"

Face troubled and thick with lines, his father still found a smile somewhere and gave it to his son. "Of course. This is a good thing. So long as you do not keep Mr. Daniels up all night with your stories, you and Hans. *Ja*?"

"No, Papa, we will be good."

"Come and help me fetch my things," Ethan said to Nathan. "And perhaps you can assist the good sergeant with his pack while you're at it."

"Ja." Nathan looked at the tall and husky sergeant. "Sir, may I carry your things to your room?"

"Aye." The sergeant was able to crack a smile. "I could use a hand, right enough."

Nathan shouldered the large pack, missed a few steps, and staggered down the hall from the kitchen, making his way to Ethan's bedroom. Ethan kissed Rose on the forehead and followed, trailed by the sergeant. In his room Ethan scooped up his three rifles, giving one to Nathan to carry, and picked up his Bible and the rose quilt that was spread over his bed.

"Thank 'ee," said the sergeant. "Sorry to put you out but it won't be for long."

"Not long at all."

"Orders, Mr. Daniels. If you'd ever served you would understand the significance of such things to a soldier."

"What makes you think I haven't served?" Ethan was half a head taller than the sergeant. "Grenadiers aren't the only troops in the county, sergeant. We have a colonial militia."

"So what are you saying, Mr. Daniels?"

"When I was a young man in the Virginia colony every fit man drilled with the others after church on Sundays. We had occasion to deal with Indian assaults and slave uprisings and always stood ready to protect our homes and farms. What makes you think the Pennsylvania militia aren't ready to defend their farms and homes from invasion?"

"Invasion? We are the king's troops, Daniels."

"You don't belong here." Ethan's voice was so quiet the sergeant barely heard it. "I thank you for your past service. But now it's best you move on as quickly as possible."

The sergeant straightened his back as if he were on parade. "We move on when our task is finished. Not before then."

"Your task?" Ethan's voice went even lower so that Nathan, who stood listening to the exchange between the two men, could not hear it. "Give your men to understand that whosoever lays a finger on Rose Lantz will never live to see England again."

"What, sir? My men know their place. They will not harm a hair on her head. We are British regulars."

"Not so much as to march her to a gallows. Not so much as to bind her to a stake. Not so much as to pile firewood at her feet. Do you take my meaning?"

"We can call up a thousand men, Daniels."

"Not in three days you can't. I say to you what I said to your Archibald Kendall who is fond of telling everyone he is appointed by King George II—beware how you tread."

He left the room with Nathan carrying the longest of the rifles.

"Is that too much for you?" asked Ethan.

"No, sir. It's just right for me. When can I have one of my own do you think?"

"You're twelve now, aren't you?"

"Thirteen this year, sir. Fourteen in 1730."

Ethan laughed. "Fourteen. Well, that sounds about right. What kind of wood do you want on it?"

"Just like this, sir. Curly maple, if you please, sir."

"We'll see what we can do, Fourteen in 1730."

Rose was showing four soldiers up the stairs to the attic on the third floor when Ethan and Nathan started up the staircase behind her. She glanced back. Nathan grinned as he held the rifle up to her.

"It is the longest one, sister. And I will get my own when I am fourteen."

"Oh, will you?" She looked at Ethan. "Who is going to do that for you, I wonder?"

"Mr. Daniels. Long Hunter."

"What a surprise. I thought it might have been Jakob Ammann."

"Oh, no, it wasn't Jakob Ammann."

She smiled at him and Ethan. "I'm glad you set me straight on that, Nathan."

Once she had shown the soldiers the attic and closed the door on them she leaned against it and closed her eyes.

They have charged me with witchcraft just like they did Lydia. Why don't I feel more fear? It does not seem real, perhaps that is it. How can this happen to our religious community two times in a row?

"How goes it with you?"

She opened her eyes and a rush of warmth went through her. "Ethan."

"Are you very much afraid?"

"Strangely, I'm not. Why is that? Perhaps I haven't grasped the reality of it yet."

"I do not like to see fear in your eyes."

"Why, is it there?"

"No. And I don't want it to come." He squeezed her shoulder gently. "It's important you understand nothing is going to happen to you."

"You keep saying that but you can't control heaven and earth, my love. Look at the predicament we are in now. Soldiers under our roof and at our table."

"If it came to it I would put you on Delaware and we would ride west to the Great Mountains or north to New France—there are no British troops in either place and none would molest us. We could live in peace."

"Are you serious?"

"I am."

"We should be far from our kin and all we love."

"You would be alive. That's what matters."

She leaned her head against his chest, happy with the firmness and strength and forest scent she found there. "I don't see how you would get me away without both of us being shot."

He placed his arms around her. "Leave that up to me."

"Perhaps I will be set free at the trial like Lydia was."

"The trial is Kendall's stage and he is the chief performer. There is no liberty for you in that direction."

"Well, now I confess I am scared just a tinge."

"I have some affairs to attend to. Will you be milking this evening?"

"Of course."

"Alone?"

"Hans and Nathan often join me."

"Make sure you are on your own. No Hans, no Nathan, no soldiers."

She rubbed her hand over his deerskin shirt. "Hans

and Nathan are easy enough to deal with. I don't believe I can do much about the soldiers."

"Be there alone. I will be back before dinner. Now Jakob and the others wish to pray with you downstairs. But first it is my prayer I want to give you."

As he held her he put one of his hands on her head. He did not press down hard but she felt the weight and the warmth from his palm and immediately the scratchings of fear inside her stomach disappeared. He prayed in German and English, repeating the phrase that Jesus had spoken, *I will never leave you or forsake you.* She almost fell asleep against his chest. By the time he had said *amen* she wanted him to pick her up, carry her down the stairs and out the door, and ride away with her to the distant mountains he had once told her were white as a Pennsylvania snowfall.

"I have to go now," he said.

"I'd rather you didn't," she murmured. "I feel safer when you are around. I feel like I'm in a palace in a fairy tale."

"I won't be gone long. But it's necessary I go."

He kissed the top of her head and went down a flight of stairs, darted into the room he now shared with the boys, came out with one of his rifles, and carried on down the last set of stairs and out the front door. She lingered at the top of the staircase, wishing to be alone a few minutes. The soldiers laughed behind the attic door and downstairs she could hear Jakob Ammann and Pastor Ulrich speaking back and forth with each other. She traced a pattern on the banister with her finger.

I should be asking you to deliver me from evil but Ethan has already prayed about that and Grandfather will be praying about it in a few minutes. It is always difficult for Ethan and I to find time alone and now it will be even harder. Does it seem strange for me to make a request for a trysting place? In three days I go on trial just as Lydia did but I have no hope I will be acquitted as she was acquitted. A few intervals of love between myself and the man you gave me would be so welcome. The fear always departs when he holds me and kisses me, why, Lord, there is no room for it, you know all this better than I, you know what he does to me, you know the good he puts in me. Please let us have that barn to ourselves, yes, ourselves and the milking cows, let us have that place for our tryst, without soldiers, without little brothers, without Mama or Papa poking their noses in. This is not a big prayer and many would look at me strangely if they heard it—You could die three days hence, Rose Lantz, why are you bringing such trifling matters before the Lord? Pray about your life. Pray about your soul. *But his love is not a trifling matter to me. And when we are close it seems that you do touch my life, you do touch my soul, not just my emotions, not just my womanhood, all of my spirit, anything and everything that returns to you at death. So when I ask you to secure a trysting place for us I am asking you to secure a place for all that matters to you, not just our hearts, not just our flesh, not just our dreams, but everything that lives forever. And somehow I need a place for that on this earth.*

Two soldiers went with her when she walked out in the April evening to milk the dairy herd. One stood guard on one side of the barn doors and one stood guard just inside. As her eyes adjusted to the dimness she saw

Ethan already at work, bent over as he sat on a stool. He turned his head and smiled as she came towards him.

"What took you so long?" he asked.

She sat at the cow next to him. "Well, you won't believe it, but the soldiers love Nitz the cat."

"The black cat? The witch's cat?"

"Yes. They ask for cream for their coffee and they give it to Nitz. She will get fat."

"So she has never had it so good."

"Never. Neither have the boys. The soldiers let them hold their muskets—"

"Uncocked?"

"Uncocked. They give them their hats to wear. The sergeant let Nathan put on his red uniform jacket for a few minutes."

Ethan got up and emptied his pail into the large milk can behind them. "My quarrel is not with them. My quarrel is with the one who is giving them orders. Though it is true my feelings towards the sergeant and his Grenadiers have not been of the warmest nature."

Rose did not look up at him. "They still watch me like a hawk even if they feel sheepish about it. And I heard the sergeant telling his corporal they would put the stake in place tomorrow morning."

Ethan stopped behind her. "You heard that?"

"Yes."

She heard him set down his bucket.

"Come with me a moment," he said.

"I'm not finished with Charlotte."

He pried one of her hands away from the cow. "Please."

He led her to a far corner of the barn. The soldier

could still see them but that did not stop him from hugging her tightly.

"You are precious to me, Rose."

"Of course I know that."

"Word of stakes being put in the ground is a knife in me. It will put the cold and the darkness in you as well."

"When you hold me as you are now I do not feel the iciness or blackness. It is like the Lord is comforting me through you."

"Then I will hold you for as long as you let me."

"Oh." Rose gave a short laugh. "That could be for a very long time. I don't think our milk cows would be in favor of that."

"You matter a great deal more than they. I pray for you but I know in my heart we are not to put our trust in men and their courts. I have taken other steps."

"What steps?"

"When everything is in place I will tell you."

She ran her hand over his chest. "They have taken your horses."

He drew back so he could see her face. "When?"

"Just before I came to the barn. I knew you'd be here because they had all three of your mounts and were leading them away."

"Where did they take them?"

"I don't know. The sergeant said we were not permitted to use our horses or buggies either. No one may leave the farm now until the trial is finished."

He looked at her a few moments and then pulled her into his arms again. "Kendall seeks to shut down every avenue of escape or any possibility of getting help. But I have two legs."

"They will not let you off the farm, Ethan."

"Not even on foot?"

"Not on foot, not by horse, not in a carriage."

"How can they stop me from slipping away at night?"

She curled her fingers in his deerskin shirt. "They'll shoot, Ethan."

"And miss."

"They won't shoot at you."

Ethan drew back a second time, his face rigid. "How can you tell me they are playing with your cat and playing with your brothers and then say they plan to shoot a member of your family if I get away from them?"

"Only the sergeant knows. It haunts him. I see that in his eyes. It would not be one of the boys, of course, nor my mother, not even me. But the sergeant would have my father shot on Kendall's orders and he follows orders. Isn't that what he always says?"

"He told you this to your face?"

"Yes."

"Alone?"

"He followed me to the smokehouse where I had gone to fetch a ham."

"And you come to me in this barn so calm and with your hair and dress fixed so pretty? After such dark threats?"

She half-smiled. "My head says I should be screaming out to heaven for my life and the lives of those around me. But inside I am as flat calm as a pond on a windless day. I can't explain it. I don't feel like dancing. Yet I don't feel like weeping either."

"How brave you are. I admire you. Didn't I see this

same courage the night the mob came against the farm here?"

"The closer you are to me the stronger I am."

"Thanks to Kendall and the soldiers it appears I am not going anywhere. So you will see a lot of me. Maybe too much."

"There's no such thing as too much of you, Ethan Daniels. But what about all your plans? How will they come to fruition now that you can't move about freely?"

"God and I will worry about that. You can worry about what that soldier standing there will think when I give you a Virginia kiss."

"Oh, no worries there." She slipped her slender arms about his neck. "Go right ahead."

On Saturday morning an eight foot high stake was pounded into an area behind the barn that was mostly rock and loose stone. One soldier got on the shoulders of another with a mallet and swung away while two other soldiers held the stake in place. After that they built a small platform at the side of the house about six feet off the ground. Then the soldiers took up their posts at various locations around the farm. In the afternoon Jakob Ammann and Pastor Philip and Pastor Ulrich arrived to pray with Rose and her family and stay for supper. On Sunday morning the stake was gone. The Grenadiers had to make another and put it up, pounding it in while buggy after buggy arrived for the worship service that was being held at the Lantz home. Jakob grumbled about desecrating the Sabbath and wanted to know why it was being erected before there had been a trial. A soldier remained at the stake the rest of the day and another through the night. The church prayed for Rose at great length, many crying out to God and shedding tears.

"Did you think removing the stake would make a difference?" asked Rose as she and Ethan milked side by side Sunday evening.

He did not say anything for a few moments.

"It does make a difference," he finally replied as milk squirted into his bucket.

"How?"

"It keeps them on edge. It keeps them uncertain."

"And that helps?"

Ethan glanced at her. "Did worship help you today?"

"I am supposed to say yes, aren't I?"

"Not with me."

"The singing helped. And the preaching. Of course it helped. Everyone is so kind. They care so much. They pray so hard. But Lydia was not there. Or her family. Several other families were not there either."

"I did not see Pastor Ulrich."

She got up with her bucket and stool. "No, you did not."

"It seems to trouble you more that Lydia was not there than the fact your trial starts tomorrow."

Rose stood still, bucket and stool in her hands. "We made a covenant months ago. Long before she herself was arrested. That we would always be there for each other. So I tried to honor that. I thought she would too."

"Did she ever speak to you about it?"

"Once. You were still unconscious. She brought me the rose quilt you sleep with. She told me she could not go through the witch hunt pain again. That her parents forbade her to spend time with me lest she be brought to trial a second time when charges were laid against me."

Ethan stopped milking and had turned around to face her. "So you understand that, don't you?"

She looked up at the rafters of the barn. "Our people were persecuted in Switzerland, Ethan. Many were put to death, yes, even burned at the stake. But we stayed together. Some left our church and would not stand with us. I have heard that Jakob Ammann's own daughter would not follow him here to the colonies and has returned to the churches that persecuted us. I—"

She hesitated and her fingers were at her eyes.

"I did not—I did not think my best friend would be one of those who refused to stand by us in a time of suffering. I did not think she would be one of those who—who hid away and kept out of sight so no one would remember her and no one would point the finger. I felt she would do anything in her power to defend me as I tried to do for her."

Ethan did not take her to the far corner of the barn but came to his feet and embraced her in full sight of the soldier. Long yellow and scarlet beams of sunset lanced through cracks in the barn wall and striped them both from head to foot. She cried as he held her.

"That is why you have me," Ethan said. "God must have known. How could he not? So he made sure you had another voice, another friend, another defender."

"But Lydia and I made a covenant with one another."

"So have you and I."

"We are not married. We may never be blessed with marriage."

His fingers were under her chin. "Marriage is good.

I look forward to it. But I don't need to wait until marriage to make a vow."

"We who follow Jakob Ammann do not put our faith in vows."

"You'll put your faith in this one. The Bible tells us no one shall separate us from the love of God. Do you believe that?"

"Of course." The tears were running freely down her cheeks. "But that is the Bible. Those are the words of God."

"Well, these are the words of a man who follows God. *If you die, I die with you. If you live, I will live too. I choose life.*"

She blinked to try and clear her eyes. "I don't understand what you are saying."

"Live or die, I'm with you, Rose Lantz. Either we both live together or we both die together. There's nothing in between."

"You can't say that to me."

"I just have."

"I don't want you dying for me."

"I'm not going to have much of a life unless you share it with me. So it's heaven or earth tomorrow. I don't care which one so long as I'm with you. I'd like to have a little bit more of earth but if not, why, heaven would do just fine."

She laughed despite herself, tears on her face and hands. "You really are crazy. *Verruckt.* I saw that from the beginning. Running around in the woods with your long hair and wearing deerskins."

"Living off pinecones and nuts and wild berries."

"Roots too."

He smiled. "Never plowing a strip of land. Never seeding a crop."

"Never settling down."

"Howling at the moon, living with wolves."

She buried her head in his chest. "I should have known better. I should never have let you carry me that day on the road. I should never have let you milk cows with me. I should never have let you kiss me—that was the worst."

"It was, wasn't it?"

"It was terrible. It went on and on. Meanwhile men were coming with clubs and torches and guns."

"Still—a long kiss seems to settle the nerves."

She laughed. "It didn't settle mine. It woke them up."

"It woke up your good nerves. Not your fears. It drove your fears away."

"Your love for me is too big, that's all. Between your love and God's love there's absolutely no room for anything else."

He touched her Quaker cap with his lips. "Men are coming again with torches and guns."

"So that is your excuse to indulge in another long kiss?"

"It's not an excuse. It's a necessity."

"Truly?"

"It might even be a commandment." He began to kiss her wet cheek. "One does not lightly disobey commandments."

She returned his kisses. "Now you and God are joining ranks against me."

"We always were."

He found her mouth and his kiss filled her with light

and heat. She lost all track of time and forgot about the stake and the trial and Archibald Kendall and the witnesses who would stand up and rail at her. Instead there was only the love of God and the love of Ethan Daniels and the peace that came with it as well as the fire. It seemed only a matter of hours before she was back in the barn milking the cows and the dawn was making fine golden slits in the dark. And Ethan was taking her in his arms again and beginning another kiss, her lips sweet with the cream he had splashed on her mouth, his strength a band of iron around her that could not be broken, his beauty something she clung to with both hands, something she could not lose, a loveliness even in the face of death that was the best thing God had ever given her through Jesus Christ her Lord.

"How did you sleep?" he asked her.

"Not so well. I prayed a lot. I read the Bible. Falling asleep was difficult."

"Let me pray for you."

"I'd like that."

"And I have these verses, commonly spoken, but no less powerful for that. *Even though I walk through the valley of the shadow of death I will fear no evil for thou art with me. Thy rod and thy staff they comfort me. Thou preparest a table before me in the presence of my enemies. Thou anointest my head with oil. My cup runneth over.*" He kissed her tears. "Remember I will never be far. Even if you look for me and cannot see me I will not be far. I shall be close. God shall be closer. Neither of us will forsake you. Put your trust in that. Despite what you may see or not see, I will be at your right hand."

"Thank you, my love."

"Now let me pray."

His words were strong and beautiful like forests or rivers or a long line of green hills that disappeared into a blue distance. But he did not have a chance to finish before Sergeant Gunn entered the barn.

"Bind her hand and foot," he ordered the soldiers with him.

Ethan's face took on hard lines as he looked at the sergeant. "Why do you need to do that?"

"Orders." The sergeant's face was equally as hard. "He's here and all of Lancaster County with him."

Ethan and Rose stepped outside of the barn and saw wagons bearing scores of redcoats coming up the lane from the roadway. Behind them was a black carriage trimmed in gold that Judge Hallowell often used. Following the carriage were hundreds of people on horseback, in buggies or in wagons or on foot.

"No wonder he wanted to have the trial here," said Rose. "Now the whole county can watch."

"Bind her, I said."

The gray in Ethan's eyes was a storm lit with lightning as the corporal tied rope around Rose's ankles and wrists. Ethan put his hand on the soldier but two others shoved him back with their muskets.

"Don't interfere," growled the sergeant.

"Are you proud of your actions this day, Sergeant Gunn?" seethed Ethan.

"I do my duty."

"So you don't mind if I do mine, sergeant?"

"Ethan." Rose turned to him. "Please. No more talk like this."

Soldiers on either side of Rose held her by the arm and helped her across the farmyard since she could barely move her feet. Redcoats were forming a square around the platform that had been erected and Archibald Kendall, taller and leaner than she remembered, emerged from the black and gold carriage as two ranks of soldiers formed a pathway for him and presented arms. People from her church were driving their buggies to one side of the house while farmers and townspeople gathered by the platform. The soldiers who held her made their way quickly through the crowds and up the steps to set her facing the men and women and children. She saw her parents and her brothers for a moment. Their faces were white blurs to her.

"We should like to pray with Rose Lantz."

She looked down, hands tied in front of her, at Jakob Ammann talking to Sergeant Gunn and a captain, Pastor Philip and her father beside him. The captain shook his head.

"I'm sorry, sir. Should the accused be condemned you may certainly pray with her then. As it is she must stand on the platform alone. No one may go to her but the soldiers that are ordered to. And the king's representative himself, Mr. Archibald Kendall."

"I shall bring this up with Mr. Kendall."

Again the captain shook his head. "My men have him closely guarded. His own instructions to me were quite clear—he doesn't want anyone approaching him before or after the trial."

"Captain—"

"I'm sorry, sir. I must look to my troops."

Jakob looked up at her as soldiers escorted him away

from the platform. "We are praying, my dear girl. It does not matter where we stand, whether we are close to you or far. Prayer is not measured by such things."

"I know, Grandfather. Thank you."

"Remember how our people held to their faith in Switzerland. Remember our God."

The soldiers kept the crowd well back from the platform. Rose looked over the faces for Ethan as the April morning warmed and the sun rose higher in the pale blue sky. At first he was easy to spot, head and shoulders above those around him, but as more people arrived and moved back and forth and put children on their shoulders, he seemed to disappear. She closed her eyes as she felt prickings of fear in her stomach and chest.

Aus den Tiefen rufe ich, oh Herr dich.

Out of the depths I cry to thee, oh Lord.

Archibald Kendall mounted the steps. The soldiers had placed Rose at the far end. Kendall remained as distant from her as he could. Everything he wore was black. He removed his church steeple hat.

"The Lord be with us!" he said in a loud voice. "Justice will be served today for Lancaster County. The Lord himself has declared it to me. Your long season of sorrow and suffering has come to an end. You shall be free. The curse will be lifted and your spring crops and calves and foals shall thrive. God himself shall bless thee and shine upon thee." He returned his hat to his head, looking immediately twice as tall and forbidding as he had a moment before. "Justice must not only be done, good Christian men and women, good citizens of King George II, it must also be seen by all of you to be done. That is why I have arranged that this important trial be held here, at the accused's own home. One reason is so that the town itself may not be tainted any more than it has been. But the other is so that all who wish to see how his majesty's justice is meted out may be able to do so. The courtroom in Lancaster is far too small to hold the numbers that swell your ranks today. Here all may observe, here all may see how the work of the devil is laid low by the laws of God and the laws of the king. I shall not keep you long. Our witnesses to the work of witchcraft in this region are ready to tell us, before God, what they have seen and heard and I, in the name of God and King George II, am ready to pass judgment on the basis of the testimonies they render. May the Lord's will be done."

He nodded his head at the first person in a long line of women and men that had assembled within the perimeter the redcoats maintained. Sergeant Gunn stood at the head of the line and he directed a man beside him to go forward. The man climbed the short set of steps and stood beside Kendall, dwarfed by the witch finder's tall frame.

"Speak your testimony, sir." Kendall stepped back and put his hands behind his back.

The man, someone Rose did not recognize, hesitated, glancing back at Kendall, who nodded his head roughly.

"Go ahead, man, tell us what you know of witchcraft and the devil's work in Lancaster County, Pennsylvania. Face your Christian neighbors squarely, sir."

The man looked to his front, twisting his small brown cap about in his hands. "Well, I—"

Sergeant Gunn cupped his hand to his ear. "Hey?"

"Speak up!" barked Kendall.

"Well!" The man almost shouted. "I seen this Miss Rose Lantz once day from me wagon on the road and she was picking herbs and such to make potions and she would change back and forth from a black cat to her human form right in front of me eyes!"

"Are you sure it was her?" asked Kendall.

"Yes, sir. I've seen Rose Lantz here and abouts since she was a child. It's a shame that she's taken to this."

"What else can you tell us? Have you ever seen her familiar?"

"I believe I have, sir."

"Is this it?"

The sergeant lifted a cage by his feet. Nitz the cat was in it.

"Leave her alone!" Rose could not hold back her outburst. "She's done no one any harm! She's one of God's creatures!"

"One of God's creatures?" sneered Kendall. "Indeed?"

"Let her go! You have no right! *Sie Gottlose!*"

You wicked man!

"Ah, casting your spells in strange tongues, Rose Lantz? It won't work. The Lord has blessed me in a particular way for this divine mission. Otherwise I should have perished years ago." He flicked his fingers at the man standing with him on the platform. "Thank you. The next witness, Sergeant Gunn."

I am sorry, my Lord, but he made up his mind about me before he left England. What does it matter if I cry out? Perhaps a few people will see the folly of this trial. Perhaps I will shake a few stones loose.

"What is your name?" Kendall asked a young woman who had come onto the platform.

"Martha Goodman, sir."

"Tell us what you have seen. Tell all of Lancaster County what you know."

"She flew, sir."

"On a broom?"

"No, sir. All on her own."

"On her own! She must possess extraordinary powers to do that. Are you sure it was Rose Lantz?"

"Yes, sir. She has a distinctive look. Her hair is very long, perhaps the longest in the county. It streamed behind her like a streak of fire."

"Fire?" Kendall raised his eyebrows as high as he could. "You mean there were flames?"

"As God is my witness. She trailed sparks. It was easy to see for the night had no moon. She went back and forth across the sky."

"What was the purpose of that?"

"She—why, she seemed to be catching things with her tongue."

"Her tongue? Was it long?"

"Yes, sir."

"Like a toad's?"

"Exactly like that, sir, yes."

"Can you tell us what she was catching?"

"She would keep them in her mouth. And then disgorge them into a large cauldron when she landed. Out came all manner of insect and firefly and moth. Even a bat."

A gasp swept the crowd and Rose saw faces turn towards her in shock and disgust and anger.

"How is it the witch did not see you and turn you into a worm or snake?" asked Kendall.

"I was well back behind a great live oak, sir, and there was a running stream between us."

"Ah."

"And I was saying the Lord's Prayer under my breath the whole while."

"Thank God, thank God. Very good. You may step down, yes, very good, you may rejoin your family. Who do we have next, Sergeant Gunn?"

Kendall brought up witnesses for over an hour. Rose had done all the things Lydia had been accused of—souring milk, drying up wells, ruining barley crops, giving children the fever—and Kendall stopped the steady stream for a minute to explain that people had mistakenly laid these charges at Lydia's door when, in fact, all along Rose had been guilty of the offences.

"Including the death of Adam Peachtree," he intoned. "Aye, the tragic, devilish death of a good family's son. Rose Lantz, all the time it was Rose Lantz who cursed you fine people—English, Quaker, German, it made no difference to her as it makes no difference to Satan. Wherever he can do the most evil there he will go, rich, poor, young, old, man, beast, he is no respecter of persons or their crops or livestock, so long as he can inflict the most damage possible and drive a wedge of pain between man and his God."

Rose could see Jakob Ammann from time to time, and her father and mother, but for a long time she could not find Ethan no matter where she looked. Then he appeared again, tall, straight, looking at her steadily, one of his rifles slung over his back again, his hands resting on the barrel of another, its stock firmly set against the ground. She wondered that she had the presence of mind to smile at him, while witness after witness accused her of the vilest deeds any witch had ever done, and she wondered that he had the grace to smile back, but his smile was obvious and beautiful. Her mind screamed at her to be afraid but she could not find it in her spirit to panic or despair.

I love you.

She moved her lips and mouthed the words.

I love you, Ethan. Ich liebe dich.

She was not sure he had seen or understood. But he was close enough that she could tell the moment he began forming vowels and consonants, taking his time, doing it over and over so that her smiles became fuller and more frequent.

You are my dream, Rose Lantz, you are my lady. I thank God for you. I love you with all my heart and all my strength.

Then he mouthed the phrase: *You will be free. I swear to God you will be free.*

"Do the proceedings amuse you, Miss Lantz?"

His voice and its tone did not alarm her. She finished a smile and turned her head slowly towards Kendall. "What proceedings?"

"You are on trial for witchcraft and murder."

She looked around her. "I see no court."

"Indeed? This is the court, Rose Lantz, and I am the judge."

"I see no judge."

Scraps of laughter blew from one end of the huge crowd to the other. Kendall took off his hat, seemed to look into for the words he was going to speak next, then planted it firmly back on his dark head.

"We have no need for further witnesses." He nodded at the people swarming against the long ranks of British soldiers. "We have heard enough. The witch mocks us. She will not be mocking us an hour from now." He squinted at the sun and glanced at Rose. "I am your judge whether you think it is so or not so. You have no power here. We will not do your bidding. You will do ours."

"Don't you think if I could fly that I would fly away right now?" She stared at him. "Why don't I do that?"

"You have no power here. I told you that. This is an assembly of good Christian folk."

"What, sir? I curdled their cream, blackened their crops by day or by night, gave their infants the fever, made sure their calves and horses were stillborn while they sang hymns in church and preached from the Bible, yet here where there are no hymns or sermons or prayers I cannot fly? It should be an easy thing for someone of my powers. If I had those powers."

The silence from the crowd was the silence that waited for an answer.

"I have bound you, Miss Lantz."

"Bound me? With a charm?"

"With prayer."

"But their prayers could not bind me. Why should yours?"

"I have been granted special graces from the Almighty. I am clothed in unique giftings. I am the righteous judge. As fine as these people are they did not have my powers or my righteousness while you were plying your dark arts. That is why they could not hold you."

"Your powers? Your righteousness? You make it sound like you are God."

The murmuring among the men and women brought a glint into Kendall's eyes.

"I am not here to bandy words with you but to pronounce judgment based on what the witnesses have declared. That is what I will do now."

He stepped forward on the platform so that he was closer to the crowd. "Good people of Lancaster County, permit to pray before you a moment and seek God's guidance for the decision I must render in the next few minutes." He bowed his head.

No one stirred. Even the children seemed to grow quiet. Rose closed her eyes and prayed her own prayer. When she opened them again Ethan was standing as close to the soldiers as he could get and his eyes did not leave her. Neither of them smiled again. But neither did they look away from each other.

"The Lord has spoken."

Kendall returned his hat to his head with a pat.

He looked down at the sergeant. "Gag her."

Gunn frowned. "Sir?"

"Gag her. She is too free with her tongue and my declaration of the Lord's judgment must not be compromised."

Gunn glanced at his captain. The captain's face was blank. He gave a slight nod of his head. Gunn drew a large scarlet scarf from his uniform pocket, came up on the platform, and crossed over to Rose.

"I am sorry, Miss," he said quietly.

"You have no more choice in the matter than I do, sergeant." She gave him a small smile. "I shall always remember you for the cup of water you gave me that night."

She could see a struggle in his face. Then he placed the scarf around her mouth three times and tied it off at the back so that its ends dangled over the front of her right shoulder. He walked off the platform.

"Thank you, sergeant," said Kendall.

Gunn did not respond as he stepped onto the ground and took up his position again.

Rose's eyes were fastened on Ethan.

I see you, my love, I see you. Even though I can no longer form words with my lips I can tell you what I wish to tell you with my eyes.

Ethan returned her gaze. His lips took their time. *Your eyes are as beautiful as sunrise. You know that. The scarf sets them apart like a veil. They are precious stone. That I have taken from the clearest mountain stream.*

"In both testaments of the Holy Bible we are commanded to shun witchcraft. Indeed, we are told that we shall not suffer a witch to live." Kendall's voice was strong and steady as he addressed the gathering. "To the testimonies of honest witnesses that have been given this morning we must add that Rose Lantz was able to bewitch the first court that presided over the charges brought against Lydia Beiler. That she was able to turn away, with a flick of her hand, a hundred men who descended upon her home that night to seek justice. That she was able to raise a man from the dead, not by means of prayer, but by means of her unholy arts. That she has eluded all attempts to discover her and end her vile enchantments for years."

Kendall did not look at Rose but extended his long arm and one long finger and pointed. "There she is at last. The queen of witches who has brought no end of misery upon your heads and the heads of your children. Cleverly hidden within the ranks of a religious community. She brought her dark arts from Europe as a child, a child who had been sold to the devil while an infant. When she came of age she was loosed upon our English colonies in America to wreak as much havoc as possible. Who knows how far her evil would have spread had you not sent for me? Who knows how many more would have lost not only their crops and calves but their lives? But now the devil's games among you are ended. Now justice will be served."

Finally he turned and looked at Rose. "The testimony of every witness was clear. Everyone has heard their words. What you have done in secret is now proclaimed from the rooftops. I find you guilty, guilty, thrice guilty, nay, a thousand times guilty. A place has been prepared for your execution. Only fire will cleanse this township from your wickedness. You and your familiar shall burn together and the land will be pure again. There will be nothing to bury. Your ashes will scatter to the winds. May God have mercy in your soul."

He faced the sergeant and the captain. "Do your duty in the name of God and king and country."

The captain nodded. "Yes, sir. Sergeant Gunn, take two soldiers and bring her down from there."

"Sir," replied Gunn.

"Corporal, take two dozen men and make a pathway for the sergeant to take the condemned to the stake."

"Yes, sir."

At first the two soldiers handled Rose roughly but Gunn snapped at them and they settled down, taking her carefully across the platform and onto the ground and along the corridor created by two ranks of redcoats. The faces of men and women that appeared on either side of her as she was hustled through the crowd were unrecognizable to her. Some leered. Some had no expression at all. Others looked as if they had been crying.

Ethan, where are you?

They took her to the far side of the barn where soldiers had been guarding the stake all night and all morning. One of her father's large carts was harnessed to one of their black geldings. Three soldiers were bringing all kinds of deadwood in from the forest and piling it high around the tall stake.

It is not real. It does not feel like anything I have experienced before in this world. Someone will snap their fingers and my hands will be free, and my feet, and I will be able to speak through my mouth. Ethan will put his arm around me. Mother will ask me to milk the cows before supper. My love will take me in his arms there and kiss me and I shall thank God for my life.

"Put her up at the stake." Sergeant Gunn gave one of the soldiers a coil of new rope. "Get Smith and Baldwin to help you. Not too tight. She's not going anywhere and the fire will render your knots useless in a matter of minutes."

"Yes, sergeant. Where shall we place the rope on her body?"

"Secure her legs. Then wind it about her arms and chest a few times. Go easy now, d'you hear? She's someone's daughter regardless of what she's been charged with. Her parents are watching so mind how you do what you do."

"Yes, sergeant."

Rose was half-carried and half-dragged through the mounds of brush and rotten logs and her back pressed against the wood of the stake. It dug into her back through her dress. The rope was thick and bristly and it cut into the skin at her ankles. Seven times they wrapped it around her arms and upper body. It became difficult to breathe. Sticks and branches were heaped as high as her waist. One soldier placed thick logs on top of them.

"Here." Sergeant Gunn leaned over and untied the scarf from her mouth.

She pulled in a deep breath. "Oh, thank you."

The struggle was still going on in the sergeant's face. "I will ask if you may be shot. Sometimes that mercy is granted. Then you will not have to bear the terrible pain the flames inflict."

"Do you think the witch finder will grant me such a blessing, sergeant?" she asked.

"You don't know about a man like him. I will speak with my captain first."

"Thank you."

"God bless you, Miss Lantz."

"He has, Sergeant Gunn. It has been a wonderful life in so many respects. I should have liked quite a bit more of it."

He nodded. “Aye.” He turned away. “I will talk with my captain.”

She watched soldiers form a ring around the stake about fifty feet from her. Their bayonets had been fixed but she noticed that none of the muskets were cocked. Hundreds boiled in from the farmyard. She could not see Ethan or her mother or father. Then she noticed Jakob Ammann with the sergeant. He and Pastor Philip and her father came towards her and the soldiers let them through. Her father tried to touch her hands but the firewood was stacked too high and deep for him to reach her.

“Meine Tochter.” Her father’s cheeks were wet. *“Meine Tochter, wie wir lieben dich.”*

“I know, Papa.” She felt the burning in her eyes and the heat as water cut across her face. “I love you too. And Mama. And my brothers. And all the families in my church. With all my heart.”

“You go to God.” The skin on Jakob’s face was like bone. “Nothing shall stand in your way. No angel can prevent you. Christ’s love is enough. You go to God just as so many of our faith have gone in the past. This is a day of injustice and unholiness but the Lord will prevail. You shall dwell at his right hand. Your treasure is stored up in heaven.”

“Danke, Opa.”

“We will care for your family.” Pastor Philip, bald, with his thick brown beard. “They shall lack for nothing.”

“I’m grateful, pastor.”

They began to pray for her, first Jakob, then Pastor Philip, then her father. Sergeant Gunn appeared and asked them to return beyond the circle of soldiers. He waited until they were out of earshot.

"There will be a sharpshooter," he said softly. "D'you see the window high up in the barn? In the hayloft?"

"Yes."

"There will be a soldier there presently. The best shot in the company. As soon as the wood is ignited he will fire. You will feel nothing after the bullet hits home."

"The witch finder agreed to this?"

"The captain made the decision. We did not include Mr. Kendall."

She stared at him. "Will this not go ill with you?"

"The sound of the fire will be very loud and it will be very loud very quickly. There will be all manner of snaps and pops. He will not hear the musket."

"I know what musket fire sounds like, sergeant. So do the others. And it will come from behind. Kendall will most certainly hear it."

"Perhaps we shall be lucky."

"I will immediately slump forward on the stake."

"Fainting from the terrible heat and from inhaling the smoke."

She smiled with one side of her mouth. "You've thought of everything. But Kendall may still suspect."

The sergeant's face was set in thick lines. "Neither of us is much concerned about that. Neither should you be. Just keep your mind on your prayers and on those you love."

"Bless you, sergeant."

He nodded, turned his face from her, and walked away.

She looked for Ethan but there were too many people, too many heads with too many hats.

Where are you? Where, my love? I know you have tried your best to save me but now I only want to see your face one last time.

Rose caught movement at the hayloft window. A scarlet coat, the long dark shape of what looked like a rifle, not a musket, the fast gleam of bright blond hair.

What a strange thing to thank you for, my Lord, but better a clean bullet strike than flames which burn and burn.

Kendall arrived with six or seven soldiers forming a bodyguard around him. He took up his position near the ring of redcoats who surrounded her and kept back the crowd. For a moment Rose glimpsed Mrs. Peachtree at his right shoulder. There was no happiness in her face. She looked drained and half-dead. Kendall had his hands behind his back as he gazed at Rose. He nodded at the corporal who was at attention nearby. The man had a torch in his hand. Kneeling, he struck flint against a square of metal. Sparks fell onto the torch. Dark with oil, its top flared with red and yellow. He picked it up. The soldiers stood aside and he passed through between them, walking towards her with the torch blazing.

It does not seem right that you should come back to life only to have me die two months later. But who can understand the dark periods in our lives, who can understand the whys of the hurts and the sufferings? I hope you will find love again, Ethan. I just wish I had been your bride. I so badly wanted to be my beautiful man's bride.

The corporal stood in front of her. Their eyes met. He looked away. His knuckles on the fist that held the torch were empty of blood.

"It is all right," she said to him. "I forgive you. Do your duty and God bless you."

He looked back at her, startled. For a long moment he did nothing. Then he lowered the torch to the tips of the branches closest to him.

I love you, Ethan. Through all death and through all of heaven, I love you. It will never end. It can't.

The wood at her feet burst into spears of fire.

Father, into your hands I commit my spirit.

Volume 9

The Rescue

"Oh!"

A sudden wave of heat from the flames made Rose twist her head sharply to the right. At the same moment the stake splintered where her face had been with a loud crack.

The sharpshooter missed! Please God, let him try again!

"Hey! Hey!"

She lifted her head despite the heat and saw dozens of horses galloping around the barn towards the circle of redcoats. Ethan was on the first horse, his dapple gray Delaware, and horse and rider leaped over two startled soldiers. The other redcoats scattered to the left and right as other horses broke the line. Behind them men on horseback and men on foot were swiftly herding the crowd to the other side of the barn.

"Shoot the colonials! Shoot them!" she heard Kendall shout.

Muskets banged. Soldiers knelt and aimed. The men on horseback fired from the saddle or jumped down and shot their long rifles once they hit the ground. White smoke from the burnt powder billowed over everyone's heads.

Ethan was at her side, two rifles slung over his back. "Hold on!"

He threw a thick blanket from his saddle onto the flames closest to her, smothering them.

Then he cut at the rope with his long knife. Strand after strand popped open and parted.

"Ethan! Who are those men?"

"Colonial militia."

"There is a soldier in the hayloft of the barn. He was ordered to shoot me as an act of mercy."

"We saw his shot. Spencer and Hutch went into the barn to take care of him."

"Ethan, no. He was trying to save me from the pain of burning alive."

"I know it. They will call upon him to surrender or shoot to wound."

He cut the last rope and seized her in one arm. Throwing her onto the gray he leaped up behind her, grabbed the reins, kicked in his heels, and Delaware sprang ahead towards the bushes and trees. Rose heard a zinging go past her ear, it was like the sound of a wasp, then another. The horse galloped into a cluster of oak trees and Ethan swung down, reaching up with his arms. Rose pushed herself off the saddle and fell. He caught her and held her.

"Are you all right?" he asked her. "Are you hurt?"

"I don't feel anything."

He quickly looked over her, examining her face and dress and hands. "The hem of your apron and dress are scorched. You will need new ones."

Rose was still dazed by the fire and Ethan's rescue. "New ones? That shouldn't be a problem."

Gunfire crackled behind them. Ethan took her face in his hands and kissed her on the lips with as much force and passion as she had ever felt from him.

"I must go," he said. "Stay here until the fight is over. I will come and get you."

"What if a soldier finds me?"

"Here." He slapped a pistol into one of her hands and his knife into the other. "If the pistol misfires use the knife."

"Ethan, I can't kill a man."

"Wound him." He jumped onto Delaware. "The redcoats will be too busy to look for you. Stay low. Stay hidden. I will be back for you."

"Ethan, Ethan, be careful."

A grin burst over his face. "Of course I'll be careful. I want to collect a proper kiss for saving you."

He galloped towards the barn and a cloud of smoke lit by snatches of yellow fire. Rose saw that most of the people and their children had quickly gone to the other side of the barn but some farmers had remained behind, unslung rifles from their backs, and begun to fire at the Grenadiers. Horses ran across the fields in a panic, one barreling towards her. She slipped behind a tree trunk. It shot past, splashed through a stream, and kept going.

To her front the shooting continued. She saw several red uniformed soldiers lying in the dirt and at least one militiaman. Flames were swarming over the stake where she had been tied and the dark smoke from that blaze made it even harder for her to see what was happening. She caught a glimpse of Ethan in his buckskins swatting a musket out of a young soldier's hands and knocking him to the ground with his fist. Then the mixture of smoke from the guns and smoke from the stake with its tall pile of firewood rolled over him. Still there were stabs of yellow light.

Still there was the boom of muskets and the crack of rifles.

To her shock she saw Archibald Kendall emerge from the haze of smoke, stumble and lose his hat, bend to pick it up, drop it, then run bareheaded towards the oak trees she was hiding in.

Oh, God, no, do not test me in this way, do not bring him to where I am.

But Kendall came straight for her tree as if he knew she was there. Reaching the oak he braced two large hands against it, gulping in air, sweat lancing down his face. Then he lifted his head and saw her.

"You!" he panted. "Witch!"

He lunged for her with his long arms.

Rose dodged and ran farther into the trees. He lumbered after her with his long strides.

"Did you think you could escape God's judgment?" he roared. "Did you think you could cause all this mayhem and get away? God has led me right to you!"

At first she kept ahead of him but it was difficult to run through the tall grass in her long dress. A hand gripped her neck from behind, squeezed, and flung her to the ground.

"There are other ways to kill witches besides fire. In

Europe they sometimes strangle them before they burn them. I can do that."

He loomed over her.

"Don't!" she cried. "I am not a witch! I have never harmed anyone and I don't wish to harm you either!"

"Oh, you will not harm me. I am fully protected from your sorcery. And you will certainly never harm anyone else again."

He threw himself on top of her.

"But first a kiss. A kiss from the witch. It would be a shame to let all that beauty go back to the dust from which it came without a final kiss from a Christian man. Who knows? It might prove to be a special grace for you. It might gain you a few minutes' respite from hell."

She twisted her head away from his lips. "Don't! In the name of God, don't!" He slapped her twice across the face. Her lower lip broke and bled.

"You do not use God's name, witch. And you do not presume to tell one of his servants what he may or may not do with the likes of you."

He forced his mouth down on hers.

She slammed him in the side of the face with the flintlock pistol Ethan had given her.

He drew back, snarling, snatched the pistol from her hand, and threw it away. "Are you done with your witchcraft? Must you resort to pistols and muskets? Why don't you turn me into a frog?" He leaned over her again. "Now where was I? Oh, yes. Bestowing a special grace on you so that you may be spared the fires of hell."

His mouth was back on hers and he began to choke her at the same time with his large hands.

She thrust the knife into his shoulder.

"Arrrrrr! Now what have you done?" He slapped a hand to the wound. "You really are a devil, aren't you?"

"Just leave me alone and I'll do nothing more."

"Leave you alone? Why, I've only just begun. I'm keen on blood sport. It brings out the best in me."

He grabbed at the knife in her hand but she twisted away and plunged it into his leg. Howling, he clamped both hands to his thigh. Blood squirted from his mouth where he had bit his tongue.

"Enough! No mercy! I was a fool to offer it! No kiss, no grace, no life!" He wrapped his bloody hands around her throat and threw the weight of his whole body behind the grip.

Rose saw double of him, watched him waver, watched him fade. She stabbed with the knife again and again, barely able to call out to God to help her, barely able to cry out to God to forgive her, not sure if she was striking him, not sure if the knife was even in her hand anymore. The choking continued and she kept on swinging her arm as she grew weaker and weaker. Finally she let her arm drop.

He was not on top of her anymore.

Panting, drawing as much air into her as she could, Rose propped herself up on her elbows.

Kendall was sprawled beside her, bleeding from wounds in his arms and legs and stomach. There was even a slash across his face. He did not move. He did not speak. He did not groan. But she could hear his breathing.

Lord, forgive me. Christ, forgive me.

She found the knife at her side, wiped its blade clean on the tall grass, and cut at the apron over her dress.

When she had several long strips she knelt by Kendall and began to bandage his arms and legs. She cut a wider strip from her dress, including a part that was scorched, and bound it around his stomach wound, pushing him up onto his side so she could tie it under his back.

His chest rose and fell but he made no sounds.

Rose wiped away the blood on his face. "Lord, lay not this sin to his charge. Archibald Kendall thought he was doing the right thing by hunting down witches. He had not read your Word properly. He did not understand." She cleaned up a small nick on his neck. "And I pray you do not lay it to my charge either. I did not know what else to do. I did not know how to stop him."

"Rose! Rose!"

Ethan's voice. Frantic.

"Here!" She sprang to her feet. "I'm over here!"

The thud of hooves. Ethan on his gray. Followed by two officers in scarlet coats bright with gold braid who rode dark brown horses.

"Ethan is a prisoner," she said under her breath and fresh fear darted through her.

Ethan leaped from Delaware and caught Rose up in his arms. "What has happened to you?" He looked at Kendall's body. "Did he attack you?"

"Yes, yes, I'm sorry, I didn't know what to do." Tears sliced through the blood and grime on her face. "He was choking me, he—"

"Shh. All right. It's all right."

She looked at the officers. "I'm sorry. He said he would strangle me. He had his hands on my throat. I just swung at him with my knife."

"I see," responded one of the officers.

"I tried to bandage his wounds."

The officer nodded. "Captain Trimble," he said. "Does the witch finder have life in him?"

The captain climbed down from his horse and went to one knee by Kendall.

He turned him over on his back and placed a hand over his heart. "A strong beat, m'lord."

"Is there? Do you happen to have a set of chains in your baggage?"

"I do, m'lord."

"Clap them on the scoundrel before he comes to. Then throw him on the back of your horse like the sack of rubbish he is."

"Yes, m'lord."

Rose looked from one officer to the other and then back at Ethan. "What is going on? What are you doing?"

"I had to strike with the militia before these men and their troops arrived from Philadelphia. I had hoped to avoid bloodshed. But Kendall put you to the stake early. I had no choice."

"Who are they? Why have they not arrested you?"

"They have not arrested me because they came to arrest Kendall and order his men to lay down their arms."

"Ethan, I don't understand."

The officer who had given the commands to Captain Trimble doffed his hat. "Lord Ashton, my dear. Colonel in the British army. I fear you have gone through a grievous trial and nearly lost your life. Word came by fast frigate from Halifax that Kendall was a fraud and wanted in England for murder and high treason. Our troops set out immediately. A courier from your militia went to the governor imploring him to stop Kendall from doing his mischief. He reported that one of their militia captains had reason to suspect Kendall had brought women up on false charges in England and Ireland, murdered them, run their husbands and families off their properties, sold the land, and pocketed the gold. The governor said he had just found out about the matter and sent troops to arrest Kendall. The courier caught up with us. I advised him to ride ahead without delay and tell the Lancaster militia to be prepared to stop any executions by whatever means necessary."

Ethan ran a hand down the side of Rose's face, wiping away some of the blood and dirt with his palm. "The courier was a day or more ahead of the troops under Lord Ashton. We hoped they would arrive yesterday but rains east of us delayed their march. I had the militia ready to take action if there was no other means of saving you. We waited until the last minute, hoping to see Lord Ashton who we knew could not be far off. But once Kendall had you tied to the stake I gave the signal for the militia to attack. They were assembled in a woods half a mile away."

"Half a mile."

"To ensure they would not be detected by the Grenadiers."

"But what—but what if—" Rose lost her words.

Ethan cupped her face in his strong hands. "I was much closer. Dismounted and hiding only a few hundred yards from the farm. If necessary I would have gone in alone."

"You would have been killed."

"Perhaps not. I'd have had a much noisier entrance.

War whoops and howls and turning horses loose among the soldiers before I came riding in."

"How did you get these horses? How did you get Delaware?"

"I merely knocked some sense into a few corporals until they saw things my way." He smiled. "Excuse me a moment."

Still bewildered, Rose watched him help Captain Trimble hoist Kendall over the back of his saddle. Kendall's wrists and ankles were manacled. The captain climbed back on his horse.

"I hope you will stay the night, Lord Ashton," said Ethan.

"We will. Several nights. It was a fast march and my men need to recover. And it was the governor's wish we remain in the area for two or three weeks."

"We are happy to board your men at any of our farmhouses."

"Thank you. If accommodation is lacking in Lancaster I shall send Captain Trimble to fetch you." Lord Ashton smiled. "Is everything quite all right here?"

Ethan nodded. "It is. I will just make sure of it and we'll be along directly."

"Very good."

The two officers turned their horses and headed back to the Lantz farm. "How did you know about Kendall?" Rose asked.

"I simply made inquiries. Sent letters to Halifax and London. The inquiries were not blind gropings in the dark. I had heard rumors. The generals in Halifax did not even know Kendall was here. Apparently he uses other names as well. But once my description reached them they knew him for the man they had already received orders to apprehend and hang. The frigate was sent to Philadelphia. The governor sent the troops marching to Lancaster County. Our courier caught up with them. You know the rest."

"My father and my mother—Jakob Ammann—the children—"

"We had men in the crowd at your trial. It was their job to steer the people out of harm's way and they did that. No one was harmed."

"No one was harmed?"

"No civilians."

Rose put her hand to her mouth. "The sharpshooter in the hayloft?"

"Wounded."

"The sergeant?"

"Wounded. He's doing fine."

"The captain of the Grenadiers?"

"Unharmed."

"Then who was hurt?" she asked.

"A corporal and three privates were killed."

"Oh, no."

"And two of our militiamen. Others were wounded."

"No, Ethan, no. I did not want men killed on my account."

He shook his head. "They were not killed on your account. They were killed because Kendall subverted the king's justice. They were killed when we fought to restore the king's justice."

"Oh, Ethan." She cried and put her head on his chest. "I feel dreadful."

"I do not like death any better than you do. But I should have liked yours least of all."

"Did you—did you kill?"

"No. I did not. There was no need. I shot to wound. Others in our militia did not have that choice. But be at peace. The fighting did not last long. The redcoats laid down their arms."

She began to sob, grasping the front of his buckskin shirt in her fingers.

He let her cry a long time, cradling her, rocking her, gently pressing his lips against her deep brown hair, part of which was still in place, while other parts had unraveled or become tangled or been singed by the fire or caked in blood and dirt.

"I'm sorry," she finally said, the tears all over her face and chin.

"There's nothing to be sorry for. You've gone through a terrible ordeal. And having gone through it you remain the bravest woman I have ever known. Even that is not quite right. I've seen no braver man in my lifetime."

"Don't say that, Ethan."

"It's true, Rose." He tilted her chin with his hand the way he always did. "How blessed I am. I get to marry you."

She laughed as the tears continued to slip over her cheeks. "You make it sound like I am quite the prize. Look at me. Half burnt. Half beaten. Blood and mud all over my hands and all through my hair. My dress torn to ribbons."

"Eyes like gemstones. Hair like silk. Skin like pearl. Lips like rubies. The smile of an angel. A heart like God's."

"Stop it, Ethan. Always you exaggerate when you pay me compliments."

"I never stretch the truth. You are the greatest beauty in the Commonwealth of Pennsylvania. No. You are the greatest beauty in all the English colonies and you are not even English. How about that?"

She swatted his arm. "How about that? Next time it will be harder."

"It will not be harder."

"It *will* be harder. Why won't it be?"

"Because you won't have the breath."

His kiss was not too strong and it was not too soft. It was sweet and steady and filled Rose with warmth and light. It did not hurt the lip Kendall had cut open with his blows. Everything about the kiss and his touch was healing to her—the arms snug around her, the smell of wood smoke and earth and pine that was on his buckskins, the soap and sweat from his skin, the taste of his lips, the heat that went through her from his hands and his chest and his body, the sound of his breathing, the solid feeling of his strength that she knew would never hurt her but always guard, always protect, always keep her safe. Her fingers found the sides of his face and she returned the kiss with the same steady continuous flow of love he was giving to her.

Finally, slowly, he broke away.

"We must go." Ethan bent down to pick up the knife she'd fought Kendall with and tucked it under his belt. "They are waiting for us."

"Why must we go? Who's waiting for us?"

Ethan took her hand. "The soldiers. Lord Ashton. Your family. The whole county."

"The whole county? What are you talking about?"

They began to make their way through the oak trees towards Rose's farm, Ethan leading his horse by the reins.

"Lord Ashton has a proclamation from the governor to read out," Ethan explained. "It has to do with you and it has to do with witch hunts and it has to do with Archibald Kendall. Ashton wants you there."

"Ethan, I don't have anything to say. My head is still spinning."

"You just need to stand there."

"Are you sure? Because I'm not up to much more than that."

"You will do very well just standing there. I would be happy to watch you standing perfectly still."

She hugged his arm and leaned into him. "With my hair full of dirt and my face streaked with tears? I must look a fright."

"You look perfect."

"Oh, Ethan, I'm far from perfect. Especially after a day like today."

"You're perfect for me." He stopped walking. "Even after all you have been through you are as lovely as a mountain stream—clear, cool, running free, full of color. I ache for you to be my bride. I ache to love you with all the love I have for you inside of me."

Her eyes wrinkled up with tears again. "Do you mean that?"

"Before God I mean it. As sure as I stand here I mean it." He ran the fingers of one hand through hair that was soft in some places, rough and stiff in others.

Then he put his lips to the strands that lay in his palm. "I love you, Rose."

She cried harder, her shoulders shaking. "I don't deserve you. I am no one special."

"That's not true. You know that's not true. You mean the world to me."

"I'm just a little brown mouse, Ethan."

He put his lips to her throat. "No. You have a beauty as rich as the earth. And your heart is the heart of the cougar. I adore you, Rose Daniels."

"Rose Daniels!"

"Rose Daniels the sooner the better." He drew her up against him.

"I thought we were in a hurry." The tears were running freely and her fingers were touching his face. "Isn't that what you said?"

"Not that much of a hurry."

His kisses came fast and burned her skin.

"Oh, we're both hopeless." She slung her arms around his neck. "We'll never get anywhere on time once we're married."

"I don't care about that."

"No?"

"Being with you is what matters the most. That's the gift from God."

"Ethan." His kisses on her face and neck and shoulder were like fire. "You saved my life."

His mouth covered hers and he pushed her back against a thick oak tree. Now he was not steady or soft or careful. Now he was like wind and rain and blazing sunlight over her face and body. She clung to him and his love swept through her like a fast river that rolled and swirled and flashed.

"My sweet Ethan." She put her fingers on his lips. "Didn't you tell me they were waiting for us?"

"I did."

"I can't relax thinking about them standing there."

"All right." He swung up into the saddle and extended his hand. "Come on."

"Ethan, I'm wearing a dress."

"Sit to the side with one arm around me."

"I'm not putting an arm around you in front of everyone."

"You kissed me in front of the sheriff and his constables when a mob was marching on your house."

"That was different."

"Today they tried to burn you at the stake. An arm around my waist so you don't pitch face forward into the mud should be the least of your worries."

She narrowed her eyes, grasped his hand, put a foot in the stirrup, and slipped up behind him on the dapple gray, sitting sideways, but refusing to slip her arm around his chest or waist. He urged Delaware forward at a walk. They emerged from the oak trees and went across the open field towards the farm. Smoke curled up from the black ashes of the stake and the firewood that had been heaped around it. Rose stared at the spot as they moved past. A shaking went through her body and she put her arm around Ethan and gripped him tightly, leaning her head against his back and closing her eyes.

"They must have gathered on the other side of the barn." Ethan glanced at her. "Are you ready?"

Rose lifted her head. “No. I’m not. I would rather go and lie down on the bed in my room.”

“I don’t think this will take long.”

“You don’t know. It could be hours.” She rubbed his back with her hand. “Could you stop for a moment, please?”

“Why?”

“I want you to help me pin up my hair.” He laughed.

“Yes, I know it is a strange request, Ethan, but you are the only one handy and I’d rather not go back in front of hundreds of people looking like something that was dragged behind a plow.”

“I like to remove pins not insert them.”

“Yes, well, that is why I say it is a strange request, but I hope you shall do the right thing by me today.”

“I will.”

He turned in his saddle and began to gather her hair gently in his hands.

Brushing off some of the dirt and dried blood he twisted it up into a bun while Rose sat still, occasionally twisting her head to look at him.

“Do you know what you’re doing?” she asked.

“I do.”

“Don’t you want any instructions?”

“I don’t.”

“How do you know you are getting it right?”

“I had five sisters. Sometimes I was pressed into service before a ball.”

“You weren’t.”

“I was.” He ran a hand over her head. “There. Never better.” He splashed water from his canteen onto a cloth from his pocket and carefully wiped her face. "We will make you look brand new."

Their eyes were close and their lips closer as he rubbed away the mud and tear streaks and spots of blood.

"Danke, Ethan," she murmured, her emerald eyes filling with light.

"Bitte," he replied softly, wiping her forehead and eyebrows.

"There is no one in sight yet, is there?"

"Not yet."

Rose cupped his jaw in her palm. "Good."

She brushed her mouth over his, gently bit his lower lip, and kissed him. Then she nuzzled his face, placing her lips against his ear and hair and neck. Where the lace of his buckskin shirt had loosened with the fighting and hard riding she kissed his chest as tenderly as if he had been a newborn. One hand found his long braid of hair and gripped it while the other caressed his skin after she had kissed it and traced a pattern that found its way to his shoulder.

"I love you with all my heart," she said softly. "You would have given your life for me. Now you can have that life forever. Marry me, marry me soon, I cannot bear to think of being apart from you another day let alone another week or month."

"But your church—my classes with Jakob Ammann—they will not let you up and be my bride just like that."

Her lips brushed his again. "You can convince them. You can convince anyone."

"Rose—"

"Do not make me wait until October or December.

I'll die. Pick me up and carry me to your cabin. Take care of me. Cherish me. I'm your wife, aren't I? Didn't God tell you that?"

"I believe he did."

"So convince the others. Grandfather likes you. He'll listen to you."

"Rose, I haven't even been baptized into your faith."

"But you will be."

"Yes, I will but it may be months."

"It can't be months." She put her arms around his neck. "Don't you want to be with me day and night?"

"Of course I do. You know how I feel about you."

"Then make it happen. Win the fight for me and take me to your home. Not next year. Not this October. Today. Tomorrow. At the most tomorrow night."

"What has gotten into you? No matter what you think of my powers of persuasion I cannot twist the arms of all the people in your church and take you to my cabin as my wife tomorrow night."

"Why not?" She kissed his face, his lips, his throat, his chest, and laid her head on his heart. "You have done everything else you could possibly do for me. Why not this too?"

He did not say anything else and neither did she. They held each other for five or ten minutes before Ethan nudged Delaware forward, still cradling Rose against his chest. They crossed the field and passed through a few bushes and came up beside the barn, the horse's hooves crunching against the dirt and stone of the farmyard.

"There they are," said Ethan. "Ashton has assembled them around the platform you stood on."

Rose sat up straight and put both of her hands in her lap.

The same crowd had returned to the farmyard. Redcoats were on all sides of them. The Grenadiers had their muskets again and were lined up with Ashton's troops as well as the colonial militia. Lord Ashton and Captain Trimble stood on the platform where Archibald Kendall had conducted his trial. As soon as Ashton spotted Ethan and Rose he gestured to them and Ethan walked his dapple gray slowly to the front of the gathering of men and women and children.

"It is exactly as it was two hours ago," whispered Rose.

"Except you are not on trial," Ethan whispered back.

"I feel like I still am. Why should they believe Lord Ashton or the governor?"

"I believe Ashton is capable of making it all perfectly clear."

Ashton continued to beckon to them until Ethan and Rose stood on the platform beside him and Captain Trimble. Delaware's reins were held by one of the Grenadiers.

"How are you, my dear?" asked Lord Ashton.

"Well enough, sir, though I'm not as strong yet as I'd like."

"I shall not be long. The proclamation is brief and to the point. The governor did not have the time for flourishes or niceties." He smiled at her. "Considering what you have been through you look none the worse for wear."

"Thank you, Lord Ashton, that's very gallant of you, but I fear I'm a wreck."

"I assure you, Miss Lantz, that you are not."

He faced the crowd. His voice strengthened as he began to read the parchment he had unrolled in his hands. The words rang out from one end of the farmyard to the other.

Archibald Kendall is a fraud. And not only a fraud but a murderer. He has falsely accused women and men of witchcraft, bullied people into testifying against them, burned the accused at the stake or hung them, stolen their land, and sold it for a profit. Moreover he has done this in the name of King George II and is therefore charged not only with fraud and murder and theft but treason. His penalty will be swift and just—he himself will be hung from the neck until dead in the town square.

Rose Lantz is innocent of all charges. She cannot and will not be accused of witchcraft again. Any persons who attempt to do so will be charged with mischief and maliciousness. From henceforth all charges of witchcraft in any part of the Commonwealth of Pennsylvania will be brought to the governor's attention and no trial will go forward until he has personally examined the evidence against the accused. He and he alone has the power to dismiss the charges or appoint the judges who will preside over the trial.

There will be no penalties exacted against those who have aided and abetted Archibald Kendall, willingly or unwillingly, in his attempted murder of Rose Lantz. However if the matter should come up again, and individuals make any effort to bear false testimony against Rose Lantz a second time, penalties will indeed be inflicted and they will be severe.

By order of the governor and in the name of King George II.

The crowd was silent.

Rose touched Lord Ashton's arm. "Sir, where is Archibald Kendall?"

"He will be brought forth when we march back to Lancaster."

"When—when do you intend to execute him?"

"Three days hence. Until then he will be in the public stocks day and night and all manner of food or refreshment shall be denied him."

"Is there any possibility of clemency?"

"Clemency?" Ashton stared at her. "You really are a different sort of woman, aren't you?"

"I don't want his blood spilled on my account. Let him have an opportunity to reform."

"Reform? He murdered more than a dozen women, some as young as fourteen, as well as three or four men. His blood is spilled because he himself spilled the blood of the innocent. As the Bible commands so will we obey. It is not on your head, Miss Lantz. It is on his."

"May I speak to the people?"

"Of course. Are you sure you're up to it?"

"I have to be."

Lord Ashton stepped to one side.

Rose looked out over the faces. "It has been a very hard day. Not only for me but all of you, for my parents, for my church. Men have been shot and killed. Men have been wounded. How sorry I am for all this. You must believe me, not just the governor's edict, when I tell you I am no witch and I have never tried to do any of you any harm. I have prayed for you. I have sought to love you all in the name of the Lord Jesus Christ. There is no crime in that, is there?"

The men and women remained quiet while the children began to whisper and play with each other.

"I am not a witch. I am a Christian woman. But even if I were a witch you should not have treated me in this way. The law came with Moses but grace and truth came with Jesus Christ. The law of Moses has had its day. It is no longer your master. The Lord Jesus Christ is. And he is the Lord of Love and Grace. Put me in jail for a while if I am a witch. Counsel me. Admonish me. Pray with me. Forgive me, yes, forgive me, for who in the Bible did Jesus not forgive? Who? Prostitutes he forgave, and thieves, and adulterers, and liars. So forgive me if I am a witch and then say, as our Lord said to a woman who had sinned, *I do not condemn you. Go and sin no more.* You know our Lord's teachings as well as I know them. If any of you have never sinned or done your neighbor any harm then burn all the witches. But if you have ever done any kind of wrong and begged the Lord's forgiveness then forgive those accused of witchcraft as well." She stretched out one of her hands. "But I myself am no witch. I only wish to be your friend. Let me be your good neighbor again. Let all my people be your good neighbors again. We mean you no harm nor do we mean to harm your children any more than we would harm our own children. We only want to live among you in peace and raise our crops and love our families. Please."

She hung her head, suddenly awkward and embarrassed by all that she had said.

"You may step down, Miss Lantz," said Lord Ashton. "God go with you. You are free."

She knew she was going to start crying again. "I can enter my home and no one will stop me?"

"No one."

She glanced back at Ethan. "Will you come with me?"

"I will be right behind you," he answered. "You step down first."

"Why?"

"Because it is your right, woman above all other women. It is your right before God."

Rose did not understand what Ethan meant but he was not making any move towards the steps so she took them one at a time.

"Captain Trimble," Lord Ashton said quietly. "Yes, m'lord."

Trimble bellowed, "The king's soldiers will present arms!" He paused a moment.

"PRESENT ARMS!"

The Grenadiers, Ashton's troops, and even the militiamen, who knew little about such drills but watched the redcoats like hawks, followed Trimble's command instantly. They brought their muskets from their sides, thrust them up in front of their chests and above their heads at arm's length, then brought them down a foot and stamped their boots against the ground with a loud crack.

Rose stood in front of the redcoats and the militia and put a hand to her mouth.

"I don't understand," she said to Ethan who had joined her. "They are saluting you."

"Saluting me? I can't imagine why they would do that."

"I can."

Her father was there and her mother and brothers, taking her hand, kissing her, embracing her.

"God be praised, child," her father said, tears slipping down his face into his beard. "God be praised."

Her mother hugged her. "That he should snatch you from the very fire. We will love and serve him forever."

"Yes, Mama."

Jakob Ammann smiled and nodded, his hand gripping her arm just above the elbow. "So you are blessed. We are blessed. A day begins in tribulation and ends in the glory of God. I want the church to gather in your home and give thanks but not yet, not until you have rested."

"Oh, Grandfather, have them come now, I can lie down after we have had a service of prayer and praise."

"No, no. Are you sure?"

"I want to do it very much. I want it as much as I want you to marry Ethan and me, Grandfather, and after what he has done for me today I want to marry him more than anything in the world."

Jakob Ammann's face tightened. "*Ja, ja.* He did great things for you." Jakob looked at Ethan. "You are to be thanked, young man, yes, we thank God for you."

Ethan nodded. "I could not do anything other than I did."

"I know that. It is who you are. God uses it." He put a hand on Ethan's shoulder. "But it is not our way. The shooting, the fighting, the wounding, the killing, no, it is not the path our people take. God has you on a different path and I do not say it is not what he wishes for you. But for our people his will is something else altogether, a walk of peace, a pilgrimage that knows nothing about the taking up of the sword or the shedding of blood."

Jakob Ammann looked from Ethan to Rose and shook his head. "I am sorry, my children, so sorry. I am not ungrateful for what Ethan has done. But you two cannot marry. It is out of the question. God has another husband for you, my Rose, and for Ethan he has a different sort of life than a life with us."

Volume 10

The Wedding Quilt

Rose sat up in bed in the dark. Nitz was in her lap.

"Oh, Nitz. You think it is time for milking? Is that why you have jumped up? But the clock says three. That is too early even for me, the early bird." She began to stroke the cat's fur, smiling.

The lightness in her heart lasted only a moment. Soon the memories of the day before rushed into her mind.

Lord, it is not so good a world I wake up to. The man who saved my life, my love, my heart, is taken from me. How am I supposed to love another? What man is out there who is like him?

She put her head on Nitz's. "What do I do without him? Is there a man among our people I can love like Ethan? No, Nitz, no."

The cat purred loudly.

"You will have to let me kneel by the bed, Nitz. That is the only thing I can think of to do right now."

The cat protested but Rose did not go far so Nitz

rubbed herself back and forth across the kneeling woman's head, curled up on the bed, and returned to her purring.

Our Father who art in heaven. Our Father who art in heaven. Our Father who art in heaven.

"I am not getting anywhere, Lord," Rose whispered. "I might as well do the milking early. If you have anything to say to me you can say it to me in the barn. My mind is too restless in here. I need to do something with my hands."

Nitz followed her down the staircase and out the door. The morning was dark and cool and the cat was happy to slip into a barn warm with the bodies and breath of the cows. She found a patch of clean straw not far from Rose, licked herself for a few minutes, and went to sleep.

I cannot think what to do about Ethan. Lord, how can I accept this ruling? How can I live with another man and call him my husband while Ethan is alive and well?

How could I bear to hear another woman is in his arms? You ask too much. I can't bear it, I can't.

In an hour she was done. Her father was surprised to see her pouring milk into the large can when he walked into the barn.

"Daughter, what are you doing here so early?"

"I could not sleep. And I could not pray. So I decided to milk."

"It was a very difficult day for you. Rest does not always come easy after such a day."

"No, I suppose not."

"The pastors are gathering here this evening to pray

with you. Jakob Ammann told us your soul would be troubled and that you would need comfort."

"Yes? He told you that? Well, why wouldn't he tell you that? He is the source of much of my trouble."

"Shh, shh. What are you saying?"

"He forbids me to marry the man I love with all my heart. The man who has saved my life. Do you seriously think I will ever be content with someone else, Papa?"

"In time. As God leads."

"As God leads? Well, he has led me to Ethan Daniels. And that is where I am staying put. If he wants to lead me away he will have to tie a good strong rope around my heart and tug with all his might."

"Rose! Do not speak so of the Almighty!"

Rose waved her hand. "I am quite sure he can handle it. He could handle Moses and Samson and David. Not to mention Peter and Paul."

She marched out of the barn. "I am going to town. Will you drive me?"

He followed after her. "What? To town? So soon? I cannot believe it is safe. People's spirits have not settled down."

"Well, we have more than enough soldiers now to help them settle their spirits and settle them quickly. Do we have the large water skin still?"

"*Ja*, so but why do you need it?"

"Archibald Kendall has been all night in the stocks. He needs water."

"What? Kendall? Have nothing to do with that evil man."

"We love our enemies. Isn't that what our Lord Jesus teaches us? We forgive our enemies. Isn't that what

Jakob Ammann teaches us? So I must fill the large skin with water from the well and take it to him. Also some bread. It is all I can think of to do right now. It is the right thing so I will go to town and see it done."

"No, no, no."

She paused as she opened the door to the house. "So if you will not drive me, if you will not let me be a Christian, I will do it myself."

"I forbid you to take the horse and buggy."

"Then I will walk."

"You will not walk."

"I will walk, Papa. I am a grow woman, not a child, and I will follow my God where he leads me. Do you want to now stand in the way of God as well as my marriage to Ethan Daniels?"

Her mother was in the kitchen. "Hush, you two. What is all this fuss about?"

Mr. Lantz shook his head and took off his hat. "She will go to town and take water to Archibald Kendall."

"What?"

"She tells me it is God's will."

Rose went down the hall. "Is it still hanging up in the closet here?"

"Is what hanging?" asked her mother.

"The large water skin."

"Yes, yes. But no. No, Rose. You cannot do this."

"Of course I can do it."

"The soldiers will not let you."

"Oh, Mama, what do they care? They are going to put him up on a scaffold anyways. What is a drink of water?" She was out of sight. "Not that he should go up on the scaffold, should he? Would our Lord have that?"

Mr. and Mrs. Lantz glanced at one another.

"Slow down, Rose," cautioned her mother. "You will break the wheels of the cart you are pulling."

"I don't mind if I break a cart," came Rose's voice. "If it saves a man's life, if it saves a man's soul, what does a cart matter?"

She returned to the kitchen with the large skin her father had turned into a water bag. "I will go and fill it. Am I walking, Papa? Or are you driving me so I can do the will of God?"

Her mother put her hands on her hips. "The will of God?"

"*Do good to those who persecute you.* Have I not heard these words at our worship services since I was a little girl?"

"Ja, ja," responded her mother, "but—"

"So I will fill the water skin and I will go to town on foot."

"You are not going to town on foot and you are not going on an empty stomach. The boys are up now so we will have breakfast together. Then Papa will drive you. And keep an eye on you at the same time. Harness the mare, Father."

Rose was heading out the door. "Papa does not need to keep an eye on me."

"Of course he does. Who knows what the *Englisch* will try to do to you next?"

"Nothing at all with two hundred redcoats here." Rose paused and looked back from the doorway. "Besides, God has appointed someone else to watch over me."

"God has appointed? Who has God appointed?"

"Ethan Daniels."

"Ethan?" Mrs. Lantz's voice rose in exasperation. "No one knows where he is."

"I know where he is, Mama."

"Oh, yes? And where is that?"

"He is in my heart. Where I go he will be there with me. And Ethan would never let any man harm so much as a single hair on my head."

She left for the well, closing the door.

Mr. and Mrs. Lantz glanced at each other in confusion once again. Nathan and Hans came tumbling down the stairs.

"What is going to happen today, Papa?" Nathan wanted to know.

"Will it be as exciting as yesterday?" asked Hans.

The sun was rising as Rose's father drove her along the road into town. The stocks were in the square. No one else was about as Mr. Lantz brought the buggy to a stop and applied the brake. Rose climbed down and went to Kendall whose hands and head drooped against the stocks they were locked into. Rose knelt and gently put her hand under his chin.

"Mr. Kendall. I have water for you." He said nothing. His eyes were closed.

"You must be chill." She took her large thick shawl from around her shoulders and draped it over his. "That will help."

She poured water from the skin onto her palm and rubbed her moist fingers over his dry and cracked lips.

"What—what—are you doing?" mumbled Kendall, his eyelids flickering. "Who is it?"

"Rose Lantz."

He stared, his eyes suddenly wide. "The witch."

"That's right. Rose Lantz, the witch."

"It's poison." He tried to spit but his mouth was too dry. "You're poisoning me."

"Mr. Kendall, if that is so, it would be the first time our well water did anything but bless. We have the sweetest water in Lancaster County." He watched as she rubbed her fingers over her own lips.

"You see? I haven't dropped dead. And neither will you. Are you ready for a drink?"

"As God is my witness, I'd give my soul for a cup of water."

"I am certain he is your witness, Mr. Kendall, and mine as well. But he does not want your soul in exchange for a drink. That is the devil's work. His only desire is to love you and bless you and heal you."

"How can you say that? You despise me."

"I don't. As God is *my* witness, I don't." She placed the spout of the skin against his lips. "I have other things on my mind that trouble me. Now drink up. But slowly."

Kendall gulped at the water, half of it running down his chin onto the cobblestones.

Rose's father came and stood by the stocks. "You left the bread in the buggy. I have it here."

"Thank you, Papa. I will let him drink his fill first."

Kendall jerked his head back. "You're her father. I recognize you."

"I am."

"Why are you here? Why would you come to me with bread? I would have burned your daughter at the stake yesterday."

Mr. Lantz gazed at him a moment. Then he cleared his throat.

"Our Lord commands us to forgive. He forgave us our sins on the Cross. We are to forgive others their sins against us. That is how it works."

"That is not how it works. Everyone knows those Bible verses. No one lives by them. No one."

"We do."

Mr. Lantz dropped to one knee and held out the loaf of bread.

"Do you want some now?" he asked. "Is your thirst quenched? Are you hungry?"

"Before God, yes, yes."

Mr. Lantz broke off a piece and held it up to Kendall's mouth. Kendall took it in his teeth, chewed noisily, and swallowed.

"Carefully, my man, carefully, *ja*?" warned Mr. Lantz. "We don't want you to choke."

"Why not? I am going to choke on a rope in a few hours. I'd sooner die with a piece of bread lodged in my throat."

Rose held the water skin to his lips again. "I do not wish you to die at the end of a rope."

"You don't? *You don't?*"

"No, sir."

"What do you want? The stake? A cauldron of boiling pitch? Will you have me drawn and quartered?"

"I'd have you live. Serve out behind bars what you owe the families you grieved. Come to repentance. Give your life back to God for the lives taken. Receive a life back from him in return. Begin again."

Kendall spluttered on the water. "Begin again? Do you believe that? You talk like Quakers or Puritans."

"We are neither."

"What are you? I don't understand you."

"We follow Jakob Ammann as he follows Christ."

"Who is Jakob Ammann?"

"An elderly gentleman. Our leader. Our shepherd."

"Where is he?"

"I wouldn't be surprised if we see him here at the stocks this morning. He will come and pray with you."

"I don't want anyone to pray with me," snarled Kendall.

An egg suddenly hit Kendall's face and broke open, spewing egg yolk over his skin and mouth. A second one cracked into his eyes. A stench filled the air.

Rose and her father jumped to their feet. A small crowd of children and adults were standing a few feet away with eggs and tomatoes and stones, hurling them at the stocks. A stone spun off the wood with a sharp snap while another made Kendall cry out as it struck his head.

A man laughed. "How's that feel, Kendall, you dirty villain? Play with our lives, will ye? Burn our citizens, will ye?"

"Stop it!" cried Rose. "He's been an afternoon and a night and all morning in the stocks! That's enough!"

"Beggin' pardon, Miss Lantz, not enough, not near enough. Ye should know that better than anyone in Lancaster."

"I know that rotten eggs and stones are not what our Lord had in mind when he commanded us to turn the other cheek. Put those rocks down."

"We won't, Miss, no, before God, we won't. He deserves the rough end of the stick before the rope pulls the soul out of him."

Tomatoes and eggs and stones showered Kendall and smacked into Rose and her father.

"Enough!" shouted Mr. Lantz, throwing up his hand. "Enough!"

"Not enough, not nearly enough," jeered another man. "Not for him or the likes of you who should know better than to sympathize with the devil." He pried up a loose cobblestone. "Put your backs into it, boys! Teach all three of them a lesson!"

Sticks and clumps of mud hit Rose and her father and raised purple welts on Kendall's face. She covered her head with her hands and threw herself in front of her father, who stumbled and almost fell as small boys pelted him with rocks.

"No more!" Rose suddenly came at them, ducking her head. "No more! Leave us alone! In God's name, leave us alone!"

As she rushed the crowd she was surprised to see the men and boys stare at her, drop their stones and eggs, and begin to back away, the boys breaking into a run. She stopped as they all scattered, some going down one street, some another, the men glancing over their shoulders at her.

Why, I must look a fright.

She felt a pricking along her back. Slowly she turned around. "Ethan!"

He was leaning on one of his rifles. "How goes it with you, Miss Lantz?" She hurled herself into his arms.

"Oh, I thank God you are here. I love you so much and I've missed you terribly." A smile played over her lips. "For a few moments I thought they were afraid of me."

Still holding the rifle, his arms went around her. "Of course they were afraid of you."

"About as much as you are."

"I find you terrifying with egg yolk on your face."

She brushed at her cheeks. "Oh, no, is there much of it?"

"Enough for a good man's breakfast."

She laughed and slapped him on the arm. "Stop it."

He kissed her. "The egg tastes fine."

"I'm sure it's not." She tugged him by the hand. "I must see to my father and Mr. Kendall."

"All right."

They went to the stocks together. Mr. Lantz was bent over and wiping Kendall's face and hair with a cloth soaked in water. Egg and tomato and mud covered his coat and hat and there were bruises on both of his cheeks. Rose took her own cloth and began to clean off her father's clothing. Then she knelt and examined his bruises as he continued to wipe blood and egg yolk off Kendall's face and hands.

"Does it hurt much, Papa?"

"I thank God, it doesn't, no."

"You must put some ice on these bruises."

"What I must do is tell Jakob Ammann what is going on." He stood up and nodded at Ethan. "Thank you. I fear you should not be here with my daughter but once again the Lord has used you in our lives by bending our rules."

"So it seems."

Mr. Lantz looked at Rose. "Do you intend to stay here?"

"I feel compelled to protest Archibald Kendall's execution." He turned to Ethan. "Will you watch over her?"

"Though it should bend all the rules in Lancaster County."

Mr. Lantz hurried to his buggy as sunlight filled the square. "I will bring the leadership as swiftly as possible."

Rose went on both knees beside Kendall. "How are you?"

"I have a headache." He scowled up at her and Ethan. "What are the pair of you planning to do?"

"I don't have much of a plan, sir. I woke up with no idea what to make of this difficult day. Finally it came to me I was to forgive you."

"Why forgive me? I have no intention of forgiving you."

"What you do is between yourself and God. But I must forgive."

"Must? That is your religious community's ritual?"

Rose smiled. "That is my God's heart. My God, Mr. Kendall, and yours."

"Not mine. If he ever was mine he rejected me as his own years ago."

"He didn't, Mr. Kendall. Today will bear me out."

"How will it do that? I'm to be hung."

"You won't be hung."

"I won't? How will you stand up to the British army?"

Rose placed a cloth of cold water against a bump that was rising on his forehead. "I'm not sure."

"Or the hangman?"

"I don't know."

Kendall bared his teeth. "I don't care. I don't want your sympathy, I don't want your God, send me out of this world and get me far away from this miserable human race."

Rose stood up, dusting off her dress. "No." She glanced at Ethan. "What's so funny?"

"I was wondering whatever happened to the mouse."

"What mouse?"

"The Rose Lantz mouse."

"There never was one."

"I knew that. I'm not sure you did."

She folded her arms over her chest. "Well, I know now. Are you disappointed in what I've become?"

"Me?" He laughed. "I've never been happier in my life."

"No?" She could not keep the smile off her own face. "Yet we are forbidden to be with each other."

Ethan was leaning on his rifle. "See how well that's working. Your father has ordered me to guard you."

"I admit the forbidden part has not come together very well. For which I thank God." She reached out and touched his arm. "I'm so glad you're here."

"I was waiting for you."

"No, you weren't."

"I was. For well over an hour. Back against that building there. I was certain you'd come."

"How could you be certain? I didn't even think of making my way here till I was milking the cows. And now that I'm here my whole idea seems ridiculous. But I had to do something. I couldn't think of what to do to save us so I thought of what I could do to save Archibald Kendall."

"It stands to reason your mind would work that way."

"Oh, yes? You think you know me that well?"

"I was waiting here, wasn't I?"

"Well, if you know so much, Ethan Daniels, what do we do next?"

"Wait on Lord Ashton and Captain Trimble."

"Wait on them? The hanging is three days from now."

"It isn't. Friends close to Lord Ashton tell me he intends to deal with Kendall today. He thinks there will be trouble if he waits too long."

"I don't believe that."

"They will come soon."

"Soon? This morning?" Rose put her fingers to her mouth. "What can we do?"

"Pray."

"Yes, pray. And then what?"

"Stall."

"Stall? How do we stall?"

He shrugged. "You are good at making speeches in courthouses and public places. Make another."

"A speech on what?"

"Forgiveness. Mercy. Clemency. Christ's Sermon on the Mount. Turning the other cheek. Isn't that why you're here this morning?"

"You think Lord Ashton would listen to another speech?"

"By me? No. By you? Yes. For a while at any rate. It will buy us just enough time, I think."

"Enough time? Enough time for what?" She saw how soft the gray in his eyes was.

"Why, it is just over seventy miles to Philadelphia," he replied. "Fresh horses along the way would allow a good rider to make the trip in a handful of hours."

"Seventy miles? Fresh horses? What on earth are

you going on about?" Heat came into her face. "What are you staring at? The egg yolk I missed?"

"I'm staring at you. God alone knows how beautiful you are."

The heat intensified. "God alone?"

One corner of his mouth lifted in a crooked smile. "Well, he let me in on the secret."

She put her hands to both sides of her face. "Oh, I thought I was over all this schoolgirl nonsense. When will I stop letting you do this to me? I'm as red as—as—"

"As red as a redcoat." Ethan lifted his curly maple rifle in his hands. "Here they come."

No fife or drums played. The Union Jack, composed of the cross of St. George and the cross of St. Andrew, was not unfurled from its staff. The men marched four abreast behind Lord Ashton and there were about fifty of them. He sat erect on his dark brown horse, walking his mount up the main street towards the square, sunlight flashing off his scarlet uniform and gold braid. Captain Trimble rode right behind him. The tramp of the soldiers' boots brought people into the street and drew more and more of them towards the square.

"Do you have your speech ready?" asked Ethan.

Her face was still crimson. "Of course not."

"Well, think of something quick. We need another half hour."

"A half hour, Ethan? What do you think I am? A long-winded politician from New York?"

The crooked smile returned to his face. "An hour would be even better."

"An hour! You have a high opinion of my powers!"

He glanced at her, the smile still there. "Indeed I do."

"Well, I don't know where you get it from."

His gray eyes remained on her, as if a sparrow had alighted in front of them. "How perfect you are," he said.

Her face flamed again.

"We're not getting anywhere. You must stop complimenting me. I need to pray."

"Go ahead and pray. I won't say a thing, Beauty."

"Beauty. You won't say a thing. Thank you very much."

"You're welcome."

"I wish you'd take this seriously. I don't want a hanging."

"Neither do I, to tell you the truth, though I have no use for the man."

"What would you do with him?"

Ethan grunted. "The Tower of London for the rest of his life. You'd better pray if you're going to pray."

She bowed her head.

Unser Vater der du bist im Himmel. Unser Vater der du bist im Himmel. Unser Vater der du bist im Himmel.

"It's no use," she said. "It's just like when I tried to pray after I woke up. My mind isn't going anywhere. I need to do something with my hands."

Ethan jerked his head at Kendall. "See if he needs another drink. Or some bread."

Rose knelt by Kendall. "Are you thirsty, sir?"

"Yes. Yes, I am."

She lifted the water skin and pulled the plug from the spout. "All right. Let's do this again."

"The soldiers are almost here."

"I don't care about the soldiers."

"They'll order you to stop."

"Do you want a drink or not?"

A thin smile formed over his lips. "Doesn't anything frighten you?"

"Lots of things frighten me. But right now it's not the British Grenadiers."

"What then?"

"Trying to find the right words that soldiers will listen to."

"And hangmen?"

"*Ja.* And hangmen."

"I don't understand a woman such as yourself. I almost killed you and here you are struggling to find the right words to save my life."

"If you understood God you would understand me because he is the one who puts that sort of heart in me." She tipped the skin so that water streamed past his lips and into his mouth. "How is that?"

"Good. Very good. Thank you."

"*Bitte.* Some more of my mother's bread?"

"Please, please, yes."

"You there!" A loud voice snapped across the square. "The woman kneeling by the prisoner! Stop giving him food and drink at once!"

Rose pushed small morsels of bread into Kendall's mouth.

"Did you hear me?"

She recognized Lord Ashton's voice. "Stop feeding the prisoner immediately!" Rose gave Kendall more bread.

"I'll have you whipped and put in the stocks, woman!" Rose stood up and faced him.

Lord Ashton reined in his horse. "Miss Lantz!"

"Lord Ashton."

"Why are you of all people giving this murderer water and bread?"

"Because, as broken as he is, he is still made in the image of God."

"What?"

"And he deserves, like all of us, a measure of mercy and grace."

Ashton shook his head, his face a crossroads of wrinkles and lines. "Every day you baffle me more."

He glanced down at Ethan, who barred his way. "Stand aside."

"No, sir."

"No? Has the whole world turned upside down this morning? The man tried to kill your betrothed only a few hours ago. And now you defend him?"

"Him. And her. She's right. There's been enough bloodshed on account of him. It needs to stop."

"It will stop once we have him on the gallows."

"It must stop now. Give him a cell in England. Let him dwell on what he has done all his days. Let him agonize over his crimes before God Almighty. Then let him choose to die in squalor or in grace. Give him space to repent."

"He has had space to repent. He shed blood so his blood must be shed in return. I know my Bible as well as you do."

"Ye have heard that it hath been said, An eye for an eye, and a tooth for a tooth. But I say unto you, That ye resist not evil, but whosoever shall smite thee on thy right cheek, turn to him the other also."

As Ethan said these words he placed his rifle on the ground in front of Lord Ashton.

"You're mad," said Ashton.

"What I have learned from this young woman is that there is a time to kill and a time to heal, a time to break down and a time to build up, a time to cast away stones and a time to gather stones together, a time to embrace and a time to refrain from embracing. This is a time to heal. This is a time to embrace."

Rose stepped forward and stood beside Ethan, taking his hand. "*Ye have heard that it hath been said, Thou shalt love thy neighbor and hate thine enemy. But I say unto you, Love your enemies, bless them that curse you, do good to them that hate you, and pray for them which despitefully use you and persecute you, that you may be the children of your Father which is in heaven. For He maketh his sun to rise on the evil and on the good and sendeth rain on the just and on the unjust. For if ye love them which love you what reward have ye? Do not even publicans the same? And if ye salute your brethren only what do ye more than others? Do not even publicans so? Be ye therefore perfect even as your Father which is in heaven is perfect.*"

Lord Ashton sat quietly on his horse and listened. "I see," he responded.

He squinted up at the sun.

"But I am the king's servant as well as God's and I am bound to deliver the evildoer up to his just punishment before the throne of earth as well as the throne of heaven. In a way you are both remarkable, especially for ones so young. In another way, you are obstructing the justice of heaven and earth. Step aside."

Rose knelt, still grasping Ethan's hand, and he knelt

with her. The lines deepened and sharpened on Lord Ashton's face.

"The world cannot live by the words of Jesus," he growled. "For monks or nuns or parsons it is fine to do so, yes, I would even say it is necessary for our world that they live in such a fashion. But the rest of us must live in the real world and in that world there are laws that must be obeyed and if those laws are broken the people who break them must also be broken."

"The world we live in is the world we make it to be, Lord Ashton," replied Rose. "Whatever we choose to do can create a world as real as we wish."

He snorted. "What a strange faith you have. You think you can move heaven and earth by your prayers and good wishes?"

"I do, sir. Would you rather I try to move God and the people of this world by curses and cruelty?"

He smiled. "No. There is too much of that already, my dear. Stick with your love and mercy, if you please. Perhaps it will balance things out. But I must do my duty as I see it just as you must do yours." He turned his head. "Captain Trimble!"

Trimble moved his horse forward. "M'lord."

"Take four men and bring the prisoner along. Chain him to your horse and make your way to the scaffold by the barracks. Drag him if necessary."

"What about the man and the woman, m'lord?"

"Go around them and do what you must do."

"Shall I arrest them, m'lord, and chain them as well?"

"No, you shall not."

Trimble dismounted and gestured to the first four soldiers at attention behind him.

"Captain, do not do this," pleaded Rose. "Do not put the blood on your head." The captain hesitated.

"The blood is on Archibald Kendall's own head for the harm he has done in Britain and the colonies!" snapped Lord Ashton. "Captain Trimble, you will do your duty no matter how beguiling this young woman's tongue is."

"Yes, my lord."

Ashton nodded at Rose. "Perhaps you are something of a witch, Miss Lantz. But a witch for righteousness, I grant you, no matter how misled I believe you are."

Trimble handed one of the soldiers the keys to the stocks. "Release him."

"Yes, sir."

"Ignore the couple."

"Yes, sir."

Trimble handed a set of chains to a second soldier. "As soon as the prisoner is out of the stocks manacle him."

"Yes, captain."

He looked at the other two soldiers. "If the prisoner gives you any trouble make use of the butts of your muskets."

"What about those two who are kneeling there?"

"If they try to prevent you from following orders use your muskets on them as well."

One of the soldier's eyes locked on Ethan's. He quickly looked away and went past him to the stocks.

Kendall was released. He collapsed in the dirt.

"He cannot stand, captain," said one of the soldiers.

"Lift him up. Manacle him. Take a length of rope and bind him to my saddle."

"Yes, sir."

"Don't do it." Rose reached out to grasp the soldier by the arm. "Let him be." The soldier looked at her and looked at Trimble.

"Shake her off, private." Trimble's voice was sharp. "Shake her off and manacle the prisoner."

The soldier pulled himself free but Rose clutched him again.

"In the name of Jesus Christ, let him be. You heard me quote the Bible a few minutes ago, the same Bible your mother quoted to you when you were a boy. Listen to what Jesus says. He is your Lord as well as mine. There has been enough death. Let the prisoner be."

"Private!" cried Trimble. "Use your musket!"

Ethan jumped up. "Do not touch her. Before God, do not lay a hand on her."

Trimble yanked a pistol out of his belt and swiftly cocked back the jaws holding the flint. "Stand down, sir. Stand down or I shoot."

"Captain Trimble!" roared Lord Ashton. "Do not fire!"

"My lord! My lord!"

A rider in a red uniform galloped into the square. "Dispatches, my lord! Dispatches!"

He handed a pouch to Lord Ashton as sweat rolled down his face.

A moment later one of the colonial militia raced into the square behind the dispatch rider.

"What is this?" demanded Ashton. "What is all this?"

The dispatch rider saluted. "Forgive me, my lord. Leftenant Jenkins. I have been riding hard since before dawn. Even changing mounts I have almost killed my horses."

Ashton looked at the lather on the horse's chest and flanks. "Under whose orders?"

"The governor's, sir. It is a stay of execution."

"What?"

Jenkins pointed to the militiaman who had just ridden up. "That man came to us at four in the morning with his petition."

"What petition?"

"From Lancaster. From the militia and the colonel of the militia, one Ethan Daniels, setting out arguments for clemency."

Ashton darted a glare at Ethan and opened the pouch. Rose scrambled to her feet. "What did you do?" she asked Ethan.

"What I knew you wanted and what we decided we wanted too."

"When did you send out your rider?"

Ethan glanced over at the militiaman and smiled. "Spencer rode through the night. He picked up fresh mounts along the road to Philadelphia."

"But I hadn't even thought about forgiving Kendall last night or requesting a pardon."

"I suppose I know your mind before you know it then, my dear." His eyes on her were the soft gray she loved. "Sometimes, at any rate."

"The Tower," grunted Ashton as he read the document from the pouch. "The Tower in London for the rest of his life. If it pleases the king." He looked down at Kendall who still lay crumpled in the dirt. "And may God have mercy on your soul."

His eyes flickered as they rested on Trimble. "Uncock your pistol. Do not put the manacles on the prisoner. We will march him back to the barracks and place him in the jail there."

"Yes, m'lord. I don't think the prisoner can walk, m'lord."

"We shall give him a few more minutes." Lord Ashton's eyes went to Ethan. "How is it you were able to persuade the governor? He is not a man with a soft heart."

"You may read the petition for yourself when you return to Philadelphia."

"He has included it here." Ashton glanced over a long sheet of parchment. "I see you made free use of Miss Lantz's sentiments."

"What?" Rose looked from Lord Ashton to Ethan and back to Lord Ashton again. "My sentiments? May I see that petition, Lord Ashton?"

"You may indeed. I shall be very interested in your reaction."

Rose took the sheet of parchment and ran her eyes over it, lips moving.

Several times she stopped and glanced up at Ethan in surprise before returning to her reading. Finally she finished and handed it back to Lord Ashton, who leaned down from his horse.

"What do you say to that, Miss Lantz?" he asked.

She was gazing at Ethan, her back straight and her arms at her sides. "I say that this man knows me better than I know myself."

"Truly?" Ashton tucked the governor's dispatch and the petition back into the leather pouch. "Then your marriage is off to a good start. Or a bad one, depending how you feel about living with a husband who reads your mind." He touched the brim of his hat to Ethan. "Colonel of the militia, sir?"

Ethan nodded. "So the men voted me."

"The men voted you?" Ashton barked a laugh. "We wouldn't try that in the British army." He turned his horse, glancing back over his shoulder. "Pray dine with me tonight at my headquarters, Colonel Daniels, you and your fiancée. I fancy an entertaining evening after another astonishing day."

"Are you extending an invitation?"

"I am. Eight sharp, if you please, you and Miss Lantz." He smiled at Rose. "The incomparable and inimitable Miss Lantz." He snapped a command at Captain Trimble. "Bring the prisoner. Put a soldier under each of his arms, if you must. Order the men back to the barracks."

"As you wish, m'lord."

Trimble jabbed a finger at two of the soldiers. "Get him on his feet and keep him on his feet. Follow us to the barracks."

"Yes, captain."

He mounted his horse and rode towards the troops who were still at attention. "About face!"

The formation changed direction in an instant. "Forward march!"

The redcoats began to head down the street as townspeople watched. "Captain Trimble," called Lord Ashton.

"Yes, m'lord."

"Fifes and drums, if you please. Unfurl the flags."

"What tune, m'lord?"

"British Grenadiers. Have the men sing out heartily."

"As you wish, m'lord."

Trimble rode to the front of the column. "Fifes and

drums! Break out the colors! The British Grenadiers! Sing it with a right good will, my lads!"

The drums began to beat and the fifes whistle while the men's voices thundered.

Some talk of Alexander and some of Hercules Of Hector and Lysander and such great names as these But of all the world's great heroes, there's none that can compare With a tow, row, row, row, row, row, to the British Grenadiers.

Those heroes of antiquity ne'er saw a cannon ball Or knew the force of powder to slay their foes withal But our brave boys do know it, and banish all their fears Sing tow, row, row, row, row, row, for the British Grenadiers.

And when the siege is over, we to the town repair The townsmen cry, "Hurrah, boys, here comes a Grenadier! Here come the Grenadiers, my boys, who know no doubts or fears!" Then sing tow, row, row, row, row, row, the British Grenadiers.

Rose and Ethan watched them go, the dirt rising like gold dust in the morning. Two soldiers hurried past with Kendall between them, struggling to gain his feet. He looked over as the soldiers hustled him towards the marching troops. "Why?" he demanded. "Why? Why?"

Rose turned to Ethan. "Why, my love?"

"You tell me. You started it."

"But I didn't start it. You sent the rider in the middle of the night. You are the one who knows what I'm thinking before I even think it."

He smiled. "Still, they are your thoughts that I'm thinking. So tell us why you fought to spare Archibald Kendall's life."

Rose shook her head and smiled back. *"It is the Lord's doing and it is marvelous in our eyes."* She reached for his hand. "Thank you for standing with me. Thank you for loving me."

"It is the easiest thing in the world to do."

"Surely not the easiest. Not with the predicaments I get myself into."

He tilted her chin with his fingers. "The easiest and the best."

She folded her hand over his and brought it down from her face. "Here comes Jakob Ammann."

The elderly man was making his way across the square with the pastors trailing him. When he reached Rose and Ethan there was no smile on his face. He glanced once at Ethan's rifle that was still lying in the dust and then turned his gaze on the two of them.

"We arrived shortly after Lord Ashton and the soldiers," he said. "We saw all that occurred. We heard all that was said."

"I'm sorry, Grandfather," responded Rose. "I know it was brash of me but—" Jakob held up his hand.

"I am an old man and I have seen many things. Every day the Lord is teaching me what I did not know the day or week before. Now and then something takes place I do not expect."

"Sir." Ethan bent, picked up his rifle, and faced Jakob Ammann. "I realize I should not be here. I know I ought not be in Rose's company. Do not lay this at her feet. She did not ask me to be here. I was concerned for her safety and came here by my own choice. And now, again by my own choice, I am on my way."

Jakob grasped Ethan's arm. "I told you we saw and

heard everything that took place here. Rose's words, your words. I saw you kneel, both of you kneel. I saw you lay your rifle on the ground. There are only a few things about which I am not clear." He looked from Ethan to Sarah. "Who sent the petition to the governor that the whole town is talking about now? You, Rose?"

"No, sir."

"I thought it best." Ethan leaned on his rifle. "It was what was in Rose's heart and I felt what was in her heart should be expressed to the governor."

"So the midnight ride of a militiaman?"

"Yes, sir."

"And a pardon from the governor?"

"Not exactly a pardon. Archibald Kendall will serve out his sentence behind bars. He will be imprisoned in the Tower of London. There will be no reprieve."

"But he will not be hanged."

"Not unless the king reverses the decision of his governor."

"And why did you go to all this trouble?"

"Rose was right. There has been enough death."

"Is that the only reason?"

Ethan looked steadily into the old man's eyes. "I love her. I would not see her prayers and hopes dashed."

Jakob nodded and ran his fingers through his beard. "How astonishing the ways of God. How past understanding the ways and means he uses to work his holy will."

"I must go." Ethan smiled at Rose. "We will see each other from time to time. Farewell."

Tears sprang onto Rose's cheeks. "You can't just leave."

"I must leave. But I am glad what was done was done well. God bless you."

"Wait." For the first time Jakob smiled. "You will need this."

He turned, took a bundle from the hands of Rose's father, and gave it to Ethan.

"What is this?" asked Ethan.

"You will need it to prepare your bed for your bride."

"My bride?"

Ethan unrolled the bundle.

"But that is the rose quilt, Grandfather." Rose put her fingers on it. "I made it for you. I and Lydia made it for you."

"And I am placing it back in your hands. So sometimes the Lord returns what we give away."

He took Rose's hand and put it with Ethan's.

"What are you doing, Grandfather? What are you saying?" Jakob kept his hand on both of theirs.

"Sometimes you see a piece of wood and you think it is too rough, too coarse, and you set it aside. Later you feel compelled to spend some time with it, to rub it and polish it and see what its grain is like. To your surprise the wood turns out more beautiful than anything you have seen before. It was hidden to your eyes but now you see clearly." He smiled at Ethan. "You have your rough edges, young man, yes, and we would see the rough made smooth. That is something we shall work on together, you and I, all that is rough and tumble, yes, you and I and God, we will bring everything to the throne of grace. And it is not only you who must be made smooth by the hand of God, I also have need of the Lord's good work in my heart. But I know today you are a man of God, Ethan. It is plain to me. Marry the woman you love, marry her with my blessing and God's, marry her before the church and in the eyes of the whole world. And may Christ be with you."

"What?" responded Ethan.

"What?" echoed Rose.

"Is tomorrow too soon?" asked Jakob. "After Ethan is baptized?"

"Too soon? Too soon? Oh, Grandfather." Rose threw her arms around the old man. "Thank you, thank you, from the bottom of my heart."

"Thank God, daughter. He is the one who has worked a miracle today. Yes, thank and praise him."

"I do, I do, but it is only right I give thanks to God for you as well."

"Of course, of course, we thank God for our family and friends, for the pastors he gives us, that is only natural."

Ethan held the quilt and the rifle with one hand and shook the old man's hand with the other. "I'm grateful, sir. It will be an honor to join your people. An honor and a blessing."

"This is something you still want? A path you still wish to pursue?"

"Yes, with Rose by my side, I can go anywhere and face anything. I can do what I never thought I could do before. Just as I did today—prayers of forgiveness, kneeling in the dust before armed men, realizing there are times when I must put aside the gun. It would be a joy to walk with all of you in the strong light of God."

"So for us as well, young man. I hope you do not regret it."

"Why should I regret it?"

"Oh, the *Englisch* have given us a nickname. They call us the *Amish* now. After my own name. *Ammann. Amish.*" He laughed. "It sounds strange to me. I do not think it will last. I do not want it to last, to tell you the truth."

Ethan put an arm around Rose and kissed her quickly on the forehead. "What do you think, Beauty? Will the nickname last?"

His use of his pet name for her in front of Jakob Ammann caused a blush to leap from her neck to her face. But she covered it up by hugging Ethan with both her arms and burying her head in his shoulder.

"No, no," she said, closing her eyes and pressing her cheek against his buckskin shirt. "They will not call us *Amish* long. The name won't be with us much more than a year. But you and I, our name, Ethan and Rose Daniels, what will happen to that is something else again."

"Is that what you think? How long do you expect our name to last, Beauty?"

She tightened her arms across his back. "Oh, forever, my love. In God and his Son, Jesus Christ, I believe you and I and our name will last forever."

* * * * *

SPECIAL EXCERPT FROM

When Mennonite midwife Beth Ann Overholt went to Evergreen Corners to help rebuild after a flood, she never expected to take in three abandoned children—especially with an Amish bachelor by her side. But this temporary family with Robert Yoder might just turn out to be the perfect Christmas gift…

Read on for a sneak preview of
An Amish Holiday Family
by Jo Ann Brown,
available November 2020 from Love Inspired!

"You don't ever complain. You take care of someone else's *kinder* without hesitation, and you're giving them a home they haven't had in who knows how long."

"Trust me. There was plenty of hesitation on my part."

"I do trust you."

Beth Ann's breath caught at the undercurrent of emotion in his simple answer. "I'm glad to hear that. I got a message from their social worker this afternoon. She was supposed to come tomorrow, which is why I stayed home today to make sure everything was as perfect as possible before her visit."

"I wondered why you didn't come to the project house today."

LIEXP1020

"That's why, but now her visit is going to be the day after tomorrow. What if she decides to take the children and place them in other homes? What if they can't be together?"

Robert paused and faced her. "Why are you looking for trouble? God brought you to the *kinder*. He knows what lies before them and before you. Trust *Him*."

"I try to." She gave him a wry grin. "It's just…just…"

"They've become important to you?"

She nodded, not trusting her voice to speak. The idea of the three youngsters being separated in the foster care system frightened her, because she wasn't sure what they might do to get back together.

"Don't forget," Robert murmured, "as important as they are to you, they're even more important to God." His smile returned. "How about getting some Christmas pie before we have to fish three *kinder* out of the brook?"

With a yelp, she rushed forward to keep Crystal from hoisting Tommy to see over the rail. Robert was right. She needed to enjoy the children while she could.

LIEXP1020